William and Tibby
Forever

LYNDA HAMBLEN

ISBN 978-1-64140-526-3 (paperback)
ISBN 978-1-64140-527-0 (digital)

Christian Faith Publishing, Inc.
832 Park Avenue
Meadville, PA 16335
www.christianfaithpublishing.com

Printed in the United States of America

To David

Two Hodgepodges

"Hodgepodges, nothing but little hodgepodges!" the mother cat cried, aghast at the sight of the two kittens feeding at her side. Shaking her head and sighing in dismay, she looked at the rest of her newborn litter of six. Respectably short-haired like her, they were decorously attired in either black and white or sunshine yellow. Her two hodgepodges, however, had long gray and orange hair overlaid with black stripes. Orange splotches decorated their white chests and bellies. Each also sported a wide black stripe that ran from the top of its head to the tip of its bushy silver-gray tail.

The two long-haired kittens were oblivious to their mother's reaction. They could not hear her because their ears were folded tightly against their heads. They could not see her because their eyes were glued shut. But had they been aware of her dismay, they would have paid no attention. They had more important matters to attend to. Along with the rest of the litter, they were busy kneading their mother's stomach with their white paws while they nursed. Their foreheads, dominated by large black *M*'s, furrowed in concentration as they gulped down their first meal.

After all the kittens' bellies were full, they snuggled against their mother, soothed into sleep by her warmth, the vibrations of her contented purrs, and the familiar rhythm of her heartbeat. While they slept, their mother examined her two longhairs more thoroughly. She winced at the long tufts of gray and orange hair curling out of their folded ears. What a sight those would be when their ears unfolded. Proper kittens had short ear tufts that stayed inside the ear. How would the kittens ever be taken seriously, be regarded as dignified when they grew up with tufts of ear hair sticking out in every direction?

Their orange nostrils rimmed in black and the orange and gray ruffs of fur around their necks didn't help matters either. Those black stripes that flared from the corners of the kittens' eyes across the sides of their faces were the worst, though. The poor kitties looked like they were wearing masks. And were those black spots on the sides of their mouth? She peered more closely. Yes, those *were* black spots—four rows of them on each side. With a white whisker sprouting from every one!

Out of curiosity, she began counting—one . . . two . . . three . . . four . . . six . . . Oh dear, did five come before six or after? She was quite sure it came after. Six . . . five . . . fourteen . . . twelve . . . Growing cross-eyed and dizzy, she stopped. But she was certain she had counted sixteen spots on one side alone. Trying to do the math on her toes, she came up with thirty spots on each face. Or was it thirty-four? Goodness knows she had never been good at doing sums. Besides, she was growing too sleepy to think straight. She could figure it out tomorrow.

Yawning, she wrapped herself protectively around her six kittens. Although they were snugly ensconced on a blanket in a deep box at the back of a shed, she didn't want to take a chance on the cold of the February day sneaking over the top of the box and chilling them. Yawning again, she closed her eyes.

Suddenly she gasped, startled out of her doze by a horrendous realization. Her two hodgepodges looked like . . . like . . . No. She couldn't bring herself to say it. But the thought persisted. She turned her head for another peek at them. There was no doubt about it.

They looked like tiny raccoons. It was the masks on their faces that did it—the masks and those black stripes and their bushy tails.

Raccoons! An animal no self-respecting cat would ever want to resemble! Disagreeable, peevish creatures they were, particularly if encountering a cat. How in the world had she given birth to kittens that looked like such creatures? Her only hope was that their looks would change as they grew. Otherwise, they would never find a home when it was time for them to venture forth into the world. Well, there was nothing she could do about their appearance. If they didn't find homes, they would simply have to live with her for the rest of their lives. With that disquieting thought, she tucked her head under her tail and fell asleep.

For a week, the kittens nursed, slept, and mewed for their mother. If she was in the box, they slept nestled next to her. When she left the box to eat, hunt, or take a much-needed break, the kittens blindly squirmed until they found each other. They continued squirming until they were all piled into one warm heap, whereupon they fell asleep.

Each time their mother returned from her outings, she sniffed her kittens to assure herself that none were missing, silently calling them by name as she did so. She had named them according to the order in which they had been born. One of the longhairs was named Kitten Two; the other, Kitten Six. Only after she had assured herself that all her kittens were present and accounted for and that no impostors had been foisted off on her did she lie down to let the kittens nurse. After they had drunk their fill, she gave each one a vigorous bath with her tongue before settling down to her own nap.

The kittens had been introduced to their first baths immediately after their birth. Alarmed at first by the strange sensation of their mother's sandpapery tongue, each had mewed in fright. But after only a few wet licks, each kitten realized that a bath wasn't so bad after all. Now they looked forward to the rasp of their mother's tongue on their fur. As she gave them a bath after every meal, they had a great many baths to look forward to every day.

Life continued this way until about a week after they were born. One morning during breakfast, Kitten Six suddenly felt a rhythmic vibration that seemed to begin somewhere inside her middle and run upward to her throat. Startled, she stopped nursing. The vibrations stopped. She started nursing again. The vibrations began anew. Kitten Six had begun to purr. Within minutes, the other five kittens had joined in. Their mother purred in response. Before the hour was over, she could identify each kitten's purr. From then on, their box was one of purring bliss.

When they were almost two weeks old, the kittens woke to feel something stroking them gently on their backs. The kittens didn't know what was touching them, but they knew that it wasn't their mother's tongue. All the while, a harsh noise, unlike their mother's soft meows, assaulted their ears, which by then had unfolded. The noise consisted of a jarring chaos of sounds, such as "Oh, aren't you a darling little kitty cat!" and "Oh, look. These two have long hair."

The kittens squirmed and mewed loudly in protest, but to no avail. Fortunately, however, the ordeal soon ceased. Afterward, to soothe them, their mother, who had been watching over them the whole while, gave each a bath. After she had given the last comforting lick to the last kitten, she said, "Don't be afraid. You've had your first encounter with humans. Two of them. They belong to me. They feed me and provide me with a warm, dry place to live. They've been to see you every day. But you were too fragile to touch until today. You'll become used to them in time. Right now, though, you need a nap. When you wake up, you'll be in a much better mood." The kittens were more than happy to snuggle against their mother, absorbing her warmth, feeling her heartbeat, and listening to her purrs. Within minutes, they were soundly asleep.

When the kittens were around three weeks old, they awoke one morning to find that they could open their eyes. They spent a few minutes opening them wide and closing them tightly, enchanted with their newfound ability. Then they began to look around. How big and blurry their mother was! How tall and blurry the sides of the box seemed! And what beautifully colored, blurry fur they had! When the humans, who by this time had become daily visitors to their box, arrived later that day, the kittens tried to see what they looked like as they bent down to stroke them. But all they could see were two huge, pinkish blobs.

By the end of the third week, the kittens were beginning to totter around their box. They could also see more clearly. One day, they glanced up to see two huge, misshapen creatures peering down at them. The only fur the poor creatures possessed was on top of their heads. Even their ears were tuftless and mashed flat against the sides of their heads, instead of growing on top of them, like proper ears should! Worse, the two creatures had no whiskers! And why did they walk and stand on their hind legs while their front ones hung uselessly at their sides? The kittens mewed in horror.

They were even more horrified when the two misshapen creatures picked them up gently with their front paws and inspected them closely while making the harsh sounds the kittens had grown used to. "Gracious, how they've grown! And look at these two long-haired ones. They look a little like tiny orange and gray raccoons. Aren't they adorable?"

Mewing desperately for their mother, the kittens frantically wriggled, struggling to get down, but to no avail. After the creatures finally departed and the kittens had regained some semblance of their wits, their mother said, "How did you like your first sight of humans, my little ones? They take getting used to, don't they? They mean well, though. They've been wanting to hold you ever since you were born, but they had to wait until you were big enough. And they can't help how they look. After a while, you won't even notice their appearance all that much. In fact, you may even begin to think humans are appealing, in an endearing sort of way.

"The small one is a woman. The other is a man. I prefer the woman myself. Her voice is softer, and she smells nicer. She's the one that feeds me and provides me with a warm place to sleep. She gave me this box with a blanket in it for you to be born in. She stayed with me while I was giving birth to make sure I was all right. She saw you come into the world. One day, each of you will have a human of your own to take care of you like she takes care of me. But first, you have more growing to do."

The kittens looked at each other, unable to believe what they were hearing. With a worried look in his eyes, Kitten Two shook his head. "I knew it. Something bad is going to happen. No good can come of anything that sounds and looks like a human. And I hate to mention it, but they don't smell as good as cats."

Kitten Six said, "Why would we want a human to take care of us when we have you? You give us all the milk we want. You keep us clean and make sure nothing harms us. I'm staying with you."

"Kitten Six is right. I'm not going anywhere," said Kitten Four.

"Me, neither," chimed in Kittens One and Five.

Kitten Three nodded. "I'm staying put too."

Their mother laughed. "But soon you'll be big enough to eat cat food and keep yourselves clean. You'll also be able to protect yourselves. You won't need me anymore. You'll be ready to go forth into the world to live your own lives with your own humans. But don't worry. Humans will grow on you. Soon you won't mind their petting and holding you. You won't even mind the way they smell.

"Besides, I'll be having more kittens one day. I can't possibly take care of them and you too. No, when it's time for you to leave, I want you to behave like the courageous kittens I know you are. Don't run and hide. Don't cry. Make me proud. Go to your new homes with heads and tails held high. Promise me."

Saddened by the thought of one day leaving their mother but wanting above all to live up to her expectations, the kittens promised that they would try their best to be brave when the day came. But at the moment, that day seemed a long way off. Right now, they had more pressing matters on their minds, such as learning to run and jump. First, though, they had to master walking without tripping over their paws.

Before long, not only were the kittens walking, they were also leaping and pouncing on one other. Soon they were climbing out of their box to wrestle, roll, and tumble on the concrete floor of the shed. Becoming braver and more adventurous with each passing day, the kittens began exploring the dark recesses of their home.

One day they discovered some boxes stacked in a corner. They took turns hiding behind them, leaping out to pounce when an unsuspecting brother or sister walked by. They also discovered a ladder propped up against one of the walls. They spent hours climbing up the two bottom rungs and skydiving off. Occasionally, one ventured so far up that it couldn't jump down. Nor could it descend head first, for it began slipping and sliding as soon as it took a step. Its claws, which had gripped perfectly well climbing up, were useless for a head-first descent.

At that point, the kitten was forced to take the only recourse left. It began mewing desperately for its mother, who always promptly climbed up to the errant kitten and then holding it in her mouth by the scruff of its neck, slowly and carefully backed down.

In time, the kittens stuck their noses outside the shed. Looking cautiously around, they liked what they saw. Without further ado, they bounded into the yard, where, under the watchful eyes of their mother, they wrestled and tumbled. They pounced on every bug they saw. They chased every leaf that blew across their path. They swatted every stray bit of fluff that tickled their noses. When they grew sleepy, they trooped back into the shed, piled on top of each other in their box, and slept. All in all, they lived the life that kittens were meant to live.

By this time, they had grown used to their human visitors. They no longer shrank from their touch or flinched at their voices. They did not struggle at being held or turn up their noses at their smell. In fact, as their mother had promised, the kittens were beginning to think the humans were appealing in a bumbling sort of way.

When the kittens were about eight weeks old, the man remarked one day, "Well, little kitties, you're getting mighty big. You don't need your momma's milk any longer. Soon it will be time to find you new homes." The kittens, who were rolling and tumbling over each other, paused momentarily to glance at him. But as they did not understand what he had said, they returned to their frolicking.

Shortly afterward, the visitors brought another woman with them, one who was tall and slender, with a face that held the promise of a smile. At first, the kittens, who were engaged in a wrestling and pouncing match, paid the humans no mind. Finally Kitten Six noticed that the two women were intently observing them.

Walking over to her mother, Kitten Six asked, "Do you think that woman is here looking for a kitten to belong to?"

By this time, much to their mother's relief, the two long-haired kittens had outgrown their resemblance to raccoons, except for the stripe of black down their tails and the black markings suggestive of a mask on their faces. She had high hopes that the two kittens would have no problem finding a home. But she was not taking any chances.

So when Kitten Six asked her about the woman, she nodded. "Yes, Kitten Six, I do think she is looking for a kitten. And I also think she would be a good human for you. Faces don't lie, and she has a kind one. Go over and introduce yourself. But first, tell me good-bye."

At her mother's last word, Kitten Six's whiskers started to quiver, and her eyes grew sad. Licking her gently on the face, her mother said, "Don't cry, Kitten Six. You'll always be in my heart, like all my kittens who have left me to make their way in the world.

"Life is all about endings and beginnings. It's time for your life here with me and your brothers and sisters to end. Your new life out in the world is about to begin. Remember how I want you to behave. Head up! Tail high! Be courageous!"

Nodding acceptance, Kittens Six touched her nose to her mother's in farewell. Turning to take one last look at her brothers and sisters, she meowed good-bye. The other kittens stopped playing, overcome with the realization that the time had come for one of them to leave. Whiskers quivering, each one touched its nose to Kitten Six's.

After all the farewells were over, Kitten Six walked over to the stranger and put a paw on one of her legs. Glancing down, the woman said, "Oh look, Christie, I don't have to choose a kitten. This one's picked me. It's a little beauty. What gorgeous long hair. Such unusual markings on it too. And those tawny eyes. They look as if they're holding sunlight."

Christie said, "This is the female longhair. The other one is a male. I can tell them apart because the female has an orange blaze on her forehead. And you're right, Jane. She does seem to have taken a shine to you. Now she's rubbing against your legs." Picking Kitten Six up, Jane gazed at her face for a moment before saying, "What a sweet expression she has. I'm going to call her Tibby, my little Tibby Wibby." And with those words, Jane put Tibby into her car and drove a short distance to a small gray house on a hill.

Sardines and Cream

ONCE IN THE HOUSE, JANE put Tibby down in the middle of the living room floor. Crouching to make herself as small and inconspicuous as possible, Tibby glanced around. Already apprehensive from her car ride, she saw nothing that looked the least bit familiar—no ladders, no boxes, no other kittens. Her mother's words to hold her head and tail high promptly deserted her. Instead, ears laid flat, she dived head first under the couch until only her bushy tail stuck out. Inch by inch, that too disappeared.

There she huddled for the entire morning. The tick-tock of a clock, music from a radio, the whirr of a ceiling fan assailed her ears. The scent of furniture, blinds, and wooden floors assaulted her nose. Nothing sounded like the mewing and purring of kittens. Nothing smelled like the dirt floor, rolled up garden hoses, and empty oil and gasoline cans that she had grown used to in the shed. She longed to be back home.

Meanwhile, Jane busied herself with household chores, talking to Tibby every time she entered the living room. She mentioned Tibby's name often during these one-sided conversations so that Tibby could learn to associate herself with the sound of her name. Frequently, she stood in front of the couch while she was talking so that Tibby could become used to her smell.

At lunch time, Jane took two shallow saucers out of a kitchen cabinet. Into one, she spooned a sardine. Into the other, she poured a small dollop of cream. When finished, she set the saucers onto the kitchen floor and left the room. Soon the kitchen was filled with the smell of sardines and cream. The scent slowly wafted into the living room.

Halfway drowsing, Tibby suddenly roused. She sniffed the air intently. Her mouth began to water as the tantalizing smell tempted her nose. Gathering up her courage, she stuck her head out from under the couch. The smell became stronger. She stuck her neck out. The smell beckoned her even more insistently. Glancing around to make sure nothing lurked nearby waiting to pounce, she cautiously crept the rest of the way out and followed her nose to the two saucers on the kitchen floor. In one was a white liquid that smelled a little like her mother's milk. In the other was something that smelled deliciously unlike anything she had ever eaten.

Approaching cautiously, as all cats are wont to do when confronted by something new, Tibby tested the liquid tentatively with the tip of her tongue. It tasted smooth and creamy, better—almost—than her mother's milk. She lapped it up. Next, she dared a cautious nibble of the sardine. To her delight, it tasted even better than it smelled. Forgetting her manners, she gulped the rest of the sardine down and then licked both saucers clean.

With her stomach full and her taste buds satisfied, she sat down on the kitchen floor to wash her face, like all well-brought-up kittens do after they have eaten. First, licking her right front paw, she rubbed it against her mouth until there was no trace of sardine left. Then she did the same for both sides of her face and her ears. After she had finished, she yawned and stretched leisurely, first the front half of her body, followed by the back half.

"So how did you like your little snack of sardines and cream? I thought that might lure you from under the couch."

Glancing up, Tibby saw Jane. She didn't understand Jane's words, of course, but she recognized the affection in her voice.

Wanting to thank her for the excellent meal, Tibby purred and rubbed against her legs. After she felt she had properly expressed her gratitude, she ran into the living room, where she hopped onto the couch for a long nap.

When she awoke, she stood up and stretched while yawning prodigiously. She was in the middle of her second yawn when she noticed Jane rocking in a recliner. Bounding off the couch, she leaped into her lap. To her delight, Jane began to rub her gently behind the ears, just as her mother had done with her tongue during her baths. At the same time, she made soft sounds, almost like her mother's purrs. Tibby decided to call her Second Mom.

Tibby lost no time in making herself at home in the small gray house on the hill. She explored all the nooks and crannies, delved into all the closets and cupboards, investigated any open drawer, and peered into the washer and dryer. Second Mom knew that cats are full of curiosity, wanting to know the whats and wheres of everything in their world. Knowing that cats were drawn to high places, she allowed Tibby to jump onto whatever she wanted—bookcases, bureaus, desks, the top of the computer, even the kitchen counter. Tibby also tried out all the chairs and couches to find out which were the most comfortable for lounging. She slept on all the beds to see which was the softest.

When she tired of exploring, she busied herself with the toys Second Mom had given her. She had a fuzzy white mouse with red eyes and a red tongue to chew and shake, a box to jump in and out of with the mouse, a plastic ball to bat around, and a paper sack to hide in so that she could leap out and pounce on Second Mom's feet if they wandered by.

For a week, Tibby was the soul of contentment. But as the excitement of her new surroundings wore off, she became aware that there was one thing she wanted that she didn't have. Sardines and cream would taste much better if she had another kitten to share them with. And another kitten to play with was much more fun than any toy could ever be. Most of all, she missed having another kitten to curl up with when she went to sleep. In short, she longed for one of her litter mates.

Tibby grew so lonely that she stopped chewing on her mouse. She stopped jumping in and out of her box. She picked at her food, turning away from even her sardines and cream. She was so lonely that she would have returned to the shed if she could have. But she didn't know the way back. So she began spending her time lying with her head on her front paws, staring out the long living room windows, hoping that a lost kitten might wander up the driveway.

Second Mom grew concerned. She felt Tibby's nose to see if it were hot and dry, sure signs of a sick cat. But Tibby's nose felt cool and moist. Her ears looked clean, and her eyes were clear. Second Mom pried open Tibby's mouth to see if her gums looked healthily pink. They did. Second Mom sighed in perplexity. Suddenly, her face brightened. Tilting Tibby's head back slightly, she peered more closely into her eyes. Just as she had suspected. They no longer held the sparkle of joyful anticipation they once had. Instead, they looked sad. She exclaimed, "Tibby, you're lonely, aren't you?" Tibby, sensing the concern in Second Mom's voice, looked up at her, meowing faintly.

Taking off her apron, Second Mom put on her hat. "Tibby, I'll be back in a few minutes. And when I return, I'll have a surprise for you."

Second Mom drove to the shed where she had found Tibby. By this time, there were only two kittens left. One was black and white. The other, a gray and orange longhair with black stripes, resembled Tibby. The black and white kitten was running around in circles chasing its tail. The one that looked like Tibby was sitting quietly, a solemn expression on its face and in its eyes.

Second Mom looked at the black and white kitten and then at the gray and orange one. Back and forth she looked, back and forth. At last she picked up the gray and orange one. Looking at its face, she exclaimed, "What a serious-looking cat you are! The other one is so playful that someone is sure to take it. But you're so glum

17

looking, no one will probably ever want you. So I'll take you. I'm going to name you William, my little glum-wum. Let's go home to Tibby, William."

While Second Mom was gone, Tibby continued to stare out the living room windows. She was still staring out them as Second Mom drove up the driveway and climbed out of the car holding a kitten. Tibby sat up. Not only did Second Mom have a kitten, she had a kitten that looked familiar. Without further ado, she ran to the front door, reaching it just as Second Mom opened it, calling out, "Tibby, I'm back."

Putting William down, she spotted Tibby, her tail twitching excitedly, her eyes shining with excitement. But Tibby had eyes only for her brother. "Oh, Kitten Two, I'm so glad to see you! I've been so lonely! I hope you're going to stay!" Then she began licking her brother to show him how glad she was to see him.

Wresting himself free of his sister's tongue, William said, "I think I'm staying. And I don't think my name's Kitten Two anymore. It's William. That's the sound my human makes every time she looks at me." He frowned. "I know what *Kitten Two* meant. It meant I was born second. But I can't figure out what my new name means. Do you know?"

His sister shook her head. "No, I have no idea. And I'm not called Kitten Six anymore. My name's Tibby. I don't know what that name means either. But I like it. It suits me, don't you think?"

William repeated, "Tibby." After considering the sound of her name for a moment, he nodded. "Yes, it does suit you. It has a soft, round sound, and you're soft and round." Frowning, he added, "What kind of a place is this? Will I like it here? Is the food good? Are there any comfy places to sleep?"

Tibby assured William that there were plenty of comfy places to sleep. "And you'll love the food. We have sardines and cream every day. All we want. Any time we want. All I have to do is meow and Second Mom gets them for me." This was not exactly true as Second Mom was careful to give Tibby only small portions of each once a day, for a snack. But Tibby wanted her new home to sound as inviting as possible.

After solemnly digesting this delightful bit of untruth, William asked, "Who's Second Mom? And what are sardines and cream?"

"Second Mom's the woman who brought us here. She takes care of me, so I call her Second Mom. And sardines and cream are the most delicious food I've ever tasted."

Just then William and Tibby heard a voice. "William! Tibby! Here are some sardines and cream for my two little kitty cats."

Smelling the food, William and Tibby lost no time in making a beeline to the kitchen where they found two saucers of sardines and two of cream on the floor. Just as Tibby had done, William approached the saucers cautiously and sniffed. Smelling nothing alarming, he decided to try his unfamiliar fare. By the time he had taken his first lap of cream and his first nibble of sardine, he knew that Tibby was right. He has just eaten the most delicious food he had ever tasted.

After licking their saucers spotless and cleaning their faces, both kittens thanked Second Mom for their treat, butting their heads against her legs and purring. Then Tibby, with William following closely, raced to Second Mom's bedroom. Once there, Tibby, contented that she had William to snuggle against, and William, happy to be living in a house that had soft beds and sardines and cream, curled up on Second Mom's bed for a long afternoon nap.

When William woke, Tibby was still asleep. Hopping off the bed, he headed for the kitchen on the chance that another treat of sardines and cream might be waiting. To his disappointment, there was no evidence anywhere on the floor of a snack—no saucers, no sardines or cream. Then he spotted Second Mom, her back to him, busy at the stove.

Meowing to attract her attention, William sat down on the floor where he had eaten his first snack, hoping that Second Mom would figure out that he wanted another one. Suddenly he heard the back door open. Springing up, he dashed into the utility room, where he glanced frantically about. Spotting a dark space between the freezer and the wall, he wedged himself in it. Then noticing another dark space underneath the freezer, he crawled into it, crouching as low to the floor as possible.

Breathing a sigh of relief in the close darkness, he became aware of voices in the kitchen. One he recognized as Second Mom's. It was soft and higher than the other, whose deep timbre somewhat resembled the voice of the man who had made regular visits to the shed. Settling himself more comfortably, he began listening. Even though he couldn't understand what the voices were saying, he enjoyed hearing their rise and fall.

"Hi, hon," he heard Second Mom say. "You're home a little early, aren't you?"

"A little," resounded the deep voice. "My last appointment didn't show. What did you do with your day?"

"Well," said Second Mom after a slight pause, "I went after a playmate for Tibby."

"You did *what?*"

"I went after a playmate for Tibby. I told you that she had stopped eating and playing. This morning, I realized she was lonesome for another kitten. So I went back to the Mosses and got her brother."

"I wish you hadn't done that, Jane. You know one cat at a time is about all I can deal with."

"But, Dave, Tibby was so excited when I came in with William. That's what I named him—William. Tibby ate all her lunch for the first time in days. And both have been sleeping together all afternoon on our bed. I can't take William back. Tibby would be heartbroken."

"All right, all right. I get the picture. I don't want to have to live with two heartbroken females in the same house at the same time. William can stay. Not that you need my permission. I've lived with you enough years to realize you usually end up getting what you want."

"Oh, thank you, thank you, thank you!" William heard Second Mom exclaim. "You won't regret having two cats, I promise. They'll be so adorable together that you might even start liking them."

"Don't ask too much of me. Just having them in the house is enough. Getting to like them is going a bit far. This new cat, what did you say his name was?"

"William . . . William, my little glum-wum. I call him that because he's so serious looking. And he has beautiful, long gray and orange hair with black stripes. Just like Tibby."

"Why did you get a kitten that looked like her? Isn't that kind of like having two of the same cat?"

"There were only two cats left. One was a frisky black and white kitten. I knew eventually someone would take it. But William was so solemn looking that I didn't think anyone would ever want him. So I took him. Besides, they don't look exactly alike. William's left ear is orange, and Tibby has an orange blaze on her forehead. And she has a black spot, sort of like an inkblot, on the back of both hind legs. I can tell which cat is which, coming and going."

"Well, we certainly wouldn't want you to get confused about which was which, coming or going. That would be a catastrophe." William thought he caught a teasing note in the deep voice.

"Oh, you," said Second Mom, laughing.

Drawn by Second Mom's laughter, William crept out from under the freezer. Peeking cautiously around the doorway to the kitchen, he saw Second Mom peck the man on the cheek. Puzzled, William wrinkled his forehead. Why was Second Mom tasting the man's cheek? Was this how humans showed that they liked one another? Why didn't they touch noses instead like cats did? That way, cats could also smell one another to make sure they had the right cat.

Just then, Second Mom turned around and saw him. "William, why are you being so shy? Come here, little glum-wum, and meet the man of the house."

Responding to the invitation in Second Mom's voice, William stepped out from behind the freezer. He was not interested in meeting the man of the house, though. Instead he rubbed his head on Second Mom's legs, purring all the while.

Laughing, Second Mom gave him a pat on the head. "I bet you're hungry for some supper. And Tibby too." Raising her voice, she called, "Tibby . . . Tibby . . . time for supper."

Tibby, who was still half-asleep on Second Mom's bed, heard her name. Lifting one eyelid a fraction of an inch, she heard her name again. Opening both eyes, she hastily leaped off the bed. Speeding down the hall and through the living room, she skidded into the kitchen. There she found William already absorbed in his food. Soon both cats were crunching and munching side by side as the kitchen filled with the sound of their purrs. And that is how William became part of the family who lived in the small gray house on the hill.

Beasts, Vets, and Vaccinations

As with Tibby, Second Mom let William explore the closets, delve into cabinets, jump into any open drawer, and peer into the dishwasher and dryer. She knew that cats are full of curiosity, wanting to know the whats and wheres of everything in their world. One of Tibby and William's favorite places to hang out was the kitchen, especially when Second Mom was in the kitchen preparing their snack of sardines and cream. Their eyes followed her every move intently then, from taking the tin of sardines out of the cabinet, opening it, and placing one sardine apiece in two saucers to taking the carton of cream out of the refrigerator and pouring two small dollops into two other saucers. Almost before she could set the saucers on the floor, they had their noses in them, tails twitching excitedly in anticipation of their treat.

With Tibby there to show him the ropes, William was not long in feeling completely at home. He learned the best place to laze in the morning sun, where to hide when the vacuum cleaner was on the prowl with Second Mom in close pursuit, and how to bound from the floor to the kitchen counter, then to the top of the refrigerator, and from there to the top of the kitchen cabinets. From this vantage point, he could observe all that was going on in the kitchen, the living room, and the dining room, as there were only kitchen cabinets and counters dividing the three rooms.

When William and Tibby weren't sleeping, leaping, or exploring, they busied themselves playing with their toys. William's favorite was a fuzzy green mouse with yellow eyes and tongue. He enjoyed taking it in his teeth, throwing it into the air with a shake of his head, and catching it in his mouth on the way down. After giving it another good shake, he usually retired to a corner to chew on it or to guard it from Tibby with his paws.

Tibby's favorite toy was a brown cardboard box. She liked jumping into it with her white mouse and then shaking and tossing the mouse into the air before settling down to give it a good chew. She also liked hiding in the box so she could jump out at William when he walked by. Occasionally, William joined her with his mouse. He also liked hiding in the paper sack that Second Mom had provided them. If Tibby failed to notice he was in the sack, he rustled it to catch her attention. When she heard the rustle and spied the sack moving, she immediately rushed over to it, pouncing on it until he came out. When the two tired of their toys, they chased each other through the house. William chased Tibby for a while, and then Tibby chased William. Life was indeed a glorious adventure in the small gray house on the hill.

Not all was play, however, in the gray house on the hill. For instance, there was the business of names. When they lived in the shed, their first mom had told them the names of everything in their world. They learned the meows for *mother*, *brother*, *sister*, *box*, *shed*, *dog*, and *mouse*, along with many more.

Now they had to make up their own names for everything new they encountered. The refrigerator they named the cold box. Likewise, the oven became the hot box. The kitchen cabinet that held their food they named the sardine box. Second Mom's bed was called the soft blanket that smells like Second Mom.

They also had to contend with the two beasts that lurked in the garage. The two cats were fascinated by the appearance of these

24

creatures. They had legs that rolled rather than walked. They had no ears but too many mouths—one in front, one in back, and two on each side. They had no fur, leaving their shiny, brilliantly colored skin exposed to the elements.

The cats were of two minds about the beasts. Fearful creatures they were. Both remembered very well their trips to Second Mom's house in one of the beasts. Tibby had hidden under the front seat the entire journey, ears laid back, howling desperately and wishing that she had never left home. Second Mom had to prize her out when they arrived at her new home. Then and there she had resolved never to get into a beast again.

On his trip, William had leaped into the floorboard, crawling under and over Second Mom's legs before jumping onto her lap. From there, he had leaped onto her shoulder and into the back floorboard where he remained only a few seconds. Eyeing the back window ledge, he jumped onto the back seat, springing from there to the ledge. Then he twisted around and around a few times before propelling himself into the back seat again and thence onto the floorboard once more. There he had remained for the rest of the trip, lashing his tail and meowing piteously. He too had resolved never to get into such a monster again.

Thankfully, the beasts were safe enough asleep, which was a great deal of the time. Almost every morning, though, the man who lived with Second Mom opened wide one of the beasts' mouths and climbed inside. Within seconds, the beast roared to life, growling and shaking with menace before rolling slowly down the drive to the road. Once in the road, it sped up dramatically and was soon out of sight. Once or twice a week, Second Mom climbed into the other beast. Then it too roared to life and rolled down the drive, soon to disappear.

William and Tibby were convinced that every time the beasts roared out of sight, it was with the intention of devouring their occupants. Thankfully, however, the beasts always thought better of their behavior and returned with their prey unharmed. The cats were waiting for the day, though, when one of the beasts failed to do so. They could only hope that when that day came, it was the man and not Second Mom who was eaten.

William had been living at Second Mom's not quite a week when one morning, Second Mom walked into the living room where the kittens were playing to announce, "William Gwilliam and Tibby Wibby, today I'm taking you to the vet for checkups and shots."

Of course, William and Tibby did not understand what Second Mom was saying. But there was something in the tone of her voice that made William drop his toy mouse and hurry over to Tibby. Engrossed in swatting a plastic ball around the room, she had paid not the slightest attention to Second Mom.

"Tibby, did you hear those sounds? *Vet . . . checkups . . . shots.* I've never heard those sounds before. Do you think they mean something bad?"

Tibby, in the midst of a swat, stopped, paw in midair. Looking at William's anxious face, she sighed. "Oh, William, you're such a worrywart! Why do you always think the worst is going to happen? I'm sure those sounds don't mean anything bad. They're probably sounds for something delicious like sardines and cream."

The more Tibby thought about this, the more convinced she became that she was right. "Second Mom always says *sardines and cream* before giving us some. So if she says *vet* and *checkups* and *shots,* they probably mean something good too. Something good to eat." William's questions answered to her satisfaction, she gave her ball a resounding thwack.

William, however, was not convinced. "I don't know, Tibby. *Sardines* and *cream* . . . I like those sounds. They sound alike. *Sardines . . . cream . . .* But *vet . . . checkups . . . shots . . .* I don't like those sounds at all. I know they mean something bad."

William's concern proved to be well founded. Second Mom was back in the room within minutes carrying a small cage-like box with a wire door on one side. Placing it on the floor and opening the door, she turned to William and Tibby with a big smile. "Come look at your cat carrier, William and Tibby. You're going to the vet in it."

Second Mom did not have to invite William and Tibby to look at the carrier. As soon as she put it on the floor, William stopped worrying and Tibby stopped swatting, their entire attention riveted on the unfamiliar object before them. Cautiously, they crept within a step or two of the carrier. Necks craned, ready to flee at the slightest provocation, they sniffed at it. Not recognizing its scent, they each stretched out a front paw and batted at it tentatively to see if it would bat back. It just sat there, so William crept closer until he was near enough to stick his head inside. He quickly withdrew it, deciding that inside the carrier was a place he didn't particularly want his head to be.

Tibby was a bit braver. She crawled all the way inside before deciding she wanted out. But it was too late. Seeing an opportunity, Second Mom, without warning, bore down on William. Swooping him up, she stuffed him inside the carrier next to Tibby. Then she slammed the door.

William and Tibby looked at each other in disbelief. Second Mom had shut them in a box! They were prisoners! Faces pressed against the door, eyes filled with anxiety, they began to yowl and howl in protest. They yowled and howled even harder when Second Mom picked up the carrier and carried it to the beast that was lurking in the garage.

They continued to yowl and howl as Second Mom drove down the driveway and headed the car toward town. Trying to calm them, Second Mom began talking in a soothing, low voice. "I'm sorry you're so upset. I know I should have given you time to get acquainted with the cat carrier. But you had so much else to grow used to that I didn't want to overwhelm you. Besides, by the time I got William, you were already a week overdue on your first vaccinations. And after today, the vet's going to be gone for two weeks. So I couldn't wait any longer. Please forgive me. Please."

Although she talked to them like this the entire trip, they were still yowling and howling when, fifteen minutes later, Second Mom pulled up in front of a building bearing the sign, "Hood's Pet Clinic." Nor did their protestations lessen as Second Mom took the cat carrier out of the car and entered the building. They continued without letup as Second Mom, after signing in at the reception desk, sat down in the waiting room with the carrier at her feet. Soon everyone in the waiting room was looking at the cats in consternation. Some even shook their heads as if to say, "What poorly behaved kittens! Don't they have any manners?"

A few people even put their hands over their ears. At this, Second Mom's face turned red. Bending over the carrier, she said, "Please, William and Tibby, stop making so much noise. You're annoying everyone. Nothing bad is going to happen. Behave yourself. You'll be home before you know it."

Even had they understood her words, the two kittens were in no mood to be good little kitties. In fact, William and Tibby did not let up their protestations until they were in an examination room and Second Mom had opened the carrier. As soon as they saw the open door, they cautiously stepped out. After eyeing the unfamiliar room and finding nothing to their liking, they looked for a place to hide. Finding none, they silently backed into a corner, huddling together as closely as possible while waiting nervously to see what was going to happen. Picking them up one at a time, Second Mom tried to reassure them. But by now even Tibby had no doubt that she did not like the meaning of the sounds *vet*, *checkups*, and *shots*.

Suddenly a door swung open. A large man in a white lab coat entered the room. Looking at two files he had in his hand, he said, "Well, well, what do we have? Two little kitties, William and Tibby. Here for checkups and vaccinations. And which one is which?"

Scooping Tibby up, Second Mom put her on the examining table in the middle of the room. "This one is Tibby, Dr. Hood. Tibby, this is your vet."

As soon as Second Mom let go of her, Tibby tried to jump off the table, for it felt cold and slippery. She knew that nothing good could possibly happen to her there. Second Mom grabbed her just as she leaped, placing her firmly back on the table. Looking at a scale at one end of the table, Dr. Hood said, "Two pounds," and then scribbled briefly on a notepad. While he was writing, Second Mom put Tibby back on the floor. Then she picked up William, who was still huddled in the corner, nervously watching the proceedings. He shuddered as his paws made contact with the cold, slippery table.

Dr. Hood looked at the scale again. "Two and a half pounds. You're a big boy, William." But William was not in the mood for the compliment he sensed in Dr. Hood's words. He was too upset by the callous treatment he had endured all morning.

Worse was to come. Dr. Hood proceeded to prod and poke at the sides of both kittens, shine lights into their eyes and ears, prize open their mouths to look inside, and then, worst of all, push thermometers up their rear ends! Surprised at the last invasion, both kittens screeched in outraged indignation.

"To check your temperatures and see if you have worms," Second Mom explained to her kittens. She realized they wouldn't understand a word she said, but she felt obliged to offer them an explanation, nonetheless.

Taking the thermometers with him, Dr. Hood left the room. William and Tibby breathed sighs of relief. The man was gone. They could go home. But no, the door swung open again. And there the man loomed, holding two eyedroppers filled with yellow medicine. He walked over to Tibby, who was still on the exam table. Firmly holding her head in one hand, he held one of the droppers against one side of her mouth. Tibby clenched her teeth, determined not to cooperate. But her efforts were in vain. Well versed in persuading recalcitrant kittens to take their medicine, Dr. Hood pressed the dropper against her teeth. Tibby automatically opened her jaws wide. Dr. Hood quickly squirted the medicine in, and down it went. He repeated the same procedure with William. Then he gave each three vaccinations. William and Tibby did not even protest the slight sting of the needles. Next to everything else they had undergone that morning, a mere sting was nothing.

Having finished with the kittens, Dr. Hood said, "That's all for today, William and Tibby. I'll see you back here in three weeks." After giving each a pat on the head, he disappeared again through the swinging door.

Before William and Tibby could grasp the fact that their ordeal with the vet was over, Second Mom had picked up Tibby and deposited her back into the carrier. Once more, Tibby started yowling and howling vociferously. William, seeing Tibby's fate, sprang off the examining table, landing in the sink of a nearby counter. Eyeing the top of a cabinet, he crouched. Tensing his muscles, he wriggled his back end, trying to get a grip on the smooth surface of the sink with his back claws. To his consternation, they scrabbled uselessly. Before he could make a second attempt, he found himself in Second Mom's arms being stuffed into the cat carrier for a second time. His yowls and howls immediately resounded with Tibby's.

Only when Second Mom set them free upon reaching home did their cries cease. Incensed at all she had undergone, Tibby turned her back on Second Mom as soon as she stepped out of the carrier. She refused to let herself be petted or consoled for the rest of the morning, moving out of Second Mom's reach every time she approached. William was so unsettled that he wriggled under the living room couch, taking refuge there until the smell of lunch persuaded him to come out.

He found Tibby already crouched over her saucer of food, her hungry stomach, like William's, having triumphed over her indignation. After finishing lunch, both rubbed their faces on Second Mom's legs while purring in contentment, forgiving her for their traumatic morning. Then they settled down on her bed. After licking each other's face and neck, they curled up together, yawning hugely. Both were almost asleep when William sighed. "Well, it was a bad morning all the way around, no two ways about it. I've been telling you that something bad would happen one day. Today it did. Do you think we'll be put in that box again? Or have to ride in that horrible beast? Or be taken back to that awful place?"

Tibby said, "No, William. Second Mom would never do anything like that to us again. When she saw what that man was up to this morning, I bet she didn't like it one bit. She probably just stayed out of politeness."

"I don't know," said William gloomily. "She didn't seem too upset to me."

"Well," consoled Tibby, "if Second Mom makes the sounds *vet* and *checkups* and *shots* again or gets the cat carrier out, we'll hide under this bed. It's really dark under there. She'll never find us. So don't worry." Then never one to worry herself, she closed her eyes.

William, however, remained doubtful. He knew in his bones that there would be more trips in the cat carrier to the vet's. Nor did he think that Second Mom would have any trouble finding them under the bed or anywhere else when it was time to go. But at the moment, he was too tired to care. He would worry about that after his nap. Curling closer to Tibby, he closed his eyes.

Tibby's Downfall

IN SPITE OF TRIPS TO the vet, William and Tibby considered themselves most fortunate, indeed, to be living in the gray house on the hill. They couldn't imagine snacks any tastier than sardines and cream or a softer bed than Second Mom's for long afternoon naps with each other.

Of course, William and Tibby didn't always take naps on Second Mom's bed. Occasionally, William fell asleep on top of the kitchen cabinets. Sometimes Tibby took a catnap in the large crystal bowl on the dining table. But for serious afternoon sleeping, Second Mom's bed was definitely best. Second Mom never disturbed them when they were asleep. She knew that sleep ranked high on a cat's list of priorities, right underneath food, which was at the top, and being petted, which was second from the top.

By the time the two cats had explored, played, leaped, and chased all morning, they were more than ready for lunch. After polishing off their meal, they cleaned their faces before settling down for their afternoon nap on Second Mom's bed. Afterward they had a snack of sardines and cream. As soon as they had licked their saucers clean, they ventured outside.

William and Tibby liked being outside at Second Mom's almost as much as they liked being inside. There were butterflies to swat, bugs to catch, grass to crouch in, and trees to climb. Sometimes they hid from one another in the shrubs around the house, leaping out and pouncing when the other walked by. They called this game hide-and-pounce. If they grew tired, they took a catnap on the sundeck, eyes half-open to make sure nothing happened in the yard that didn't meet their approval.

If Second Mom was outside, they stuck to her side, poking their noses into whatever she was up to, be it working in her flower beds, reading on the sundeck, or bird watching with her binoculars. Birds flew in and out of the trees in Second Mom's yard all day, so many that sometimes the two kittens grew dizzy trying to follow them with their eyes. One of the trees held a bird feeder. Sometimes William and Tibby tried to sneak up on the birds eating the seed that Second Mom had scattered on the ground under the feeder. They never caught one, though. The birds were much too cautious and quick. Besides, the bells on the kittens' collars announced their presence well in advance.

Once, however, William did manage to snag a red tail feather from a cardinal. Feeling pleased with himself, he proudly showed it to Tibby. Miffed that she hadn't snagged a feather yet, she said, "It was probably getting ready to fall out anyway." Turning her back, she flounced away, head held high, vowing to snare a tail feather herself. Soon.

Some afternoons, if the weather was especially pleasant, Second Mom walked with her two cats down the hill in her yard to the creek that skirted one side of the yard. There the two kittens prowled in the tall grass and weeds bordering the bank, sniffing wild scents that stirred their blood. Tibby was positive she smelled foxes and coyotes, although she had not the least idea what a fox or coyote was, much less what one smelled like. But her First Mom had warned her about them, so she was ever on the alert for their presence. William thought that she was probably smelling rabbits and moles.

Sometimes Second Mom took a blanket and a book to the bank. Lying on the blanket in the shade of the hill, she read while William and Tibby played at being grown-up cats. Occasionally, they dashed over to the blanket to rub their faces against her legs before plunging back into the tall grass and weeds. At other times, Second Mom watched them for a few minutes before heading back to the house. But she always returned before long to fetch them. The two cats were never ready to leave, but they obediently followed Second Mom's summons, stopping occasionally to cast wistful looks back.

After supper, William and Tibby usually meowed to go out again. As darkness fell, they entertained themselves by chasing lightning bugs and climbing to the top of the window screens to catch the moths hovering there. They never caught any, though, because the moths saw the two cats long before there was any danger. They would have stayed out at night for hours, but Second Mom was strict about their being inside after darkness had completely fallen. "The foxes and coyotes will be out soon. They would love to have William and Tibby for supper. Then I wouldn't have my two kitty cats anymore," she explained when they meowed plaintively to stay out a little longer.

When they came back inside, Second Mom readied them for bed. First she brushed them from head to paws, saving their bushy silvery tails for last. During this part of their bedtime ritual, William and Tibby purred ecstatically, especially when she brushed the sides of their faces and their bellies. After brushing their tails, Second Mom checked them for fleas and ticks, parting the fur on their necks, their backs, their faces—anywhere she thought the varmints might have set up housekeeping. Sometimes she even checked their necks twice. She knew that fleas especially liked to congregate there.

Only when she was completely satisfied that no fleas were chewing on her cats and no ticks were sucking them dry of blood did she turn her attention to the inside of the cats' ears, on the lookout for dirt and mites. She also examined the pads of their paws to make sure they weren't scraped or cut. This part of getting ready for bed was not as enjoyable as being brushed, but William and Tibby endured it with good grace.

Last, Second Mom put a small dab of cat toothpaste on two small cat toothbrushes. Prying William and Tibby's mouths open, she brushed their teeth. Both cats hated having their teeth brushed, but they were resigned to it. It was a small price to pay for living with Second Mom in the small gray house on the hill.

Besides trips to the vet and tooth brushings, the only bad part about living with Second Mom was having to share her with Hon. Hon was what they called the man who lived with Second Mom. They called him Hon because that was what Second Mom called him. She was always making sounds such as "Hon, supper's ready" or "Did you have a hard day at the office, hon? You look tired." Although William and Tibby had no idea what the sounds meant, they recognized the love in her voice when she said them.

After making these sounds, sometimes she kissed Hon's forehead and looked at him with adoration, just as she looked at William and Tibby when she petted them. They felt that the affection and care she spent on Hon could have been better spent on them.

In fact, William and Tibby couldn't figure out why Second Mom needed Hon at all. He was much too big to sit in her lap. And he never purred or rubbed against her legs after being fed, even though she spent much more time preparing his meals than she did theirs. But the moment Hon walked through the door in the evening, Second Mom stopped what she was doing, even if she were petting or playing with them, to rush over to Hon and kiss him. Then she took his hat and coat so that he could sit in his recliner and relax.

One evening while he was in the recliner, Tibby jumped onto the kitchen counter. Springing up, Hon slapped a newspaper down beside her, yelling at her to boot. Frightened half out of her wits, Tibby leaped to the floor. To add insult to injury, Second Mom, busy in the kitchen, didn't even scold Hon. She merely wiped off the counter and then coaxed Tibby out from under the dining table where she had sought refuge. After giving her a reassuring pat along with a few soothing words, she returned to the kitchen as if nothing untoward had happened.

From that evening on, Tibby was forever leery of Hon. Late every afternoon, when the time approached for him to arrive home, she grew nervously alert, asking William, "Did I hear Hon's beast drive up?" or "Is that Hon I hear coming in?" When he did arrive, she made sure to keep off the kitchen counter and out of range of him and his newspaper.

Worst of all, when William and Tibby became big cats of three months instead of little kittens, Hon refused to let them sleep any more on Second Mom's bed at night. "Sorry, sweetie. Kittens I can take. But two big cats sleeping with us is two cats too many. One or the other is always waking me up by walking on my back or sitting on my chest and staring at me. It's time for them to find another place to sleep, like all your other cats have had to do."

"It must be William who's waking you up," Second Mom said. "Tibby's afraid to go near you since you slapped that newspaper at her." At bedtime that evening, bowing to the inevitable, she dragged a laundry basket out of the utility closet, lined it with a soft blanket, and placed it on the floor beside the bed. William and Tibby watched these preparations with great interest. But when she lifted them from the bed, where they had already ensconced themselves for the night, and placed them in the basket, matters took a decidedly serious turn.

For a moment, the two cats looked at her questioningly. Then they looked at each other. Both were of the same opinion. Second Mom couldn't possibly intend for them to sleep in the basket. So hopping out, they leaped onto the bed. Second Mom, who had barely settled herself under the covers, sighed, got back up, and put them into the basket again.

Tibby and William promptly hopped back out again. This time, Second Mom was ready. She had not bothered to return to bed but, instead, had remained standing by the basket. As soon as the two kittens hopped out, back in they went. This procedure was repeated several more times. Finally, Tibby and William looked at each other again. Evidently, Second Mom did intend for them to sleep in the basket. Wanting more than anything to please Second Mom, the two settled down for the night.

The new sleeping arrangement lasted about a week. Then one night, William, dreaming that he was pouncing on a mouse, leaped out of the basket onto the bed and from there onto Hon's head. Waking with a start, Hon jumped out of bed, yelling, "That's it! Out they go!" Without further discussion, William and Tibby found themselves and the basket banished to the other side of the bedroom door.

Of course, William and Tibby had no idea what had gone wrong. All they knew was that one night, they were sleeping on Second Mom's bed; the next night, they were sleeping in a basket next to the bed; and a week later, they were sleeping on the wrong side of the bedroom door. They were convinced, though, that their exile was Hon's doing.

Yet in spite of vets, tooth brushes, and Hon, William and Tibby knew they were blessed to have Second Mom for a mother, even if she didn't like mice and couldn't climb a tree. Not for anything would they have gone back to the shed. As good as their lives were, however, William worried every day that something bad would put an end to their carefree days and their happy home.

"Oh dear," he said every morning after waking up. "I hope nothing bad happens today." Then, before falling asleep at night, he might suddenly murmur, "Well, nothing bad happened today, but wait until tomorrow."

Tibby, who was definitely not a worrier, always assured William that Second Mom would protect them from anything bad. "Doesn't she make sure we don't get tummy aches from eating too many sardines and drinking too much cream? Doesn't she brush our teeth so they won't fall out and make sure we don't have any fleas or ticks? And doesn't she make us come in at night so the foxes and coyotes can't eat us? Whatever they are. No, William, you don't have to worry. You can relax. Second Mom is watching out for us."

But William wasn't convinced. "Better to worry. Then I'll be ready when something bad does happen."

One morning, he woke up more certain than ever that something bad was lurking, waiting to leap on them. The feeling lasted through a morning of exploring the coat closet, playing with his mouse, and chasing Tibby around the dining table. It lasted through lunch and up to nap time. But as he settled down with Tibby on Second Mom's bed for an afternoon nap, William reassured himself that at least nothing bad could happen while he and Tibby were asleep.

He closed his eyes. Soon he was dreaming of sleek, fat mice; trees dripping birds; and an unending row of saucers filled with sardines and cream. Suddenly, he felt something pounce on his back. Not ready to give up his pleasant reveries, he snuggled deeper into the blanket. As he was about to reenter his dreams, he felt another thud on his back. Opening one eye, he saw Tibby crouched low and wriggling her back end, preparing to pounce again. William closed his eye, hoping that she would get the message. But she didn't. Instead she pounced a third time, this time attacking his side.

Sighing, William reluctantly gave up all ideas of finishing his nap. As he opened his eyes to see where Tibby's next attack was coming from, an angry, frightened yowl erupted from the foot of the bed. Hastily rising to his feet and bounding to the foot of the mattress, he peered down. To his horror, he saw that Tibby had caught her right leg in a crack between the mattress board and the bedstead. It was wedged so tightly that she couldn't pull it free.

Tibby glared up in fear and rage. "Help me, William! Help me! I can't get my leg out! It hurts too much! Don't just stand there! Go get Second Mom!"

William was beside himself. He had known something bad was going to happen today, and it had! Leaping off the bed, he ran out of the bedroom and down the hall to the living room, caterwauling for Second Mom. But she was nowhere to be found, not in the living room or the kitchen or the dining room. Nor was she in the utility room. She must be in the yard. How would he ever yowl loudly enough for her to hear him?

Running back down the hall to the bedroom, he cried, "Second Mom's not in the house, Tibby! What am I going to do?"

But Tibby—frightened, angry, and in pain—couldn't answer. She could only yowl more loudly. Running to the utility room again, William yowled at the back door as loudly as Tibby was yowling in Second Mom's bedroom, hoping against hope to get Second Mom's attention. But the door didn't open. Jumping up, he tried turning the door handle with his paws, a trick that usually worked for Second Mom and her paws. But his efforts proved futile.

By now Tibby was yowling so loudly that he could hear her all the way on the other side of the house. "What are you doing, William? Oh, I hurt so much! I'm so afraid! Can't you do something?"

William could think of nothing else to do but race back to the bedroom again, still yowling in fright himself. Just as he was about to give up in despair, he heard steps coming down the hall. Within seconds, Second Mom filled the doorway.

"What's going on? I came in from working in the yard and what did I hear but this horrific commotion, like two tomcats fighting! And what's wrong with you, William? Why are you running around in circles?"

She picked William up but could see nothing wrong with him. Then she realized that most of the noise was coming from the direction of the bed. She glanced at it, looking in vain for Tibby. Suddenly she spied a tiny leg sticking out from the foot of the bedstead. She screamed, "Tibby, what have you done?" Putting William back on the floor, she rushed over to the foot of the bed. Peering down, she drew in her breath sharply.

"Tibby, how in the world did you do that? How am I ever going to free you?" For a second, she looked as scared as Tibby. Then composing herself, she said, "Now, calm down, Tibby. And you too, William. Mamma's going to get Tibby out." After considering the situation a few moments, she bent down and pushed with all her weight against the mattress board, hoping to move it toward the head of the bed enough for Tibby to pull her foot free. But the board was too heavy. After several more tries, she stood back up.

Breathing hard from her efforts and chewing on her lips in concentration, she cast about for another solution. Suddenly, she snapped her fingers and bent back down. Gently grasping Tibby's leg, she tried to move it forward where the crack widened a bit. But at her touch, Tibby yowled even louder. Second Mom jerked her hand away, afraid of breaking Tibby's tiny bone.

Standing back up, she looked down at the desperate cat. "Don't worry, Tibby. I'm going to get you out of here if I have to take an ax to the bed." Glancing around the room, as if searching for an ax, she exclaimed, "I'll call Dave! He'll be strong enough to push the mattress board toward the head of the bed."

Hurrying to the phone on her desk, she had Dave on the line within seconds. "Dave, you have to come home immediately. Tibby's leg is caught between the mattress board and the foot of the bedstead, and she can't get it out. Don't ask me how she did it. She just did. . . . I know it isn't time for you to quit work, but I'm not leaving her stuck for two more hours. You have to come home right now. . . . I *did* try pushing the mattress board toward the head of the bed, but I'm not strong enough. . . . If you don't come home this second, I'm going to take an ax to our bed!"

Banging down the receiver, Second Mom returned to Tibby. "Dave's coming home. He'll be here in a few minutes. You'll be unstuck before you know it."

Exhausted from struggling to free herself, Tibby could only look at Second Mom imploringly, as if to say, "Please do something. Don't leave me like this."

Second Mom didn't leave. She and William both stayed with Tibby until Hon arrived, within minutes, just as Second Mom had promised. Taking one look at Tibby, he shook his head. Bending down, he too tried moving her leg to the widest part of the crack.

But as with Second Mom, Tibby yowled with such ferocity that he immediately stopped. Next, he too tried to push the mattress board toward the head of the bedstead. But he had no more luck than Second Mom.

After his second push, he looked around for her. "Go get the crowbar in the garage," he instructed. "Maybe I can use it to lift the board. I can't get enough leverage to move it by myself."

Running from the room, Second Mom returned within minutes with a long iron rod that curved upward in a point at one end. She handed it to Hon, who placed the pointed end in the widest part of the crack between the mattress board and the foot of the bedstead. Wedging the crowbar's curve under the board, he leaned all his weight on its handle, pushing it down.

Almost imperceptibly the board lifted the tiniest bit. In an instant, Tibby's leg was free! Jerking it from the crack, Tibby leaped onto the bed and from there onto the floor as if she never again wanted to get back on the bed, much less nap there! Bolting across the room, she dived under the chest of drawers. Overwrought and too embarrassed to show her face, she refused to budge in spite of Second Mom's pleadings and William's meows.

Finally, at suppertime, hunger nudged her from her refuge and propelled her down the hall and into the kitchen. William, who had stayed with her all this time, followed closely behind, determined not to let her out of his sight. To their surprise and delight, Second Mom had prepared a special helping of sardines and cream in addition to their regular fare. Tails twitching in appreciation, Tibby and William licked their saucers clean. When not even the tiniest morsel of food remained, they rubbed against Second Mom's legs, purring loudly in appreciation. Then worn out by the afternoon's drama, both cats jumped upon the living room couch to wash their faces and relax.

Midway through his grooming, William paused. "Well, Tib, we've been wondering why Second Mom keeps Hon around. Now we know. It's for rescuing us when something bad happens."

Tibby nodded. "Yes, William, I think you may have something there. I guess we'll have to let her keep him." Then giving a huge yawn and stretching out luxuriously, she settled down against William for a brief nap before bedtime.

5

Tibby's Night Out

SECOND MOM HAD BEEN CLEANING closets since early that morning. Midway through the afternoon, she couldn't face the dusty jumble of another closet. Even the two cats, who, tails twitching in excitement, had nosed and prodded with delighted curiosity every box and bundle that Second Mom had dragged from the closets, were beginning to droop. Taking off her apron, Second Mom announced, "We're taking a break. Let's go to the creek."

Sensing the invitation in her words, the cats' ears perked up. Once outside, they bolted for the nearest tree, climbing halfway up before looking around for Second Mom. When they saw her strolling toward the bank, they backed down to the lowest branch, slipping and sliding a good part of the way. From there, they sprang to the ground and took off. Galloping at full speed, they quickly caught up with and passed Second Mom, skidding to a halt at the edge of the grass and weeds that skirted the bank. Giving her a quick glance over their shoulders, in they dived.

Reaching the bank herself a few seconds later, Second Mom sat on the grass to watch them play. Before long, her laughter at the cats' antics and the warm sun on her arms began to revive her spirits. After watching them a while longer, she reluctantly stood up. "I have to start supper, little kitties. I'll be back after a while." William and Tibby were so engrossed in sniffing and crouching and leaping and pouncing that they hardly noticed her leave. They were in pursuit of rabbits and mice, squirrels and moles, real and imaginary. At the moment, Second Mom took a back seat to their chase.

So caught up were they in their hunt that they did not see a huge yellow cat staring intently down from a tree. The creature was twice as large as William and three times as large as Tibby. It had been silently watching them the whole time. Almost as soon as Second Mom disappeared over the hill, it leaped into the grass a few feet from them. Startled, William and Tibby froze, fur huffed up, backs arched in fear.

Lashing his tail back and forth, the strange cat growled menacingly as he crept toward them. Stopping only inches away, it sprang at William, who, turning tail, raced to the nearest tree and shot up it. He was almost to the top before he dared stop to see if the strange cat was behind him.

It wasn't. Peering down, William spotted it chasing Tibby along the creek bank, both moving further and further away by the moment. Soon the two were lost in the tangle of grass and weeds, their progress marked only by the sway of the bank's undergrowth. Finally, they were so far way that William was unable to see even that.

Suddenly, William realized that he had never been so high in a tree before. Usually he stopped before he was more than a few branches up. But this tree was tall, and William was many branches off the ground, so high that he dared not move. Tightening his grip on the branch underneath him, he tried not to think about how high he was or how he was going to climb back down. There was only one thing to do. He would have to stay in the tree until Second Mom returned. He looked forlornly toward the house, hoping against hope to see her heading toward the creek bank.

But Second Mom was nowhere to be seen. Sighing, William gripped the tree branch even more tightly and prepared to wait. And wait he did for what seemed an interminable time. Just as he was about to despair of ever feeling the ground under his paws again, he heard Second Mom calling, "William . . . Tibby . . . time to go back to the house." Moments later, he saw her striding over the top of the hill. He uttered a huge meow of relief. Second Mom would help him down. She would find Tibby. Second Mom could do anything.

Upon reaching the bank, Second Mom glanced around. "William . . . Tibby . . . come out. It's suppertime." To her consternation, no William or Tibby appeared. She called them a second time. Still no William or Tibby. Second Mom began to thrash through the vegetation along the bank, calling their names over and over. But they didn't appear. Her heart started to race. She forced herself to stand still and breathe deeply while trying to think what to do next.

Suddenly, from above, she heard a faint meow. Her heart gave a huge thump of relief. Glancing up, she scanned the trees closest to her. There were so many that at first she didn't spot William. In addition, the sun had already dropped low in the sky. The encroaching dimness made him difficult to see. Only when he gave a second meow did she locate the sound in the tall tree just to the left of her. Sure enough, peering up, she spotted William clutching a tree branch. He was so high up she grew dizzy looking at him. "William, what are you doing up there? You come down right this minute. And where's Tibby?"

William meowed again, tightening his grip on the branch as he implored Second Mom with his eyes and his meows to rescue him. But Second Mom was not about to climb the tree to get William down. He was up too high. Besides, she knew that if she did, every time he climbed a tree afterward, he would expect her to climb up and bring him down.

She said, "William, you'll have to come down by yourself. Slide down backward, the way you do when you climb a tree in the backyard. Come on now. You can do it. I know you can." Taking heart from the encouragement in Second Mom's voice, William unloosed his claws from his perch and crept cautiously toward the tree trunk a few inches before becoming overwhelmed by fear again. He froze once more, meowing piteously.

Second Mom said, "Good boy, William. What a brave cat you are! Just a few more steps." Summoning up his courage a second time, William crept the few remaining inches to the trunk, fervently embracing it in relief. Second Mom was jubilant. "William, you're almost down. The worst part's over. You won't fall, I promise. Just hold on tightly with your claws and slide down."

So William, front and back legs splayed out to clutch the tree trunk, slid down backward a little at a time, taking heart from Second Mom's voice and stopping occasionally to get a better grip with his claws. The one thing he did not do was look down. After what seemed a long time, he was on the ground. He'd never dreamed that it could feel so good beneath his paws.

Second Mom hugged William. "Oh, William, I was so scared when I saw you up there. I knew you were brave enough to get down, though. And you did! Now we have to find Tibby!" Calling Tibby's name, Second Mom walked along the creek bank where it bordered her yard and one side of the field beyond her backyard. William followed the whole way, giving an occasional meow for Tibby to show herself. But Tibby didn't appear.

Next, Second Mom and William walked around the other three sides of the field, Second Mom calling, "Tibby . . . Tibby . . . where are you? Time to come home." Tibby still did not appear. By the time they had walked around the entire field, dusk had fallen. Realizing she would never find Tibby in the dark, Second Mom headed toward the house, William still behind her. Hoping that Tibby might show herself at the last moment, both gave backward glances when they reached the back door. Their hopes, however, went for naught.

When Second Mom fed William that evening, there was just one saucer of food and one saucer of water where, before, there had been four. William felt so lonely at the sight that he barely nibbled his food. Afterward, he trooped into the living room where he despondently contemplated his green mouse sleeping under the coffee table.

Turning away, he plodded heavily into the dining room where he disconsolately regarded Tibby's white mouse hiding under the china cabinet. He sighed. Playing with Tibby's mouse was no fun without her there trying to snatch it from him.

Seeking comfort, he headed to Second Mom's room. Leaping onto her bed, he lay down. Sleep took a long time coming, though, without Tibby to curl up beside him. Yet when sleep finally overtook him, he slept so soundly that he didn't even rouse when Second Mom put him outside the bedroom door in his and Tibby's basket.

When he woke up the next morning, he glanced around, expecting to see Tibby. Then he remembered that she wasn't there. He covered his eyes with his paws, not wanting to face the day without her. Suddenly he sat up. Tibby might be at the back door right now, waiting to be let in. Leaping off the bed, he raced to the back door, meowing for Second Mom to open the door. But when she did, there was no Tibby on the back steps peering in through the storm door.

Second Mom tried to reassure William. "Don't worry, William. She's been gone only one night. I bet she's back by lunch." William, however, thinking about the cat that he had seen chasing Tibby, doubted that she would ever return. How would she manage to get away from a cat that big?

Privately, Second Mom wasn't so sure Tibby was coming back either. At breakfast, she had asked Hon, "Where could she be? She's never wandered off before. Why, she's always the first one at the back door when it's time to come in. Besides, she would never leave William!

"No, I think something got her. But what? She's much too large for a hawk or owl to carry away. I haven't seen any dogs around in a good long time. Coyotes and foxes roam at night, not during the day. I just don't know what to think."

Neither did Hon. After supper the night before, flashlight in hand, he had walked up and down the road in front of the house and crisscrossed the field that Second Mom and William had walked around earlier, calling Tibby. She never answered. At daylight that morning, before either William or Second Mom awakened, he had trudged up and down both sides of the creek bank to the back of the field behind the house and the field beyond. Again his efforts went for naught. Soaked with dew, he had returned to the house Tibbyless.

Barely touching his breakfast, William wandered through the house. He peeked under every bed, dresser, and cabinet in case Tibby had come home. Yet he knew in his heart that she wasn't in the house. She was somewhere out in the vast, scary world without him and Second Mom. What if she never came home? Unable to bear that thought, he trudged to the back door, meowing to be let out.

Once outside, he did not chase butterflies or climb trees. He did not try to catch a bird. Doing these things without Tibby was unthinkable. Nor did he hide in the shrubs waiting to pounce on Tibby because there was no Tibby to pounce on. Indeed, life without Tibby was proving to be a most disheartening affair. He had worried something bad might happen, and now it had. Lying down on the sundeck, head on paws, he looked across the yard toward the creek, hoping for Tibby to appear.

His hopes went unanswered. When Second Mom called him in for lunch, Tibby was still missing. To tempt William to eat, sardines and cream, instead of his usual lunch fare of dry cat food, were waiting for him. He realized that Second Mom was trying to cheer him up. The sardines and cream didn't taste nearly as good, though, without Tibby there to share in the treat and to purr happily with afterward. He ate all the sardines and lapped up all his cream anyway. He didn't want Second Mom to worry about his not eating. She had enough on her mind already.

After he had eaten, he cleaned his face, as all cats do after eating, no matter how discouraging the circumstances. When all traces of his meal were vanquished, he headed to Second Mom's room for a nap. Jumping onto the bed, he curled up on the folded blanket he and Tibby always shared. Closing his eyes, he contemplated how dreary life was with no Tibby Wibby to share it with.

A few minutes later, he heard Second Mom enter the room. Walking softly to the bed, she began rubbing his head and back. "Don't be sad, William. We can't give up hope yet." Looking up at her, William gave a small yip. At that instant, they heard a thump at the bedroom window, followed by a scratching noise on the screen. Second Mom turned around, not even daring to hope that Tibby was at the window. But she was! Second Mom cried, "Tibby, oh Tibby, you're back! Where have you been?"

She raced to the back door. But William reached it first. He pressed his nose to the glass, trying to reach Tibby. No sooner had Second Mom opened it than in Tibby scooted. She and William touched noses and butted heads in affection. Finally Tibby, meowing, turned her attention to Second Mom. Picking her up, Second Mom burst out crying. "Oh Tibby, I thought we would never see you again. I thought we would never know what had happened to you."

She hugged Tibby so hard that Tibby, meowing in protest, struggled to get down. Reluctantly, Second Mom set her down on the floor. Wasting no time, Tibby sprinted to the kitchen cabinet where her food was stored. Second Mom laughed. "Tibby, I don't know whether to be mad at you for disappearing or be glad that you've come back. I ought to make you go without lunch for being such a naughty cat. But I'm so relieved to see you that I haven't the heart to do any scolding."

Reaching up into the cabinet, she took out a tin of sardines. "I don't know whether you deserve any sardines and cream or not. That's what William had for lunch, though, so you can have some too." William, who had not let Tibby out of his sight since she had come in, meowed hopefully. Second Mom looked at him, laughing again. "All right, all right! I'll give you another helping as well."

She sat two saucers of sardines and two of cream on the floor. The two cats licked them clean. Afterward, purring contentedly, they rubbed their heads on Second Mom's legs in thanks before turning their attention to cleaning their faces. When each was clean to its owner's satisfaction, they bounded down the hall to Second Mom's bed.

Both were exhausted, Tibby from her night out and William from worrying about her. Curling up against one another, they closed their eyes. William sighed in contentment. Then, eyes still closed, he asked, "Where did you go with that cat, Tibby? And why did you take so long to come home?"

Tibby sat up and looked at her brother. "Oh William, I had a terrible night! That cat chased me into a corner of a big dark barn like the one in First Mom's backyard that we were afraid to go into. Every time I tried to leave, he growled and blocked my way. I couldn't escape. I stayed awake all night waiting for him to close his eyes. Finally, this morning, he went to sleep. As soon as he did, I made a beeline for home. I never looked behind.

"When I was in that barn, I thought I would never see you or Second Mom or home again. I thought I would never have sardines and cream again or sleep on Second Mom's bed."

William, sitting up, mulled over Tibby's story for a long moment before saying, "Well, Tibs, I've been telling you that something bad was going to happen. And it did."

"William, you think something bad is going to happen every day. Well, yesterday, something bad did happen. But today, something good happened. I escaped and came back home. Plus we had sardines and cream for lunch."

To show William how happy she felt to be back, she began to lick his face. William decided not to tell her that he had had two helpings of sardines and cream. She might become miffed and stop licking his face. When she had finished, both curled up together again. Before long, they were fast asleep. They slept all afternoon, barely waking in time for supper.

6

An Ending

By the time William and Tibby were five months old, they had become more cats than kittens. But Second Mom still called them her little kitties. By then, they had become so big that they had to sleep on a rug instead of a basket outside Second Mom's door. They had explored all the nooks and crannies Second Mom's house had to offer. They had poked their noses into all the cabinets and closets. They had made themselves at home on all the couches, chairs, and beds. Gradually, they began spending more and more time outdoors. Second Mom's yard—filled with butterflies, bugs, and birds, along with grass, trees, and shrubs—never failed to thrill them. The field beyond the backyard was the perfect place to wait for an unsuspecting mouse to scurry by. The creek bank, overgrown with weeds and tall grass, beckoned insistently.

One place, however, William and Tibby avoided was the road in front of Second Mom's house. They didn't like the noise of the beasts roaring by. The sound frightened Tibby so much that even if she were in the field beyond the backyard when she heard it, she raced to the sundeck, diving under it and refusing to come out for at least five minutes. Unlike Tibby, William did not race for the sundeck when he heard a beast go by, but he did pause to assure himself that the noise was staying in the road where it properly belonged. Unless, of course, the beast belonged to Second Mom and Hon. Even then, he kept a respectable distance.

Second Mom was glad that Tibby was frightened of the sound that the trucks and cars made. She didn't have to worry about her wandering into the road and getting hurt or killed by traffic. She also figured that if Tibby stayed well away from the road, so would William because he never ventured anywhere unless Tibby went too.

Second Mom found it amusing that of her two cats, Tibby, not William, was the leader. "You'd think," she said to Hon, "that being the male and bigger, William would boss Tibby around. But no. It's Tibby who decides what games they're going to play. And she's the one who chooses what tree they're going to climb. If they go to the bank or the field, she's the one leading the way. William just galumphs along behind her, going along for the trip.

"Don't you, William, my little galumphy, wumpy glum-wum?" she added, turning to William, who had just meandered into the kitchen. He had been catnapping on the coffee table in the living room, one eye half-open and one ear half-raised in case anything interesting happened. When he heard Second Mom mention his name, he had decided to investigate in case a snack of sardines and cream was somehow involved.

He meowed to show his agreement with what Second Mom had said, even though he had not the slightest idea what she had been talking about. He knew, though, that if she mentioned his name, whatever she said had to be right.

As William and Tibby had grown from kittens into cats, so had the year grown older, turning from late winter into spring, and then into early summer, with its warm weather and long days. By June, the two cats were staying out longer and longer in the afternoons and later and later in the evenings. Sometimes Second Mom didn't call them in until time for bed.

Hon warned Second Mom that the cats shouldn't be out after dark. "There are lots more foxes and coyotes around here than there used to be. Especially coyotes. Sometimes I hear them hunting in the back part of the field," he reminded her. "Just because William and Tibby are larger now doesn't mean one can't get them. Or they might wander into the road one night and get hit by a car or truck. It's hard for a driver to see an animal in the dark in enough time to avoid hitting it."

Second Mom knew Hon was right. For a while, she called William and Tibby in as soon as the sun went down. But as the days passed, she began to lessen in her diligence. Soon the two cats were staying out as late as ever. The late hours outside suited William and Tibby fine because cats by nature are night creatures who like to sleep in the day and prowl and hunt at night.

Hon cautioned Second Mom again about the late hours William and Tibby were keeping. Second Mom sighed. "I know. But this is their first summer. Everything is new and exciting. It's such a joy watching them outside at night. They have so much fun chasing the lightning bugs and jumping up on the window screens after the moths. And I keep an eye on them to make sure they stay close to the house. If I can't see them when I look out the kitchen window, I call them until they come. Besides, it will be winter soon enough. Then they won't have these beautiful evenings to enjoy. They won't want to go out as much when the weather's cold. Especially if it's raining or snowing."

One evening, as dark began to fall, William and Tibby, who were on the sundeck swatting at lightning bugs, spied a rabbit crossing the yard from the direction of the creek. Ears grew erect and bodies taut as they fastened their eyes on it.

The rabbit spotted the cats at about the same time they noticed it. Realizing that it was the object of not one cat's attention but *two,* it bolted as fast as it could toward the field beyond the backyard. In a flash, William and Tibby were after it. This time, William, being faster, led the way. Before the two cats realized it, they had crossed the field and were in the one beyond it.

Halfway across the second field, Tibby paused. She didn't like being so far away from home. Moreover, they were headed toward a road that lay beyond the second field. Not wanting to leave William alone, though, she resumed the chase behind her brother.

Diving under a fence, the rabbit dashed across the road, William close behind. When Tibby saw William wriggle under the fence, she stopped again. "William," she called, "William, come back! Watch out for the road!"

But William kept running, too excited by the chase to heed Tibby's warning or the noise that was roaring toward him. He was halfway across the road when—*zoom!*—a car plowed into his side. He bounced off the car, landing on the grassy roadside, where he lay still.

When Tibby saw the car strike William, her eyes widened and her heart stood still for a moment. Then she turned and galloped home, not daring to looking back. Once there, she hid under the sundeck, her heart beating with fear, waiting for William. But William didn't come. Before long, she heard Second Mom open the back door.

"William . . . Tibby . . . where are you? Time to come in!" Shooting out from under the sundeck, Tibby, ears laid back, dashed toward the steps. When Second Mom saw her, she smiled. "There you are, Tibby! Where's William? Isn't he with you?" She held the door open for Tibby, her eyes scanning the yard.

Tibby paused on the top step to look back. William, however, was still nowhere to be seen. Wondering what was keeping him so long, she entered the house. Second Mom continued scanning the yard, calling "William . . . William . . . where are you? Come on home. Time to come in."

But William did not bound across the yard from the field, as Second Mom expected him to. After a few seconds, Second Mom closed the door. Turning to Tibby, she said, "That brother of yours! Where could he be? Well, let's get ready for bed. Maybe by the time I get through brushing you, he'll be at the back door."

But he wasn't. Tibby had to sleep alone on the rug outside Second Mom's door. As she settled herself down for the night, curling around herself instead of around William as she usually did, Second Mom said, "Don't worry, Tibby! William will come scratching at my bedroom window in the middle of the night wanting in! Just wait and see if he doesn't."

William, though, didn't come scratching at Second Mom's bedroom window in the middle of the night. Nor was he at the back steps the next morning. By now both Second Mom and Tibby were worried. While Second Mom fixed Tibby's breakfast, Tibby checked every room of the house to make sure that William was not in one of the corners or under one of the dressers or beds or chairs.

When Second Mom called her to breakfast, Tibby reluctantly gave up the search for the time being. But she couldn't eat. A meal without William next to her, purring in satisfaction, was no pleasure. After nibbling a few bites of her food, she trooped despondently into the room. On the floor lay William's mouse. She sniffed it desolately, trying to spur her interest. Her attempt was futile. She was too heavyhearted to play with toys, especially one of William's. Since she had not slept well the night before, she decided to take a morning nap. Maybe she would be able to sleep better on Second Mom's soft bed, even if William wasn't there to curl up with her.

In the meanwhile, Second Mom busied herself with chores. "William could have wandered off by himself for a while. Cats often do, especially males," she had said to Hon that morning before he left for work. "Tibby disappeared one afternoon, remember. She didn't show up until lunch the next day. I'll keep busy until he shows up."

She was cleaning the kitchen while singing along with the radio when she heard a car drive up. Drying her hands on a towel, she glanced out the living room to see who had decided to pay her an unexpected visit. To her surprise, she saw Hon climbing out of his car. She watched as he walked to the front porch. A moment later, she heard the front door open.

"What are you doing home so soon?" she said as he entered the living room. "It's only ten o'clock."

Hon looked at her a moment without speaking. Then taking her by the hand, he led her to the couch. "Sit down, sweetheart. I need to talk to you."

"What's wrong? Did something happen at work?" Concern written across her face, Second Mom peered up at him as she sat down.

He hesitated a second before saying abruptly, "I found William this morning on the way to work. He was lying on the side of the road. He'd been hit by a car."

Second Mom grew still. Then taking a deep breath, she said, "He's dead, isn't he?"

Sitting down beside her, Hon took her in his arms. "Yes, he's dead."

Closing her eyes, Second Mom sat without moving for a moment. Then she looked toward the road. "Where is he now?"

"I put him in the trunk. I went on to work because I couldn't decide whether to bury him without telling you what had happened or to tell you the truth. Everyone at the office said that not knowing what had happened to him would be worse than knowing. So I came back home to tell you."

"Is he still in the trunk?"

"Yes."

"I want to see him."

Hon paused before answering. "I'll bring him to you. But you have to promise not to look at him. Get me a towel. I'll wrap him in it."

"Why can't I look at him? Is he all smashed in?"

"No. He has a little bit of blood on his mouth and nose. I just want you to remember him the way he was when he was alive, that's all."

Second Mom looked at Hon. Then she glanced out the window at his car. Turning back toward Hon, she said, "All right. I promise not to look at him." Rising from the couch, she went to the linen closet in the hall and pulled out the biggest, fluffiest towel she had. Walking back into the living room, she handed it to Hon. "Take this. It's my nicest one. William deserves the best." Then she sat back down on the couch, keeping her eyes away from the living room window and rocking her body back and forth to keep from crying.

Hon returned shortly carrying the body. It was completely wrapped in the towel with the ends of the towel tucked neatly in. Handing it to Second Mom, he reminded her, "Remember, you promised not to look."

"I won't," she promised again, taking the towel-wrapped body from him and cradling it in her arms. Then she burst into sobs.

Sitting down beside her, Hon wrapped her in his arms again as best he could. "I'm so sorry. I'm so sorry."

After a few minutes, Second Mom stopped crying. Taking Hon's handkerchief, she wiped her eyes. "I want to bury him along the fence line by the creek bank. He loved being down there." While Hon was digging William's grave, Second Mom held William's body, talking to it as if William could hear. "I love you, my little glum-wum. I always will. I promise you that Tibby and I will never forget you, not for one moment. And I know that one day we'll be with you again." Hugging the body to her chest, she began crying anew.

When Hon returned from the creek, Second Mom stood up. Hon reached out to take William's body. But Second Mom said, "No, I want to carry him down. It's the last time I'll hold him for a long while."

At the creek bank, Second Mom looked silently at the hole Hon had dug. Then she looked at the trees and the brushy undergrowth on the bank and at the tall grass waving in the field, still without saying anything. Taking a deep breath, she gave the towel-wrapped bundle a last hug before handing it to Hon, who knelt and gently placed it in the grave. Standing back up, he took the shovel and covered the body with dirt as Second Mom watched silently, bereft of tears. Nor did she cry or speak on the way to the house. But as they were going in the back door, she paused and looked back toward the creek. Turning to Hon, she said, "I should have woken Tibby and shown her William's body. How is she ever going to understand what's happened?"

A Beginning

Aᴄᴛᴇʀ ʙᴇɪɴɢ ʜɪᴛ ʙʏ ᴛʜᴇ car, William knew nothing for a long while. He didn't even feel his body land on the grass at the side of the road. When he finally roused, he found himself in a large field, much like the one beyond Second Mom's backyard. He had no idea how he had gotten there. The last thing he recalled was chasing a rabbit across a road with Tibby close behind him, shouting at him to stop. Now she was nowhere to be seen. What had happened to her? And where was that rabbit? More important, where was home?

With these thoughts whirling inside his head, William stood up and glanced around. Beyond the field, he saw a woman standing outside a square white house. But the woman was not Second Mom. She looked much too short and plump. Then he heard her calling, "William . . . William . . ." William started in surprise. How did she know his name? Well, no matter. If she knew him, she might be able to help him find his way home.

As he wound his way through the field toward the woman, he noticed that the grass he was treading on was the greenest he had ever seen. And the most ticklish to his paws. And the sweetest smelling to his nose. It was also overrun with grasshoppers leaping higher and crickets chirping more loudly and beetles chewing faster than any he had ever run across before. Why hadn't Second Mom ever taken Tibby and him here? What fun they could have had stalking and chasing and pouncing and leaping!

Bedazzled by the smell and feel of the grass, as well as by the extraordinary amount of life teeming in it, William continued his steady pace toward the woman. He paused momentarily when he felt a small creature scamper onto one of his front paws. Glancing down, he saw a mouse, the fattest, sleekest mouse he had ever had the pleasure of meeting, looking up at him. Its soft, dark eyes held no fear, only curiosity. Suddenly, as if it had thought better of itself, it scurried away. William considered giving chase but decided against it when he heard the woman call again, "William . . . William . . ."

Reaching the woman's yard, he paused, his attention riveted to a tree at the yard's edge. And for good reason. It had the greenest leaves he had ever seen. Even better, its branches were full of plump birds, much plumper than those in the trees in Second Mom's yard, all singing louder and more beautifully than any he had ever heard. And their feathers! Never had he seen feathers so brilliantly colored—fiery orange, sunshine yellow, emerald green, indigo blue, dark purple, and vivid scarlet. He thought momentarily about trying to snag a tail feather from an unsuspecting bird to show Tibby later, but the woman's insistent call urged him on.

When William finally reached the woman, he noticed that she had short, curly red hair, blue eyes that crinkled at the corners, and a wide, welcoming face. A feeling of security and happiness spread though him just looking at her smile. He butted his head against her legs to say hello. As he did so, the woman bent down and rubbed him behind his ears. "Hello, William. I've been waiting for you."

To his surprise, William understood not just his name but every sound the woman had made. When Second Mom spoke to him, he had to rely mostly on her tone to understand what was being said. He wondered if this woman could understand him. Looking up at her, he said, "Meow, meow?"

The woman laughed. "Yes, William, I can understand every sound you make. Just as you can understand mine. In heaven, every creature understands all the other creatures. God planned it that way."

"Who's God?" William asked.

"God's the Creator of the whole universe and everything in it. He has many names, such as Jehovah, Allah, the Great Spirit, Brahman, to name a few. But all the names refer to the same God, the God that made you and me and the grass and the trees and the birds and the mice. He made everything you've ever seen or felt or heard or tasted or smelled. He lives here in heaven. But you can't see or smell Him or touch or hear Him because He doesn't have a body. He's a spirit. And He knows everything. He's the one who told me to be on the lookout for you today."

William glanced around. "Heaven? Is that where I am? In heaven?"

"Yes, William, that's where you are."

"Well, where is heaven? How far is it from Second Mom's? Is it down the road? How long will I be here?"

"Heaven is no place, William. It just is. And you'll be here forever. You'll never leave."

As William considered the woman's last statement, desolation welled up in his eyes. "You mean I'll never go back home? I'll never see Second Mom and Tibby again?"

Smiling gently, the woman bent down to pat William on the head. "No, William, you won't ever go back home. This is your home now. But you'll see Second Mom and Tibby again. Heaven is the place where all creatures' souls go when they die. When Second Mom dies, her soul will come here. And when Tibby dies, hers will too."

William thought a moment before saying in a quavering voice, "But I miss Second Mom and Tibby. I want to be with them now. I don't want to be in heaven. And what does *die* mean?"

Sitting down on the grass, the woman put William on her lap. William immediately cheered up. He had always liked lying in

Second Mom's lap. And although this woman wasn't Second Mom, her lap fit him just fine.

For a minute or so, the woman stroked William's back. Then she began talking again. "William, heaven is a wonderful place. You have everything you need to be happy here. You have other cats to play with, mice and rabbits to chase, a warm, soft place to sleep, plenty to eat, and someone to love and take care of you. But whether or not you're happy here is up to you.

"You can choose to do nothing but grieve every day, waiting for Second Mom and Tibby to come. Or you can choose to enjoy all that heaven has to offer. If you choose to be happy, Second Mom and Tibby will be here before you know it. You see, time loses its meaning in heaven because here everything is forever. Why, when Tibby and Second Mom arrive, it will seem as if you've been in heaven only a week or so yourself."

William twisted his head around to look at the woman. "But why can't I go home and come back when Tibby and Second Mom do?"

"Because the body you had back there doesn't work anymore, William. Remember chasing a rabbit into the road last night?"

"Yes."

"What do you remember after that?"

"I don't remember anything. I just woke up and here I was. Why did I wake up in heaven and not back home?"

"Because when you ran out into the road after the rabbit, a car hit you. It damaged your body so badly that it couldn't live any longer. All its parts stopped working. That's called *dying*. So your soul left your body and came here to get a new body, one that won't ever get sick or grow old, one that won't ever die. A body that is perfect."

Intrigued by the idea of having a new body, William examined his front paws and legs; next he twisted around to inspect his back legs and tail. After that, he peered down first at his chest and then at his belly. Nothing about his body seemed any different. He was still a black-striped gray and orange cat. His chest and paws were still white, and the orange splotches on his chest and belly seemed to be in the right places. And his tail was still bushy. "I look the same to me," he said. After a moment's reflection, he added, "What's my soul?"

"You're supposed to look the same, William. You're still a solemn-looking, black-striped gray and orange cat. Only you don't ever have to worry again because in heaven, nothing bad happens. And your soul is the part of you that makes you, you, and not Tibby or some other cat. It's the part of you that Second Mom will never be able to replace, no matter how many other cats she has after you. She may find one that looks like you, but she will never find one that is you, one that has your soul."

For a moment, William felt a brief flicker of jealousy at the thought that Second Mom might find a cat to take his place. But the feeling lasted only a moment. It was silly to be jealous. Hadn't this woman told him that he couldn't be replaced?

Suddenly, he frowned. Who was going to take care of him until Second Mom came? The woman must have read his thoughts, for she said, "Now, William, until Second Mom comes, I'm going to take care of you. You see, my job in heaven is to be a cat keeper. Right now, I'm taking care of all of Second Mom's cats who have died. You'll live with them in my house. After Second Mom comes, though, you'll live with her."

"What will you do then?"

"I'll start keeping someone else's cats until that person dies and comes to heaven. Or I might get some cats of my own, cats that died at birth or that were abandoned. Or cats that never had a home or someone to love them. I'll just have to wait and see what is given me.

"But I do know that I'll always be a cat keeper. That's the job I chose when I came here. Because I've always loved cats. I couldn't have any on earth, though. I was allergic to them. I'm not allergic here because my heavenly body is perfect."

William wrinkled his brow, thinking hard about what the woman had said. After a moment, he asked, "Will you brush me every day and let me sleep on a rug outside your bedroom and feed me sardines and cream like Second Mom did?"

Laughing, the woman hugged William. "Yes, William, I'll brush you every night before bed. But you don't have to sleep on a rug outside my bedroom. You can sleep on my bed with the other cats. And you'll be able to have all the cream you want. But no sardines."

William couldn't believe his ears. No sardines? How could heaven be a perfect place if he couldn't have sardines for snacks? The woman explained. "In heaven, sardines do the things that sardines are supposed to do, like swim in the ocean. They aren't killed so that cats can eat them for dinner. In heaven, no creature eats any other creature."

Perturbed, William said, "Are you saying that I can't eat grasshoppers and bugs and mice and rabbits? What's the good of hunting and chasing and pouncing on them if I can't eat them? And what will I eat?"

"A delicious food called Heavenly Delight for Cats. All Second Mom's cats swear by it. Believe me, that's quite a few cats!"

William looked at the house that he was to live in until Second Mom came. From the outside, it seemed small. Exactly how many cats were living in it now? How many more would have to fit in it before Second Mom arrived? The thought of Second Mom brought another question to mind. "What do the other cats call you?"

"They call me Third Mom because I'm taking the place of their Second Mom for a little while. Would you like to call me that too?"

Third Mom was exactly the name that William had in mind. So that problem was easily resolved. But a larger one presented itself. "Do you have a hon like Second Mom does?"

Laughing again, Third Mom gave William a kiss on his nose. "No, I don't have a hon. I have a sweetie pie, though, who, I'm sure, is much like Second Mom's hon. He'll be showing up for supper before long. Right now, he's planting corn. Everyone has to work in heaven. He farms."

William's ears pricked up. Did everyone mean cats? When he lived with Second Mom, all he had had to do was eat, sleep, and play. Afraid of the worst, he asked, "What will my job in heaven be?"

Third Mom's answer was most reassuring. "Your job is to be a cat and do the things that cats do. Like running and jumping and leaping and pouncing. And sleeping and eating. Plus loving me and Sweetie Pie. And waiting for Tibby and Second Mom and Hon."

"Hon? Hon's going to come to heaven?" Perturbed, William shook his head. How could he be happy in heaven if he had to live with Hon?

"Of course, Hon's coming to heaven. Why, Second Mom wouldn't be happy in heaven if she didn't have her hon with her."

This was not good news. Hon had barely tolerated Tibby and him. How would he ever be able to put up with all of Second Mom's cats? And for forever? Third Mom interrupted his worries. "I can tell that you don't appreciate Hon. In heaven, one of the lessons that all creatures have to learn is to get along with all other creatures. So that means that you and Hon will have to make your peace one day.

"Who knows? Maybe Hon will learn to like cats so much that he will even allow all of you to sleep with him and Second Mom in their bed. At first, Sweetie Pie didn't want cats in our bed, but now they all sleep with us. He wouldn't think of having them sleep anywhere else."

Lifting William off her lap, Third Mom stood up. "That's enough questions for now. Time to introduce you to the other cats."

8

Scads and Scads of Cats

THIRD MOM WALKED TO THE back door and opened it. Out swarmed cats, more cats than William had ever seen together at one time. There were black cats and yellow cats, striped cats and calicos. There were plump cats and thin cats, sleek cats and long-haired cats. There were big cats and medium-sized cats, small cats and kittens.

Unknown to William, they had been impatiently waiting behind the closed door to meet him ever since Third Mom had called his name. Now they were eagerly intent on touching their noses to his, butting him gently with their heads, greeting him with their meows. William was overwhelmed. He plopped down with a thump, hiding his face in his paws.

Third Mom interceded. "All right, kitties, give William some breathing room. Introduce yourselves one at a time."

Like the polite creatures they were, the cats immediately backed away. After a few seconds, one stepped forward to introduce itself, then another stepped forward, and then another, until all had touched their noses to his, told him their names, and said, "Glad to meet you. Hope you like heaven."

In turn, William, regaining his feet, said politely to each one, "Pleased to meet you too. I'm sure I'll enjoy being here." Privately, though, he was worried. What a lot of cats for him to remember! First to introduce themselves were the two cats who had been given to Second Mom on her fifth birthday, a gray and white one named Miss Paws and a tan one named Suki. There followed two huge, scruffy stray cats, Black Bart and Big Tig, that Second Mom had adopted when she was a little older. Black Bart was entirely black down to his nostrils and paw pads, while Big Tig, a white cat with black stripes, looked like a menacing miniature tiger.

Next, William met two small black cats, Dorca One and Dorca Two. William had no idea how he was supposed to tell which was One and which was Two, for they looked exactly alike. Every time he encountered one of them would he have to sniff at her to know which Dorca he was dealing with? What if he forgot which smell went with which cat? Would she answer to the wrong name or ignore him? Something told him she would probably choose the latter.

Interrupting his worries, two calicos named Prissy and Callie introduced themselves. Their black, white, and orange fur was arranged in such irregular, huge splotches that William could barely resist laughing when he met them. To his relief, they didn't look so much alike that he couldn't tell them apart. Prissy was large and motherly looking, whereas Callie was smaller boned and looked rather flighty.

Two orange tabby cats, who also looked alike, stood next in line. Each introduced himself as Tom. William was relieved that he wouldn't have to remember which was One and which was Two. Just plain Tom was evidently good enough for both.

Three kittens, all smaller than William, stood last in line. William immediately liked the white kitten called Little Cat and Sweet William, a short-haired, black-striped gray kitten that looked a bit like him. He wasn't too sure about the third one, however.

Although a calico like Prissy and Callie, she was mostly black sprinkled with a smattering of orange. Only her feet, throat, and paws were white. William found her black face set off by white whiskers and startlingly blue eyes most arresting looking. She introduced herself as Neiki, the Crazy Cat, but assured him she would answer to either name. Once satisfied that the proprieties regarding their introduction had been dealt with, she ran behind him and pounced on his tail, tussling at it with her paws and tugging on it with her sharp teeth.

Fending off her advances as best he could, William suddenly felt his stomach growl. He realized that he had eaten nothing since the night before. As if on cue, Third Mom spoke up. "That's plenty of introductions for now. It's growing dark. Time for supper. I bet William is hungry. He slept most of the day, so his stomach is probably empty. Let's go inside."

The cats did not have to be invited twice. As she opened the back door, they swarmed into the house, tumbling over one another and stepping on one another's paws in the process. Shy and unaccustomed to so many cats, especially when they were trying to crowd into the house at the same time, William hung back. Only when all the others had disappeared through the doorway did he cautiously step inside.

Third Mom closed the door behind him. Patting him on the head reassuringly, she said, "Come with me to the kitchen, William, and have the best meal you've ever tasted." William doubted that. Sardines and cream were the best food he had ever tasted. How could Heavenly Delight for Cats be any better?

In the kitchen, William found the other cats lined up, each one standing in front of two bowls. At one end of the line waited two extra bowls. William decided those must be his. Third Mom filled one of the bowls for each cat with what William supposed was Heavenly Delight for Cats. Then she filled the other with a small amount of what William hoped was cream. He cautiously touched his tongue cautiously to the liquid. It was cream! Purring contentedly, he lapped up the rest.

Still hungry, he decided to chance the food in his other bowl. Sniffing it warily, he took the tiniest nibble he could manage in case it proved inedible. But once more, Third Mom was proved right. It was the most delicious food he had ever tasted, much better than sardines, though he hated to admit it. He polished off the Heavenly Delight in short order, the other cats munching, lapping, and purring contentedly along beside him.

After they had finished eating, all the cats, William included, rubbed against Third Mom's legs, purring their thanks for their fine supper. Just like at home, William thought, then felt an overwhelming rush of homesickness. As if reading his mind, Third Mom picked him up for a hug. Immediately, William felt happier.

When she put him down, he wandered into the living room where the other cats were washing all traces of supper from their faces. Knowing his own face could use a good cleaning, he joined in the ritual. After every face had been washed to its owner's satisfaction, the cats relaxed, some on the floor, some on the couch, others on the chairs or in the five cat hammocks scattered around the room. Not yet feeling at home and not wanting to seem too forward by choosing a soft, comfy cushion to reside on, William crouched underneath a small table near the kitchen doorway. While they let their meal digest, Third Mom busied herself in the kitchen.

Suddenly, the back door burst open. A moment later, a man entered the kitchen. William peeked at him from underneath the table. His eyes widened in amazement as he beheld the largest man he had ever seen, much bigger and taller than Hon. Even more impressive was the fact that he didn't have any hair growing on his head. On the other hand, his upper lip was covered with brown hair, so much hair, in fact, that it drooped down each side of his mouth in a tight curl. William couldn't take his eyes off the sight.

Third Mom gave the man a hug. "Hello, sweetie. Did you have a hard day?"

"Not too hard. What's for supper? I'm starved!"

"Your favorite. Imitation meat loaf, green beans, tomatoes, mashed potatoes, and cornbread. And for dessert, blackberry cobbler with cream. I picked the berries this morning. It's almost ready. Go wash up."

Seeing Third Mom and Sweetie Pie together reminded William of Second Mom and Hon. Hon was probably coming through the door about now, and Second Mom was rushing to him to take his briefcase. At the thought, he felt another spell of homesickness, but it lasted only a moment. Mostly, he felt a warm glow, knowing that he was going to be happy here and that one day soon he would see Second Mom and Tibby. Maybe next week. Third Mom had said so.

In the midst of these ruminations, a worrisome thought reared itself. Sweetie Pie hadn't noticed the new cat in the house. Perhaps there were so many cats that another one wasn't that obvious. When he did notice, what would happen if he decided one more was one too many? Where would he go? Out into the vast, endless space of heaven where there would be no one to love him or for him to love? His glum-looking face took on an even glummer aspect.

He need not have worried. Spotting William underneath the table, Sweetie Pie approached him. Bending down, he gave the newcomer a friendly pat. "Hello, stranger. What's your name?" William's voice managed to croak out his name in a nervous quaver. Smiling in reassurance, Sweetie Pie called into the kitchen, "I see we've added another cat to the household. How many does that make now?"

Third Mom, who was busy putting the supper dishes on the dining table, smiled reassuringly at William. "He makes fourteen. With no telling how many more to go."

William held his breath. Fourteen cats in one house and on one bed! He wasn't quite sure how many fourteen was, but it sounded like a whole lot of cats, the same whole lot that were lounging at this moment in Third Mom's living room. Again, he was worried for naught, for as Sweetie Pie was washing up at the kitchen sink, he said, "Fourteen, huh? Won't be long before we'll have to have a bigger bed. And a bigger house."

As Third Mom and Sweetie Pie sat down to eat, William noticed that all the other cats rose and made their way to the dining room, where they sat down in a semicircle around Sweetie Pie's chair, fixing their eyes on him. Concluding that they were staring at Sweetie Pie's amazing-looking head and face, William joined them.

Sweetie Pie ignored them during the meal, concentrating instead on the food on his plate and an occasional remark made by Third Mom. But after he had finished eating, he rose and gave each cat, William included, a rub behind the ears and a tiny bit of imitation meatloaf. William was astounded. Hon had never given him or Tibby anything to eat. Nor had he ever rubbed them behind the ears! Or patted them on the head!

After supper, while Third Mom cleaned the kitchen, the cats assembled themselves in the living room again and began cleaning themselves. Once they were finished, they looked at one another, ears alert and tails twitching. Suddenly without warning, the living room was filled with a swarm of tumbling, pouncing, tussling, and wrestling cats. Amid the melee, Sweetie Pie rested in his recliner, hiding his face behind a newspaper. Every once in a while, he lowered it to glance at the TV screen. Before long, he was fast asleep, snoring softly behind his paper. Just like Hon does, William thought, as he tussled with one of the Toms while trying to keep his tail out of the way of Neiki's teeth.

When Third Mom sat down in her recliner in the living room and picked up a magazine, the cats immediately rushed over to her, tripping over one another to be first in her lap. William was afraid there might not be room enough for all of them, but Third Mom wriggled around until finally they were all in the chair with her. Of course, not all of them ended up in her lap. She wasn't that big. Some had to sit on the back of the chair and some on the arms of the chair. Two were draped over her shoulders. William found himself squeezed in between one side of the chair and one of Third Mom's legs, with Neiki snuggled on top of him.

Once they were settled, the cats filled the room with their contented purring. It wasn't long, though, before Third Mom, gently shooing the cats out of her lap, stood up. Walking over to Sweetie Pie, she shook him awake. "Time to get the kitties ready for bed."

Getting the kitties ready for bed proved to be an assembly-line production. To begin, all the cats lined up in the kitchen. William, taking his cue from the other cats, went to the end of the line. Third Mom then picked up the first cat in the line, one of the Toms, and placed him on the kitchen counter. After brushing his fur vigorously, she peered into his ears and eyes. Next she parted the fur on his neck, muttering as she did so, "Only place for fleas is on the cows and chickens."

Within seconds, she triumphantly uttered a loud "Aha! A flea!" She carefully picked the offending creature off Tom's neck and stared at it in displeasure before dropping it into a jar. Then she peered into the jar. "You know you're not supposed to jump on my cats. I think you need a few more lessons in goodness. Now don't get huffy. You won't have to stay in the jar for long. I'll put you out in the yard after I've checked the other cats. There may be more joining you."

William could have sworn he heard a tiny voice squeak from the jar, "I'm sorry. I'll try to do better. I promise."

Third Mom sniffed. "I'll believe that when I see it."

Only when Third Mom was satisfied than there were no more tangles, fleas, or mites anywhere on Tom did she hand him to Sweetie Pie. Picking up Callie, who was the next cat, she proceeded to give her the same thorough brushing and inspection she had given Tom. William hoped fervently that when his turn came, Third Mom wouldn't find any tiny varmints on him. How embarrassing that would be!

Sweetie Pie's job was to brush the cats' teeth. After giving Tom's teeth a thorough brushing, he picked up a tiny hand vacuum cleaner and proceeded to give Tom's fur an equally thorough vacuuming. William's eyes bugged out. He had never seen such a tiny vacuum before, much less one used to vacuum cats.

He had been terrified of Second Mom's vacuum, hiding under the freezer whenever she took it out of the utility closet. Yet Tom didn't act at all afraid of this one. He stood uncomplaining and still as Sweetie Pie diligently moved the vacuum back and forth over his fur. Nor did any of the other cats seem perturbed when it was their turn to be at the mercy of the vacuum. William hoped that he acted as grown-up as they when it was his turn.

With two worries claiming his attention, he found himself on the counter all too soon. Third Mom must have read his mind. As she parted the fur around his neck, she said, "Let's see what we've got here. You didn't bring any tiny critters with you, did you, William? Probably not. None of the others did." She brushed and searched diligently for what were to William a few tense minutes. Putting the brush down at last and handing him to Sweetie Pie, she exclaimed, "Clean as a whistle, William." William expelled a sigh of relief. One hurdle down and one to go.

To his surprise, the vacuum presented no more of an obstacle to self-respect than had Third Mom's examination for tiny varmints. In fact, the whooshing pull of the vacuum as it traveled over his fur was not only gentle but pleasant. He would be able to hold up his head after all. All that worry for nothing.

After all the cats had been readied for bed, they returned to the living room where they began discussing their day's escapades and adventures. Meanwhile, Sweetie Pie vacuumed up the cat hairs on the counter. Next, he opened the kitchen cabinet and took down a plastic bag. Rattling it to catch the cat's attention, he headed for the living room. "Time for your treat for being good little kitties. Tonight it's Mighty Mice."

William's eyes widened in amazement. Hon had never given Tibby or him a treat. Why, when Second Mom wasn't at home, he sometimes forgot their meals. When that happened, he and Tibby were forced to stand in front of the sardine box to remind him what time it was.

One evening at suppertime, when Second Mom was out and Hon was asleep behind the newspaper in his recliner, he had tired of waiting patiently. Taking a drastic measure, he leaped into Hon's lap. Hon woke up all right, yelling and jumping out of his recliner, arms flailing wildly. Clinging to Hon's shirt and pants in fright, William finally managed to spring to the floor, taking part of Hon's shirt with him. Diving under the couch, he refused to come out until Second Mom returned. Yet here was Sweetie Pie, who had fourteen cats to live with, handing out treats without being asked or reminded!

Sweetie Pie handed each of the cats five "Mighty Mice." All except William began crunching noisily on their treats. William sniffed tentatively at his. To his surprise, they smelled like mice. He bit one to see if it tasted like a mouse. It did! Maybe even better, he decided, as he noisily munched the second one.

As soon as the cats had crunched down their treat, Third Mom announced, "Time to pick up your toys. Then to bed with all of you." William couldn't believe his ears. Toys? Cats pick up toys? Yes, indeed, picking up their toys was exactly what the other cats were doing. All except Suki were carrying pencils, wooden spools, feathered birdies, plastic balls, and other assorted toys in their mouths to a low, black-and-yellow-striped box in a corner of the living room into which they dropped the toys. Even Neiki, Little Cat, and Sweet William were helping.

For some reason, Sweet William had chosen the largest toy of all to tackle, an orange wooden spool that was much larger than his mouth and that weighed almost as much as he did. But he had managed to sink his teeth into it enough to drag it haltingly along the floor to the box. Once there, though, he encountered a problem. He wasn't tall enough to drop the spool into the box without first putting his front paws on the top edge of the box. But he couldn't quite manage to grip the spool in his mouth, lift his head up, and put his front paws on the top edge of the box at the same time.

Prissy finally came to his rescue, picking up the spool with her mouth and dropping it in for him. Sweet William looked as proud as if he had dropped it in himself. William could barely restrain himself from rolling on the floor with laughter. But as none of the other cats were laughing, he thought it best not to either.

After the cats had dropped all the toys in the box, the cats trooped down the hall to Third Mom and Sweetie Pie's bedroom. On the way, Black Bart explained to William about picking up the toys.

"Think how tired Third Mom would be if she had to pick up all our toys every night. She's already tired enough from taking care of us, plus her garden and flower beds, as well as the house and Sweetie Pie. Besides, we're the ones that took them out of the box, so we should be the ones to put them back."

William felt a sense of shame overcome him. He and Tibby had never put their toys away in the toy basket Second Mom kept next to her recliner in the living room. She had picked them up all by herself. Every night. Without complaining either.

Black Bart continued. "I know how you're feeling. All of us have a lot of apologizing to do when Second Mom gets here."

William's ears pricked up at the unfamiliar word. "*Apologizing.* What's that?"

"Saying you're sorry for something you did. Like not picking up your toys or tracking muddy paw prints into the house. Or tearing up the newspaper. Or waking up Second Mom at three in the morning for a snack. Or, worst of all, yowling and howling when you went to the vet. All the way there and back and in between."

William lowered his head in more shame. He and Tibby were guilty of all those infractions. Especially the yowling and howling. And no telling what else they had done. Another thought struck him. "What if Second Mom doesn't believe us when we tell her we're sorry? What if she decides she doesn't want us when she gets to heaven?" He could well see this happening if all of the cats here had treated Second Mom in the thoughtless way that he and Tibby had. He had an idea that they had.

Black Bart smiled reassuringly. "Don't worry. I asked Third Mom that same question once. She said I didn't have to worry because Second Mom knows that cats on earth can't understand about muddy paws and not waking her up at three in the morning for snacks. But in heaven, they can understand about being considerate, so they don't have any excuses for thoughtless behavior."

"Well, if that's so, why didn't Suki help? I didn't notice her putting any toys into the box."

Black Bart snorted. "I can see you don't know Suki very well. She says that since she doesn't play with toys, she shouldn't have to pick them up."

William looked at Black Bart in astonishment. "You mean she never plays with toys. Why not?"

Black Bart shrugged. "She says toys are for kittens. And she's not a kitten. You'll find out that Suki is a law unto herself. You'll never understand her. She has a long way to go."

"Go? Go where?"

"She has a long way to go in earning her halo."

William's ears pricked up again at this second unfamiliar word. *Halo?* What was a halo? By this time, they had reached the bedroom where Third Mom and Sweetie Pie, already dressed in their night clothes, were turning back the blankets and plumping the pillows on the bed. William promptly forgot his question, so excited was he at the prospect of all the cats sleeping together with Third Mom and Sweetie Pie on a soft, cozy bed.

As he was wondering where he would be sleeping on the bed, a wave of grief rolled over him. This wasn't Second Mom's bed, and Tibby wasn't sleeping with him. She was probably sleeping alone on the rug outside Second Mom's bedroom door. He didn't want Third Mom and Sweetie Pie and the other cats to think him ungrateful, but he longed to be back home. Even if he did have to sleep on the rug on the hard floor outside Second Mom's bedroom, at least he would be sharing it with Tibby and Second Mom would be there in the morning when he woke up.

Just as William was about to burst out in a torrent of grieving meows, Big Tig's voice sounded in his ear. "I say, old man, buck up. The first night's the hardest. But since you can't go back home, you have to make the best of it. It's not as if you're never going to be with Second Mom again."

Swallowing his meows, William flashed a grateful look at Big Tig. By that time, the bed had been arranged to Third Mom's satisfaction. Taking off her house shoes and robe, she climbed in, followed by Sweetie Pie. After she had drawn the blankets over them, Third Mom raised up and looked at the cats. Patting the blankets, she said, "All right, you can get up now."

The cats immediately jumped on the bed. For a while, there was mass confusion as fourteen cats tried to find a place to sleep at the same time. Some chose the foot of the bed, some squeezed between the headboard and pillows, and some snuggled between Third Mom and Sweetie Pie. A few unfortunate latecomers were forced to lie on the edge of the bed.

Fortunately William was able to secure a spot between Third Mom and Sweetie Pie. Next to him lay Neiki. After all the cats had settled themselves and quietness and stillness had fallen over the bed, Third Mom reached up and turned off the lamp.

William closed his eyes. Feeling drowsiness overwhelm him, he gave one last little wiggle to make sure he was as comfortable as he could be. But he couldn't go to sleep. Neiki kept fidgeting, turning this way and that, sighing in frustration every few seconds. As he opened his mouth to tell her to be still for goodness' sake, she stood up and began attacking Third Mom's and Sweetie Pie's blanketed feet. At first, Third Mom and Sweetie Pie moved their feet out of Neiki's way. When this stratagem failed, they kept their feet perfectly still, hoping Neiki would finally tire of leaping on feet that didn't fight back. That ploy didn't work either. Finally, Sweetie Pie said, "Settle down, Neiki, or I'm going to put you out in the barn with the cows and chickens!" William decided that being put out with the cows and chickens must be bad, for Neiki quieted at once, squeezing back down next to William and lying still.

Sighing in relief, William closed his eyes. He had had a long day. Suddenly, he opened his eyes. He had never asked Black Bart what a halo was. He would have to remember to find out first thing in the morning. Snuggling a little deeper into the bedclothes, he closed his eyes again. Almost immediately, he was asleep, lulled by the gentle snores of Third Mom, Sweetie Pie, and the other cats.

9

A Bad Start

WILLIAM WOKE THE NEXT MORNING dimly aware of an unaccustomed weight on his back. Glancing around, he realized with a start that he was lying in a valley of blankets. Then he remembered where he was. He had spent the night between Third Mom and Sweetie Pie. He craned his head around to see what was lying on top of him. It was Neiki, sprawled on her back, her legs in the air, soundly asleep.

At the sight, homesickness once more flooded him. He longed to be curled up next to Tibby on their rug, waiting for Second Mom to wake and give them breakfast. His longing took a seat to a more pressing concern when Neiki rolled over and began cleaning his neck vigorously. Turning on his side, he dislodged her from her perch. Righting herself, she stared unblinkingly into his eyes. "Hi!"

William, who had been on the verge of telling her to go away, couldn't bear to dampen the enthusiasm in her eyes. Instead, he said, "Sshh! I think the others are still asleep."

Neiki, switching her tail in acknowledgment, promptly lay down beside him, burying her face in his side. When William tried to make a little wriggle room between them, she lifted her head. "We have to be still until Third Mom and Sweetie Pie get up. It's the rule. Or tonight we'll be in the barn with the cows and chickens!"

Sighing in exasperation, William put his head on his paws to wait for Third Mom and Sweetie Pie to awaken. He did not have to wait long. A minute or so later, he felt a stir and then a big heave on his left side as Sweetie Pie emerged from the blankets. Taking their cue from him, the other cats also began to stir, as did Third Mom. Rising from the bed, she yawned and stretched. Turning to the cats, she announced, "Breakfast." She no more had the words out of her mouth than the cats, William included, were stampeding to the kitchen in a melee of pumping legs and quivering tails.

And so began William's second day in heaven. And a good day it was, just as Third Mom had promised. A day filled with sleeping, eating, playing, leaping, and pouncing—all the activities that had occupied his days at Second Mom's.

There were a few minor differences, however, between the two moms. Just like Second Mom, Third Mom let the cats make themselves at home on all the chairs, couches, and beds. But she allowed them to lie on Sweetie Pie's recliner too. Hon's had been strictly off limits. She also permitted the cats to investigate all the closets and cabinets and climb on all the desks, tables, and counters, just as Second Mom had. However, unlike Hon, Sweetie Pie didn't yell if he saw a cat on the kitchen counter. He merely lifted the cat off the counter before wiping it clean with a damp cloth.

The two houses were different too. The utility room in Third Mom's house had a small doorway with a flap over it at floor level. "It's a cat door," explained one of the Toms. "Third Mom would never get any chores done without it. She'd have to spend all day at the door letting us in and out. And since we can go out whenever we want to, we don't have to have litter boxes. We have the whole outdoors. Except for Third Mom's flower beds." Tom concluded this last remark with a stern look at William.

"Yeah," said the other Tom. "Can you imagine having to empty and clean fourteen litter boxes a day?" William couldn't. He was so entranced by the door that he spent good part of his second afternoon at Third Mom's going in and out of it. By suppertime, he was so worn out that he could barely eat.

Third Mom's house also had a room designed exclusively for cats, with walkways and ledges to climb and sprawl on and nooks to hide in. "If it's raining, we can climb and jump and pounce, just like we were outside. And whenever we want to be alone, we can curl up in one of the hidey holes," Black Bart said. William made a mental note to become better acquainted with the room. Like whenever he wanted to escape from Neiki.

He decided that if he couldn't live with Second Mom and Tibby, living in heaven with Third Mom was next best. Not that there weren't a few challenges. First, he had to learn thirteen cat faces, as well as thirteen cat names, plus remember which name belonged to which cat. By the end of his first week, though, he had mastered most of the names and faces.

But try as he would, he simply could not remember which Dorca number, one or two, went with which Dorca face. This failing was most unfortunate, for both Dorcas tended to become miffed if addressed by the wrong name, huffing in indignation while walking haughtily away, leaving the offending cat futilely calling out the correct name. William's only consolation was that even Third Mom sometimes called them by the wrong number. If she couldn't always tell them apart, how could he possibly be expected to?

His relationship with Miss Paws and Callie did not get off to a good start either. One morning, at the end of his first week in heaven, as the two cats were ambling down the front walk engrossed in a private conversation, completely oblivious to the rest of the world, he decided to ambush them. Slinking behind the shrubs at the end of the walk, he crouched and waited. As they drew nearer, he wriggled his back end, his claws seeking a better grip in the earth. When the two cats drew near, he leaped from the shrubs. Pouncing on their tails, he meowed in his loudest, fiercest voice, "Boo!"

Fur raised and backs arched, the two victims shrieked in fear and outrage. Bolting for the nearest tree, they climbed to its top branch before recovering their wits. Glancing down, they drew back, horrified to discover how far up they were. Equally horrified at their unexpected reaction, William ran to the tree, remembering the occasion he had found himself in the same predicament. Peering up at the two cats, he called up contritely, "I'm sorry. I didn't mean to scare you so badly. Please come down. I promise I won't do that again."

Looking down again and tightening their grip on the tree, the two cats shook their heads violently. Miss Paws meowed in a terrified quaver, "It's too far down. We'll fall."

"No, you won't," William assured them. "I was up that far once. And I got down all by myself. I just slid downward a little at a time."

Despite William's entreaties, the two cats refused to come down, clinging desperately to the tree while meowing pitifully for help. In the meantime, Black Bart had wandered up to see what all the commotion was about. He was soon joined by Big Tig, who wanted to find out why William and Black Bart were looking at the top of the tree with looks of consternation on their faces. Before long the rest of the cats had gathered round the tree. Even Suki, who had seen the commotion through the living room window, had come outside to investigate. They stared openmouthed at the drama unfolding above them. Seeing none of them making a move to help matters, Miss Paws wailed down, "For heaven's sake, don't just sit there. Go get Third Mom."

The cats looked at each another, but none budged. Finally, one of the Dorcas spoke up. "You go, Sweet William. You're the littlest."

"Yeah, you go, Sweet William," some of the other cats chimed in.

Sweet William shook his head. Like the others, he didn't want to take a chance on missing any further developments. Besides, it was big vacuum day in the house, and he hated the big vac. Although none of the cats minded Sweetie Pie's hand vacuum, they all feared the big vac's fearsome noise and suction power, scattering in all directions as soon as Third Mom dragged it from the utility closet. In spite of her explanations that the vacuum was only a machine and would not harm them, the cats remained convinced that its sole mission in life was to suck them up by their tails.

At Sweet William's refusal, the other cats looked at one another. If he refused to go, then who was going to go? An interminable silence held sway. Finally, Suki spoke up in her long, slow drawl. "I think William should go. He started all this in the first place."

William hung his head. Suki was right. It was his duty to go. But he also felt it was his duty to stay with Miss Paws and Callie, occasionally throwing them what nuggets of comfort he could.

Big Tig settled the matter. "No, William should stay here with Miss Paws and Callie. I'll go get Third Mom." William flashed him a look of gratitude as off he sped around the corner of the house.

While Big Tig was gone, the other cat took bets on whether Third Mom would be able to talk the two cats down or whether she would have to get a ladder and go up after them. Most were betting on the ladder. They knew that there was no way that they themselves would climb down the tree, so they didn't see Miss Paws or Callie doing so either. Neiki doubted that even Third Mom and a ladder could get them down. The cats were much too high up in the tree. It looked like a job for Sweetie Pie.

Within minutes, Big Tig reappeared with Third Mom in tow. When she saw how high the two cats were, she tended to be of the same opinion as Neiki. Rescuing the two cats looked like a job for Sweetie Pie. But he wouldn't be home for at least three or four hours. So she would have to get them down herself. Otherwise, she would have to listen to Miss Paws and Callie for hours meowing for help. She couldn't bear that.

Fortunately, Miss Paws and Callie weren't privy to Third Mom's reservations. When they saw Third Mom round the corner of the house, they breathed a sigh of relief. Third Mom would rescue them. She could do anything. She had never let them down before and she wouldn't now.

"Third Mom," they meowed, "thank goodness you came. Get us down. We're so scared. And it's William's fault."

Peering up, Third Mom smiled reassuringly at them. "No, it's my fault. I forgot to tell William not to play hide-and-pounce with you." Turning to William, she whispered, "They're very high strung, you see. The least thing sets them off."

After giving William a consoling pat on the head, she called up to the two cats above her, "Don't be frightened, little kitties. You know nothing bad can happen to you in heaven. Just slide down slowly. You'll be all right. God will take care of you. All you have to do is trust Him. Come on now. You can do it."

The two cats shook their heads emphatically. When they weren't high in a tree, believing God would take care of them was no problem. But having faith when they were as high as they were was another matter. Better to let Third Mom rescue them. They would trust in God again when they put paw to ground.

Realizing that her pleas were of no avail, Third Mom sighed in exasperation. "I guess I'm going to have to go up after them. I could go find Sweetie Pie, but he's busy mowing hay. I hate to bother him." The cats murmured agreement. Squaring her shoulders in resolution, she set out at a fast pace to the shed, followed by a few of the cats, their tails twitching in excitement. Disappearing into the darkness of the shed, Third Mom reappeared a few moments later dragging a tall ladder with her.

Propping it against the tree, she drew a deep breath. Looking up at the two cats while putting one foot on the ladder's bottom rung, she told herself, "I know I can do this. God is with me. If I use all my wits and the common sense that He gave me, I can get them down. Even if I can't bear heights."

Taking a deep breath, she slowly started up the ladder, neither looking down or up, her attention focused on her hands and feet. Up, up she climbed, one rung at a time, hand and foot, hand and foot until she was a few rungs from the top. Expelling a deep breath, there she stopped. Below, the cats milled anxiously, attention riveted on the ladder. Above, Miss Paws and Callie were watching just as anxiously, their claws still gripping the branch where they perched.

Slowly and carefully, Third Mom reached for the farthest branch that she could touch with one hand. Then just as slowly and carefully, she put one foot on the branch nearest the ladder. Her other hand and foot followed. She was on the tree! From there, she advanced upward as she had on the ladder, one branch at a time, hand by hand, foot by foot, until she could reach out and touch the two cats reassuringly. "Stay calm, little girls. I'm going to pick you up one at a time and put you on my shoulders. Then we're going to go down together. Just hang on tight." To herself she muttered, "Now comes the tricky part." Climbing down with two scared cats at the same time, both gripping their claws into her shoulders, wasn't going to be fun. But she was going to climb the tree only once. That she had already made up her mind about.

On the ground, the other cats held their breaths as Third Mom lifted first Callie, who was closest, and then Miss Paws from their precarious perch and put them on her shoulders. They watched silently as Third Mom then sought for the farthest branch she could reach below with one foot. Thus she slowly descended the tree as she had climbed up, one foothold and handhold at a time, the two cats holding fast to her shoulders with their claws.

Within minutes, the three were on the ladder. Third Mom took a deep breath before prying each cat from her shoulder and setting it on the top rung. She looked at them reassuringly again. "You can climb down by yourselves now." Without further ado, she rapidly descended the remaining rungs, sagging in relief as she finally felt the ground beneath her feet. The two cats quickly followed, ending their rescue by jumping to the ground once they were halfway down the ladder.

All the other cats, except William, crowded around Miss Paws and Callie, meowing excitedly. "You sure were high up!"

"Were you scared?"

"Did you close your eyes on the way down?"

"I bet you were glad to see Third Mom with that ladder."

"I knew Third Mom would save you. She can do anything."

Ignoring their comments, the two marched over to William. They slowly looked him up and down as he stood shamefaced before them. At last, drawing themselves up to their full height, they spit and then hissed emphatically, "DON'T EVER DO THAT AGAIN!"

He didn't.

10

Learning the Hard Way

Fortunately, William's experiences with the other cats were of the more agreeable sort. Being a personable, soft-spoken cat, he quickly made friends with Big Tig and Black Bart. They became his favorite playmates, willing to run and leap and pounce with him to his content. And Sweet William, an adorable kitten, all fluffy and cuddly, who was forever falling over his own feet, entertained William endlessly. He never tired of watching the kitten's playful antics as he scuffled with yarn balls almost as large as he or tussled with the dining room drapes, determined to show them who was boss.

Most of all, he never tired of being a partner in Sweet William's favorite game, which was hide-and-pounce. When Sweet William sprang from his hiding place among the shrubs, William had to work hard to keep himself from laughing at his tiny, squeaky "Boo!" Instead, he pretended to be frightened, jumping straight up in the air and huffing up his fur to the kitten's unfailing delight.

No matter how hard he tried, though, he could never convince Sweet William that the kitten was not named after him. "You see, you were born first," he would patiently explain. "You lived with Second Mom for a while. Then you died and came to heaven to live with Third Mom. A long time afterward, I was born and came to live with Second Mom. Then I also died and came to live with Third Mom in heaven. Since I was born after you, you couldn't have been named after me. It's the other way around. I was named after you."

Sweet William would nod in agreement. "Yes, William, I understand." At that, William would smile, thinking he had finally convinced Sweet William of the facts. His smile always vanished, however, for Sweet William never failed to add, "But I was only five weeks old when I died. And you were five months old. So you're older, which means I was named after you." Pleased that he had figured the whole matter out, off he would gambol, proud to be William's namesake. William finally concluded that Sweet William's brain was not yet big enough to follow the logic of the matter and gave up any further attempt at explanation. Second Mom could sort the matter out with Sweet William when she arrived.

Little Cat proved more difficult to get to know. Easily distracted, she had an unnerving habit of wandering off in the middle of a conversation to chase a butterfly, swat at a leaf, or investigate a bit of fluff. Sometimes she became so absorbed in her distractions that she forgot about mealtime. Prissy, her mother, would have to find her and remind her that it was time to eat. William learned not to be offended if she meandered away while he was talking to her, a faraway look in her eyes. It wasn't that she didn't find his company enjoyable. But that caterpillar crawling through the grass demanded investigation.

William also had to make allowances for the two Toms, who were, at best, grumpy and grouchy in the mornings. After approaching them a few times for a friendly chat before breakfast and being met with nothing but grumps and growls, he realized that it was best not to talk to them until they had eaten and even better to wait until after ten. To be on the safe side, sometimes he even waited until eleven before venturing a "Good morning" to them.

Suki was the hardest one to make friends with. He could never think of anything amusing or interesting to say to her. The first time he approached her, the only conversational tidbit he could think to offer her, after clearing his throat nervously, was "Great day, isn't it?" Instead of agreeing, as William expected, in the conventionally polite way with a hearty "Yes, indeed, a great day, no doubt about it" or even a mild "Sure is," she looked at him unblinkingly with her green eyes and yawned. Feeling like a silly kitten totally lacking in experience or wisdom, he slunk away, vowing never to talk to her again.

However, politeness occasionally demanded that he at least acknowledge her presence with a meow or two. But try as he would, her imperious air coupled with her complete disregard of him never failed to tie his tongue into knots and reduce his brain to mush. As a result, all of his conversational attempts failed miserably, never going beyond the feeble "Great day" he had offered the first time.

As for Neiki, William had hoped that once the novelty of his presence wore off, her attentions might lessen. But after he had been at Third Mom's three weeks, she still insisted on eating next to him, sleeping next to him, and dodging his every footstep when he was awake. One day while playing leap-and-chase with Big Tig and Black Bart, he grew so exasperated with her presence that he could stand it no longer. Turning on her, he said, "Why don't you quit tagging along behind me all the time? You're not big enough to play with me and Big Tig and Black Bart. Go play with the other girls."

Neiki drew back, a stricken look in her eyes. Without uttering a meow, she turned away. Head and tail lowered in dejection, she trudged to the back porch steps and sat down on the bottom step. Sunning herself on the back porch, Prissy had heard William's cruel remarks. She immediately hurried over to Neiki. Sitting down next to her, she began licking her face and neck, trying to comfort her.

As soon as the words were out of his mouth, William felt sick. How could he have been so heartless? After all, Neiki's only crime was to adore him. Seeing Prissy trying to console her only made him feel worse. He wanted to apologize, but he was afraid she and Prissy might rebuff him. Besides, never in his life had he apologized for anything, so he wasn't sure what to say. "I'm sorry" didn't seem quite good enough.

He looked at Big Tig and Black Bart. To his shame, they were glaring at him with stern disapproval. Unable to stand such unspoken censure from the two cats whose approval he most wanted, he slunk under the back porch. Later that day, Prissy, who acted as mother cat not only to Little Cat but to all the other cats as well, gently reproved him. "What you said to Neiki, William, was hurtful. Be kind to her. She's new here too. She came here right before you did. When she arrived, she cried for days because she missed Second Mom so much. You're the first real friend she's made here. Before you came, she was kind of an outsider.

"The two Toms hang out together, as do Big Tig and Black Bart. Callie and Miss Paws are inseparable. And you never see Dorca One without Dorca Two. Suki doesn't seem to need a close friend, although she does try to be a mother to Sweet William. He was only a little over a month old when he arrived, with not the slightest idea about how to be a cat. Suki took him in hand, showed him how to clean himself properly, how to use the cat door, things like that. She even lets him sleep curled up next to her at night.

"And I have Little Cat. I try to be a mother to Neiki too, but she wants a cat of her own, like the rest of us. I had hoped she and Sweet William might hit it off, but I think he's a little intimidated by her. She's so rambunctious. But she's really taken quite a shine to you."

William felt worse. Determined to apologize, even if he said the wrong words, he went in search of Neiki. He found her curled up on Third Mom's bed, head on her front paws, staring out the window. Looking up when William entered the room, she tensed, as if expecting another barrage of hurtful meows.

Knowing he was the cause of her wariness, William inwardly winced. He jumped onto the bed next to her. Swallowing hard, he said, "I'm sorry for what I said this afternoon, Neiki. I won't ever say anything like that to you again. You can follow me around all you want. Even if I trip over you, I won't lose my temper. I promise. Just please forgive me."

Neiki looked at him with a sweet smile. "That's all right, William. I forgive you. Besides, it was my fault. I'm always pestering you. You just got tired of it, that's all. I won't get in your way again."

William said gruffly, "You get in my way all you want. I shall consider it an honor."

"Oh William, you say the funniest things," said Neiki, snuggling against him and laughing.

From that time on, William let Neiki sleep as close to him as she chose, even if she usually ended up sleeping on top of him, legs in the air. And just as he had promised, he allowed her to eat next to him at every meal and to follow him as closely as she wanted, even if he tripped over her.

He even let her tussle with his tail and pounce on his back as long as she did not tussle and pounce too hard, which, as excitable as Neiki was, was most difficult for her to keep in mind.

When she did forget, William simply said, "Calm down, Neiki. Or you'll have to go out to the barn with the cows and chickens." Although he had no intention of carrying out the threat, he had learned that this warning settled her down immediately. She was terrified of the cows and chickens.

After regaining control of herself, she would snuggle up to William, saying, "I'm sorry, William. I don't know why you put up with me."

William was always quick to reassure her. "Oh, you're not so bad." At those words, Neiki would give a deep purr of affection and contentment.

And so the days passed, turning into weeks, the weeks into months, and the months into years. But in all that time, William never forgot Second Mom and Tibby. Sometimes in the midst of whatever he was doing, he would stop, suddenly yearning for the gentle touch of Second Mom's hand or the soft sound of her voice. Or he would be overcome with memories of Tibby's long, soft hair and her beautiful tawny eyes. At those moments, he sought out Third Mom to ask, "Is today the day? Are Tibby and Second Mom coming today?"

Third Mom, who heard questions like this every day from one cat or another, always stopped whatever she was doing to say, "No, William, today isn't the day. But someday, I promise."

Then she would pick him up, giving him a hug and a tidbit before saying, "Go play now. Be happy."

Growing in Goodness

BESIDES THE BEWILDERING ARRAY OF cat names, cat faces, and cat quirks to contend with the first week or so in heaven, William also had to absorb a few rules. Some he learned with no trouble. The rule forbidding wiggling around or talking in bed after the lights were out and before Third Mom and Sweetie Pie woke up in the morning posed no difficulty. In fact, every morning or so, he usually had to remind Neiki about this rule. Other rules, however, such as wiping muddy paws before coming inside or not interrupting another cat while it was talking caused him more trouble.

Thanks to Black Bart's and Big Tig's help, though, he didn't chalk up too many flagrant violations. "Just remember," Black Bart counseled him, "that the rules are all about thinking of the other creature first. If fourteen cats walked in with muddy feet every day, Third Mom would never see an end to mopping the floors. And if we bounced around and talked in bed when Third Mom and Sweetie Pie were asleep, they'd be too tired the next day to take care of us."

"I see," William said. "Like the rule about not inviting other creatures over without asking Third Mom first. If each of us invited another creature for the afternoon, there wouldn't be room for them. And what would Third Mom give them for refreshments?"

Looking at each other, Black Bart and Big Tig cleared their throats. "Well, actually," said Big Tig, "that rule came about because Neiki invited a dog that she met one afternoon in the field back of the house to drop by anytime. You know Neiki. She never met a creature she didn't like. But a dog! Can you imagine?" He gave a slight shudder as he finished speaking.

"Now, Big Tig," admonished Black Bart, "you know there's nothing wrong with dogs. They're a little over friendly and have slobbery kisses, I have to admit, but all in all, they're not nearly as dreadful as we cats like to make out."

Big Tig frowned. "I know . . . I know. I'm trying to be charitable."

William interrupted impatiently, "You were telling about the dog Neiki invited—"

"Oh, yeah," said Big Tig, his face brightening. "Well, one night, we were all awakened in the middle of the night by a fearsome banging and yelping. All of us, Third Mom and Sweetie Pie included, sat straight up in bed, scared out of our wits, even though we know there's nothing to be scared of in heaven. But when you're awakened like that in the middle of the night, you're apt to be somewhat befuddled. Anyway, after we came to our senses, we rushed to the utility room to see what was making all the ruckus. You'll never believe what it was."

"The dog," said William.

"Yes," said Big Tig, "but what kind of dog?"

William sighed in exasperation. How was he supposed to know? Before he could open his mouth to hazard a guess, Big Tig exclaimed, "It was a Saint Bernard! In the middle of his nightly wanderings, he had decided to take Neiki up on her invitation. Can you imagine a dog that huge trying to get in through the cat door? That just goes to show how stupid dogs are!"

"Now, Big Tig—" reproved Black Bart.

"Well, maybe not stupid," conceded Big Tig, "but they certainly lack the common sense cats are born with. Anyway, there he was, his neck stuck in the cat door, not able to go in or out. He had practically torn the door out trying to get unstuck. It took Sweetie Pie quite a while to calm him before he could begin trying to free him."

"How did he do that?" William asked, remembering another creature that had once been stuck in a tight place.

Black Bart took over the story. "He got a crowbar from the barn and prized the door frame from the wall. Then he managed to wriggle the frame over the dog's head. That took some doing, I can tell you. What a mess! Then, of course, Sweetie Pie had to rebuild the frame the next day. When Third Mom discovered that the dog was there at Neiki's invitation, she laid down the law. Before inviting another creature to visit, we have to get her okay first. Be sure you don't forget it."

William assured them he wouldn't. And he didn't.

A few of the rules, William learned the hard way. One of them was to never chase Third Mom's pets, the ones that she had belonged to when she was a little girl. William found out about this rule shortly after his arrival. Going out to play with the other cats one evening after dinner, he spied two rabbits in Third Mom's garden. Never before had he seen such rabbits! Not only were they the largest rabbits he had ever seen, but they were also the oddest looking. They were white, and the inside of their ears were pink! And they were munching Third Mom's lettuce and carrot tops! How dare they! Play was immediately abandoned.

Crouching down, William slowly crept toward the rabbits. Sensing his approach, they reared up to look at him, twitching their noses as they placidly chewed lettuce and carrot tops. William's outrage grew. No rabbit had ever ignored him before. These two did so at their peril.

Rising from his crouching position, he streaked toward the rabbits at full speed. Midway there, he suddenly found himself tumbling head over paws. Coming to a stop, he glanced around to see what he had stumbled over. All he could see was Black Bart observing him a foot or so away. Shaking his head to clear it, he rose to his feet and sped toward the rabbits again, only to tumble head over paws a second time. Black Bart again.

Annoyed, but not wanting to get on the wrong side of a cat so much larger than he, William righted himself a second time. Then he looked at Black Bart. "I don't mean to be impolite, but I'm trying to catch those two rabbits over there. They're nibbling the lettuce and carrot tops in Third Mom's garden. So I'm going to eat them. Could you kind of . . . you know . . . stand back out of the way?"

Black Bart said, "That's what I thought. Those are Third Mom's pets, Petunia and Pettigrew Pinks. We aren't allowed to chase them, much less eat them. She has two pet chickens too, Henrietta and Mr. Combs. They live in the barnyard. We can't chase or eat them either. Or her two pet frogs, Humphries and Mr. Wilson. They live in the rock garden in front of the house.

"And while it's all right to chase other animals, like the rabbits and birds you see in the yard or field, you can't eat those either. It's all right to eat them on Earth because that's what God made cats for. But not in heaven. Didn't Third Mom explain that to you?"

William thought back over all that Third Mom had told him about heaven. He did remember her telling him that he couldn't eat sardines because in heaven, one creature wasn't meant as food for another. At that time, he had not thought about how difficult this rule might be to live by in terms of never, ever eating a rabbit again. Or a mouse or a squirrel or a bird or any other creature that he might develop a hankering for.

Not that being forbidden to eat Third Mom's chickens or frogs bothered him. Chickens looked too scrawny and stringy, and frogs had a warty, unappetizing appearance. But nice, plump rabbits. William's mouth watered just thinking about them.

In the middle of a particularly juicy thought, inspiration struck. What was the worst that could happen if he ignored the rules? Most likely a good scolding. Or having to stay out in the barn with the cows and chickens for a few days. That seemed a small price to pay for two tasty rabbits.

Wriggling his back end as his back paws sought a better grip on the ground, William tensed his body, ready to leap into action in spite of Black Bart's disapproving stare. But just as his paws were about to leave the ground, Black Bart spoke up. "How do you think Third Mom is going to feel if she finds out you chased her pet rabbits till they were hot and tired and dusty? How is she going to feel if she finds out you tried to eat them? More important, how would you feel if something tried to eat you?"

Dumbfounded, William stalled. Why, Third Mom would be heartbroken if he ate her rabbits, just as he would be heartbroken if a coyote or fox, whatever they were, ate Tibby or Second Mom. How could he have been so unfeeling? Casting one last glance of longing at the rabbits, he sighed in regret. For a brief moment, he wished that Black Bart had kept quiet. Then he turned around and headed back to the house.

Walking beside him, Black Bart said approvingly, "You've just taken your first step in growing in goodness."

"What's that?" asked William absently, his mind still on the rabbit meal he had passed up.

"Hasn't Third Mom talked to you about that yet, either? Well, if she hasn't, she soon will. According to her, none of us are perfect when we reach heaven. So we have to grow in goodness until we become perfect. Haven't you noticed how sometimes, when the light's just right, Third Mom and Sweetie Pie and Prissy seem to have a bit of a glow around their heads. Those are halos. They have them because they've become perfect."

So that's what a halo is, William thought, suddenly remembering he had heard Black Bart talk about halos on his first night at Third Mom's. Come to think of it, he had occasionally noticed a bit of a glow surrounding Third Mom's and Sweetie Pie's and Prissy's heads. At that time, he had thought it was from the sun. But now he knew. It was made from goodness, from being perfect. He decided that he wouldn't mind having a halo. "What do you have to do to grow in goodness?" he asked, picturing to himself how he would look with a halo.

"Third Mom says growing in goodness mostly means putting another creature's feelings ahead of yours and treating it like you want to be treated. Like with the rules. And that's what you just did. You put Third Mom's feelings ahead of what you wanted to do. You should be proud."

Thinking over what Black Bart had said, William was proud. He resolved that he would never chase another animal, not even wild ones, much less eat one. Then he really would grow in goodness. He couldn't wait for a rabbit to run across his path so he could show Third Mom and the other cats just how good he had become in the short time he had been here. He might have a bit of a glow already.

Before supper that night, he surreptitiously checked himself in the bathroom mirror. Yes, he determined, twisting his head this way and that, his ears did seem to have a bit of a glow around them. He felt so proud that he couldn't help boasting while the rest of the cats were eating their bedtime snacks. They glanced at one another as he described how—mouthwatering at the sight of those pesky rabbits eating Third Mom's lettuce and carrot tops—he had nobly and unselfishly put Third Mom's feelings ahead of his appetite for a rabbit.

Carried away by his own bragging, he concluded, "I bet no other cat has grown so much in goodness in so short a time. Why, I'll probably be perfect before Second Mom gets here. Just think how proud she'll be of me."

Eyeing one another again, the other cats said nothing. After a long moment, Suki broke the silence. Looking at William with unblinking appraisal, the feline drawled, "Well, I've always heard that pride goeth before a fall."

William flushed in embarrassment. Then he bristled with determination. He'd show her! And the rest of the cats too! He'd become perfect before any of them did!

Right around the Corner

Opportunity knocked sooner than expected. The next afternoon, as he and Black Bart were tussling in the catnip patch by the back porch steps, a wild rabbit ventured into the yard. Halfway across, it noticed the two cats. Stopping and standing up on its hind legs, it taunted, "Yannh! Yannh! Yannh! Can't catch me!" Seeing that its jeers had caught William's attention, it bounded into the field.

In a flash, William sprinted in pursuit, his resolution of the day before forgotten. Up and down and around the field he chased the rabbit, until, on the verge of exhaustion, he gave one last prodigious leap, snaring it in his paws.

"Hey, no fair," squealed the rabbit, struggling to escape. "Let me go."

Ignoring the rabbit's pleas, William tightened his grip. Laughing in triumph, he opened his mouth wide. Just as he was about to chomp down on the rabbit's neck, he remembered. He wasn't supposed to eat another animal. But surely, heaven wouldn't miss one rabbit! Especially a wild one that nobody loved. Emboldened by these thoughts, William opened his mouth once more. Just as he was about to chomp down on the rabbit's neck a second time, a disturbing thought entered his mind. How would he feel if he were about to be eaten by a rabbit? Why, he would be terrified! Who wants to end up as another creature's dinner? Appalled, William closed his mouth and opened his paws.

"Well, it's about time," sputtered the rabbit. It shook itself all over, as if trying to rid itself of the feel of William's paws. Then it sped away but not before turning to give a friendly wave and say, "See you soon."

William, head and tail lowered in shame, slunk toward the yard, hoping that none of the other cats had witnessed his ignominious behavior. Not after the way he had boasted the night before. He looked toward the house. No cats were to be seen. Just as he was drawing a breath of relief, however, he spotted Big Tig heading toward him through the field. Oh no, the one cat besides Black Bart he most wanted to impress! Wouldn't you know it!

However, Big Tig didn't seem to be gloating at William's downfall. Instead, reaching William's side, he said, "Don't let what happened with that rabbit get you down, William. You can't expect to grow in goodness all at once. We all backslide, even humans. In fact, Third Mom says they're the worst backsliders of all.

"Believe it or not, you're a better cat than I was when I first arrived. The first mouse I caught, I didn't feel sorry for at all. No indeed! Believe it or not, terrible as it sounds, I didn't back off after I had it in my mouth. Instead, I bit down on its neck."

William drew in his breath, horrified. Big Tig nodded in agreement. "Yep, you're right. It was a ghastly thing to do. But I'd chased that mouse for a good ten minutes. After working so hard to catch it, I was determined to eat it, no matter what. Of course, I knew that I wasn't supposed to eat other animals. Third Mom explained that to me the first day when I asked for a real mouse for supper.

"Well, when I bit down on that mouse's neck, nothing happened. So I bit down again, thinking that maybe mice in heaven were harder to kill than the ones I was used to. Nothing, again. I might as well not have had any teeth for all the difference they made on that mouse's neck. After a few more tries, I finally let the critter go. Of course, it was laughing like crazy the whole time, saying 'Stop! Stop! You're tickling me!' It knew, even if I didn't, that I wouldn't be able to eat it, no matter how hard I tried.

"Later Black Bart told me that I wasn't able to kill the mouse because there's no such thing as death in heaven. No matter how hard I tried to kill it, I couldn't because it was protected by God. Evidently, God figured that us cats would be big backsliders too. So He gave all the critters that we might want to eat built-in protection.

"I never try to kill anything I chase now. Not that I want to, anymore, of course," he added hastily. "You see, it's not enough to be unable to eat another creature. That's God's doing. You have to not want to eat them. That's your doing.

"For a while I felt bad about all the creatures I had eaten on earth—all the rabbits and mice and moles . . ." His voice trailed off in longing remembrance. Then he recollected himself. "But Third Mom told me not to feel bad about that because that's the way God made the world. On earth, I was doing exactly what God had created me to do. Besides, all those creatures I ate went straight to heaven. It's almost as if by eating them, I was doing them a favor."

William felt immensely cheered by this last statement. Big Tig was right. Cats were doing the animals they ate a favor. He needn't feel guilty or apologize to any he had eaten if he happened to run into them in heaven. Instead, they should be grateful to him.

Big Tig interrupted his ruminations. "For a while I kinda worried about the chasing. But all the other cats do it too. So it must be all right. Third Mom says it is. She says God made cats to be chasers and mice and rabbits to be chased. She says if chasing wasn't okay in heaven, God wouldn't allow us to do it. He'd figure out a way to make creatures chase-proof. Thank goodness! Having to give up eating them is bad enough. Not to be able to chase them would be too much.

"To tell the truth, I think they like being chased. They always seem to be having a good time when I catch them. They even shake my paw sometimes and say, 'Let's do this again soon.'"

William sighed. Why had God made living in heaven so complicated? Living with Second Mom and Tibby on Earth had been simple. In the midst of these musings, he thought of a question he had been wanting to ask. He turned to Big Tig. "What do you think God looks like?"

Big Tig reflected a moment before answering, "Well, Third Mom says He's invisible because He doesn't have a body. He's just a spirit."

"Oh, yeah, I remember now," said William. "Third Mom said something like that when she told me about heaven the first day I was here." He looked down at his chest and front legs. How strange it would be to not have a body, to look down where your feet should be and see nothing.

Big Tig interrupted his musings. "Third Mom did say, though, that when she was a little girl, she thought of God as an old man with white hair and a beard who lived in the sky. He carried around a big black ledger with the names of everyone in the world. If He saw someone on Earth do something wrong, He wrote it down next to that person's name.

"As for myself, I like to think of Him as a white cat with black stripes who lives on top of the tallest mountain in heaven where He can look down to see if anyone is breaking the rules in heaven. That way, He can be sure that no creature gets a halo who doesn't deserve one."

William was astounded. That was pretty much how he had just been picturing God, except He wasn't a short-haired white cat with black stripes. Instead, He was a long-haired gray and orange cat with black stripes. Did all the creatures in heaven think God looked like them? Did a flea imagine that God looked like a flea? Did a dog imagine He looked like a dog? Maybe that's why God had chosen not to have a body and be a spirit instead. He didn't want to play favorites by looking like one creature and not the others. Or maybe He couldn't decide which one He wanted to look like, so He decided not to look like anything at all.

He could have looked like one creature one day and another creature the next, though. Of course, He would have had to keep a list of what creature He had looked like on what day so none would get left out or have more turns than the others. That was probably more trouble than God wanted to go to.

One thing for sure, God was a mystery. But He was the boss, so what He said went. But if growing in goodness required never eating another creature again, then unlike Big Tig, he wouldn't bother chasing one again either. What was the point? He squared his shoulders in resolve. But, resolution to the contrary, William was a cat through and through. So whenever a mouse or squirrel or rabbit ventured by, he just had to chase it, in spite of himself. But never again did he allow himself so much as a thought about eating it.

After his talk with Big Tig, he wondered what other surprises growing in goodness would present. He was soon to find out. On Earth, he had never had to share. Second Mom had provided two of everything—one for him and one for Tibby. There had been two fuzzy mice, two plastic balls, two balls of yarn, two feathered birdies, two rolling pencils, and two wooden spools. The only toys they had had to share were a brown paper sack and a brown cardboard box. Having two of every toy worked well, especially when William couldn't find the one he wanted. Instead of looking for it, sometimes he grabbed Tibby's, even if she were playing with it. She never protested, though. She simply found another toy to amuse herself with.

In heaven, however, matters were different. Third Mom couldn't possibly have been expected to provide one of each toy to every cat. There wouldn't have been room to walk in the house! And the expense! Instead, there were only three of every toy—three fuzzy mice, three plastic balls, three balls of yarn, three feathered birdies, three rolling pencils, three wooden spools, three brown paper sacks, and three brown cardboard boxes. Counting the sacks and boxes, that added up to a toy box overflowing with toys, one apiece for all the cats, with plenty left over for good measure.

Despite this surplus, one morning, when William saw Dorca One guarding a plastic ball he wanted, he did not hesitate to grab it from her, even though a feathered birdie, two balls of yarn, and three wooden spools were lying on the floor in plain sight, begging to be played with.

To his surprise, Black Bart, who was lying next to Dorca One, stood up and, glaring at him, cuffed him lightly across the face, just like a mother cat disciplining an errant kitten. Then retrieving the ball, he rolled it toward Dorca One.

Taken aback but not dissuaded, William made a second grab for the ball. This time, Black Bart, still playing the mother, grabbed William by the scruff of his neck with his teeth and dragged him away. After returning the ball to Dorca One a second time, he stared at William steadfastly. William decided that one of the feathered birdies lying nearby would suffice after all.

At lunch, William was careful to stay out of Black Bart's way, not wanting to risk being cuffed or dragged away again. But after the meal, Black Bart took him aside to say, "No hard feelings, are there? Just remember. In heaven, no one grabs. Everyone shares, even cats. Keep that rule in mind and you'll do fine."

After pondering Black Bart's advice for a moment, William said, "But Third Mom said that in heaven, all I had to do was be a cat. And cats don't share. The biggest one always takes what he wants."

Black Bart said, "That's true on earth. But since there are so many creatures living together in Heaven, sharing is the only way for them to live in peace. That means cats, dogs . . ." At that word, Black Bart gave a slight shudder before resuming. "Fleas, fish, humans. Think about it like this. How would you like me to grab a toy from you?"

William had to admit he wouldn't like it.

"There you are," said Black Bart. "Dorca One didn't like it either. But she's small, not big enough to get it back, even from a five-month-old cat. So I got it back for her."

William nodded in understanding. It was the growing-in-goodness business again. After that dismal incident with the rabbit in the field, it wouldn't do to lag behind all the other cats in goodness now. No more grabbing. Or taking without first asking. His soul filled with remorse when he remembered how frequently he had butted Tibby away from her snacks without the least compunction. And how many times had he grabbed Neiki's Heavenly Delight after he had gobbled all of his? Never again, though.

Learning to take turns was even harder than learning to share. He saw no reason why he had to wait his turn to be fed or brushed. It wasn't as if he were grabbing something from somebody. At Second Mom's, he had always been fed first, brushed first, and petted first because he was bigger. If Tibby got in his way, he had simply pushed her aside. But one morning, when he tried breaking in line in front of Little Cat for breakfast, all the other cats glared and hissed so vehemently that he slunk back to his proper place, which, that week, was one cat from the end of the line.

Worse than having to take turns at being first in line to eat was having to take turns with thirteen other cats to sit in Third Mom's lap. At Second Mom's, William, who loved being held and petted almost as much as eating and sleeping, had always had all the stroking and cuddling he wanted. But Second Mom had had only two cats. With fourteen cats to pet and hold, Third Mom could devote only so much time to each. William, though, was never ready to jump down from her lap when it was another cat's turn to be held. Third Mom usually had to lift him firmly from her lap, saying, "Sorry, William, your turn is up for now."

Sometimes he felt overwhelmed by all the sharing and taking turns expected of him. At those times he consoled himself with the thought that he must be growing in goodness by leaps and bounds. Perfection surely had to be right around the corner.

Elvira to the Rescue

WHEN TIBBY AWAKENED FROM HER nap the morning after William died, she yawned prodigiously and then stood up and stretched luxuriously, first her front half, followed by her back half. Next, out of habit, she looked around for William. But he wasn't on the bed. Suddenly she remembered. William was missing. She felt a thud in the pit of her stomach. Lying back down, she covered her eyes with her paws. She couldn't face getting up. She intended to stay on the bed the rest of the day.

After a moment, she lifted her head hopefully. Just because he wasn't on the bed didn't mean he hadn't come home. He might be lying under the bed right now, waiting to surprise her when she awoke. Jumping off the bed, she peered under it. There was no sign of him, though, no shining eyes staring back at her, no dark blur of his crouching body waiting to spring out at her when she walked by.

Could he be somewhere else in the room? She glanced at the armchair by the window. But there was no William lying there in wait for her. Nor did she see him under the chest of drawers. Maybe he was in some other part of the house. Why, he might be in the living room right now, playing with his toys while he waited for her to wake up. She dashed down the hall to the living room, half expecting to see him there tossing his mouse in the air or swatting a ball around the room. But William was nowhere to be found in the living room either. Instead, she found Second Mom sitting in Hon's recliner. Of course! Second Mom would find William for her. Second Mom could do anything. Walking over to the recliner, Tibby looked up at her and meowed.

Second Mom glanced down at Tibby. To her surprise, Tibby noticed that Second Mom's eyes were filled with water and her face was wet. She meowed again.

"Oh Tibby," Second Mom said. "You want me to help you find William, don't you? He isn't coming back, little one. How am I ever going to make you understand?" Reaching down, she picked Tibby up and put her in her lap, stroking her gently. After a few moments, Tibby hopped down. She had to search all the other rooms in the house.

Only after she had peered under, behind, and on top of every bed, chair, couch, dresser, desk, table, and counter in the house did she return to the living room. Second Mom was still in the recliner, staring out the living room window. Jumping onto her lap, Tibby touched her nose to Second Mom's.

Stroking her, Second Mom began making alarming sounds, as if she were hurting. Water once more began pouring out her eyes and down her face. Butting her head against Second Mom's chest gently, Tibby lay down on Second Mom's lap to look out the living room window. William might appear at the window, wanting in.

Tibby and Second Mom sat in Hon's recliner the rest of the morning and most of the afternoon, Second Mom stroking Tibby's back, talking gently and softly to her, Tibby waiting patiently for William to return. If a bird skittered by on the sidewalk or hopped about in the flower bed in front of the living room window, if a butterfly flitted by the window, if a squirrel dashed across the yard and up a tree, her muscles tensed and her tail swished in excitement. But she remained in the recliner with Second Mom. She didn't want to be away chasing birds, butterflies, or squirrels when William returned.

But William did not return. At bedtime, Second Mom, looking at Hon hopefully, placed Tibby on their bed. "Until she becomes used to William's absence."

Shaking his head no, Hon said firmly, "If you let her sleep with us tonight, she's going to expect to do so tomorrow night too. She has to start learning at some point to live without William. Now is as good a time as any." Second Mom sighed, knowing Hon was right. Postponing the matter would only make it worse. So with a heavy heart, she closed the door on Tibby, and for a second night, Tibby slept alone.

When she woke up the next morning, she did not jump up and run to the kitchen to see if William were there eating breakfast. Nor did she search for him in any of the other rooms. Instead, she went to the dining room and lay down by the window, which looked out onto the backyard. When Second Mom tried to tempt her with sardines and cream for breakfast, she turned her head away. Nor could Second Mom interest her in playing. She ignored the balls Second Mom rolled across the floor. She merely glanced at the sack Second Mom rustled at her. She wouldn't even play her and Second Mom's favorite game, throw-and-chase-the-mouse. When Second Mom threw Tibby's mouse across the floor, Tibby merely eyed it before turning once more to look out the window.

She lay in the dining room all day, head on her front paws, eyes fixed on the window, waiting for William to return. And the next day and the one after that. But on the fourth day, she did not lie down by the window. Instead, she stood staring out it for a long time. Somehow she knew that William was never coming back. She looked at the birds eating at the feeder, remembering the time that William proudly showed her the feather he had snagged. She gazed at the trees they had loved to climb. She glanced toward the creek where they had spent so many afternoons. Then she plodded to the living room to look at the toys that she and William had spent hours playing with. Sighing, she returned to the dining room and lay down. But she did not look out the window.

Second Mom found her there a little later, eyes closed, as if asleep. She spent the whole day there, rousing only to nibble at her food, use the litter box, or open her eyes briefly if Second Mom came into the room to pet her. Only at bedtime did she rise. Walking into the living room, she jumped onto Second Mom's lap to be brushed. But as soon as Second Mom had finished, she padded down the hall to the rug outside Second Mom's door, lay down, and closed her eyes again.

"I don't see how she could be sleepy," said Hon. "You said she slept all day."

"She did. She's depressed."

"Depressed? Cats aren't people. They don't get depressed. Besides, what could she be depressed about?"

"What could she be depressed about?" echoed Second Mom. "What do you think she could be depressed about? She's realized that William is never coming back. She doesn't understand that he's dead, but she does know that she's never going to see him again. She's sleeping to escape her grief."

After a week of watching Tibby do nothing but sleep, Second Mom could stand it no longer. She told Hon, "I'm grieving for Tibby as much as I'm grieving for William. I feel as if I've lost her too." The next morning she marched into the dining room. "Tibby, I know that you're grieving over William. So am I. But I still have you. And I'm not letting you lie here and die. At least, not without a fight. So I've decided to do something you might not like at first. I'm going to find us another cat. Today. There's a neighbor down the road with kittens to give away. I'm driving over right now to get one."

Opening her eyes, Tibby eyed Second Mom dully before closing them again. A few seconds later, her ears twitched as she heard the back door open and close. Within less than a minute, she heard the beast in the garage roar to life, back out of the garage, and head down the hill. Shortly, she heard it return. She heard the back door open and close a second time. All the while, she did not lift her head off her paws or open her eyes.

Nor did she see Second Mom come into the dining room. But she did hear Second Mom walk over to her. Suddenly, she smelled a naggingly familiar scent. But what was it? It wasn't a mouse . . . or a rabbit . . . or a bird. It was a . . . a . . . a *cat*! But one that didn't smell like William. Her hackles rose. Surely Second Mom hadn't brought another cat into the house!

She heard a soft meow. Opening her eyes, she stared in disbelief. Second Mom was holding a scrawny black kitten with a fierce-looking face, a frowning brow, and huge, piercing yellow eyes. Placing the kitten on the floor, Second Mom said, "Tibby, I want you to meet Elvira. I know that the two of you are going to become good friends."

Glowering, Tibby rose. Arching her back and huffing up her fur, she hissed. Startled, Elvira stared up at Tibby. Then uttering a tiny squeak, she ran into the living room, where she dived headlong under the couch, just as Tibby had once done.

There she stayed the rest of the morning, refusing to so much as poke her nose out, despite Second Mom's pleading and cajoling. But as lunchtime approached, her stomach began growling. It growled and grumbled, growled and grumbled, a most distressing state of affairs for any cat, much less a scrawny kitten. Just when she thought she couldn't bear another growl and grumble, a deliciously fishy smell assailed her nose.

She cautiously stuck her nose out from underneath the couch and sniffed. The smell was even more tempting now. Next appeared her eyes darting around the room. Seeing no Tibby, she stuck the rest of her head out, her ears perked forward to catch the slightest sound of a hiss or growl. All remained silent. She decided to take a chance. Sniffing to locate the source of the tantalizing odor, she slowly allowed first her chest and front legs, then her back and hind legs, and finally her tail, switching nervously, to slowly emerge.

Looking every which way, she warily followed her nose to the kitchen. On the floor was a shallow saucer from which emanated the fishy smell that had driven her from under the couch. Creeping over to it, she lowered her head to investigate its contents. Just as she was about to take her first nibble, she spotted Tibby across the room.

Her first instinct was to dash back to the safety of the couch. She noticed, however, that Tibby was paying her no attention. Instead, she was completely absorbed in her own saucer. Looking out of the corner of one eye, Elvira began eating. The two saucers were placed far enough apart that she felt safe enough as long as Tibby was busy with her own food.

Several minutes passed as both kitten and cat ate. Before long, Tibby had licked her saucer clean. Sitting down, she began licking the outside of her mouth to rid it of its fishy smell. In the middle of her third lick, she noticed Elvira. Arching her back and huffing up her fur, she hissed. Elvira cowered, expecting to be cuffed. Instead, Tibby dashed into the living room and dived under the couch. Elvira fled in the other direction, into the utility room, where she spied a dark space behind the freezer. It looked to be the perfect hiding place for a scrawny kitten filled with terror. Squeezing into it, she lay still, heart racing, body quivering.

For the next few days, matters stood at this impasse. If the two cats happened upon each other face-to-face, Tibby hissed, Elvira squeaked, and both fled in opposite directions. But Second Mom noticed that instead of sleeping all day, Tibby now spent much of it watching Elvira, who was always up to something—swatting the window blinds, batting a ball around the room, rolling a pencil down the hall with her nose, even chasing her own tail.

Second Mom decided to leave them alone to work out their relationship. Every day, though, she moved their water and food saucers a little closer together until the cat and kitten were eating side by side, with only an occasional hiss or growl from Tibby. Elvira, who by this time had decided that Tibby's hisses and growls were much worse than her bite, did not even raise her head at the unfriendly sounds.

But aside from watching Elvira play and allowing Elvira to eat next to her, Tibby refused to have anything to do with the kitten. She would not permit Elvira to sleep with her on the rug outside Second

Mom's door. She would not play hide-and-pounce with her or chase her around the house as she once had William. And when Elvira played with the cat toys, Tibby merely looked on. Elvira didn't mind being ignored. There were enough closets and cabinets and rooms to explore; enough shelves, tables, and desks to climb onto and jump off; enough blinds to rattle and drapes to climb; and enough toys to boss around to more than keep her busy. If she couldn't think of anything else to do, she could always chase her tail. So Elvira played and Tibby watched.

Their relationship continued like this until the morning Elvira cornered a grasshopper in Second Mom's iris bed. Never having caught a grasshopper before, she wasn't quite sure what to do with it. First she swatted it in one direction. When it tried to hop away, she swatted it in the other. Tibby, who had been idly observing Elvira, tried to ignore the game. But the more Elvira swatted, the more difficult doing so became. Finally, her cat's love of the chase got the better of her. Seeing the grasshopper give a giant leap outside the reach of Elvira's paws, she leaped into action herself, snaring it in her own front paws. Soon both cats were swatting the beleaguered insect up and down the length of the iris bed.

From that day on, Tibby and Elvira were friends. They ate together, played together, and took naps together. At night, they slept together on the rug outside Second Mom's bedroom. They even gave each other cat baths. More important, Tibby shared with Elvira her vast lore of cat knowledge. She showed her how to jump from the kitchen counter to the top of the refrigerator and from there to the top of the cabinets, where she could watch unobserved all that was happening below. She taught her how to walk on a cluttered desk or dresser without knocking anything off. She shared with her the secret of how to slide down a tree backward without getting stuck or falling. She gave her lessons in catching rabbits, mice, and squirrels, as well as grasshoppers.

She showed her where to hide when Second Mom brandished the flea medicine and the best place on the couch to sharpen her claws. "But only when Second Mom's not around. She doesn't like the sound. I think it makes her nervous." She divulged to Elvira that the best place to take a nap other than on Second Mom's bed was in the laundry basket on top of clothes still warm from the dryer. She gave her lessons in how to wake Second Mom up for a snack at three-thirty in the morning by scratching at the door and meowing. "Second Mom won't complain. She'll get right up and give you a snack. But Hon's different. Sometimes he yells and throws something at the door. It sounds like a shoe. So try not to scratch or meow too loudly, so he won't wake up.

"You need to watch yourself around him. Don't ever, ever jump on the kitchen counter if he's in the room. Else he'll yell and swat at you with his newspaper." Elvira's eyes grew wide. She wasn't sure what happened when Hon yelled and swatted a newspaper, but she didn't want to be around when he did. Tibby wasn't finished with her admonitions. "Don't think about jumping on his head or bothering him if he's hiding behind his newspaper either. Unless you want him to go berserk. Believe me, you don't."

Elvira's eyes grew wide again. She had never seen anyone go berserk. In fact, she wasn't sure what happened when someone went berserk. But she was sure she didn't want to find out. Especially if the someone going berserk happened to be Hon. Hon in his normal state was scary enough.

Nervously, she cleared her throat. "Doesn't Hon like cats?"

Tibby rolled her eyes. "No, he doesn't like cats. I think he's a dog person."

"A dog person!" Elvira was horrified. "Do you think he'll get a dog?"

Tibby rolled her eyes again. "No, silly, Second Mom wouldn't stand for it. This is our house."

Tibby also cautioned Elvira about the yellow cat that sometimes prowled about on the creek bank. "Watch out for him. He's twice as big as I am. If he sees you, he might chase you into a big barn and keep you there all night, like he did me."

Elvira's eyes widened larger than ever. Forever afterward, before going outside, she always peered out the door in all directions for at least half a minute to make sure that no yellow cat twice as huge as Tibby was lurking nearby. Only when she was sure she was safe did she warily and slowly step one foot out the door. Before venturing the second foot, she looked in all directions again, trying Second Mom's patience dreadfully.

"I know that cats have a hard time deciding whether they want in or out. But Elvira's impossible," Second Mom complained to Hon. "It takes her a full two minutes to get out the door. I can't understand what she's looking for. You would think we had foxes or coyotes in the yard. She's such a scaredy cat."

"Well," said Hon, lowering the paper he had been reading to look at Second Mom, "she's a cat, isn't she?" Ignoring the remark, Second Mom wandered down the hall in search of Elvira. She wanted to give her a hug to make up for her complaints.

One afternoon, as Tibby and Elvira were prowling in the utility closet, they came across the cat carrier. "What an unusual-looking box!" said Elvira. "It has a door on it! I wonder why Second Mom doesn't take it out of the closet so we can play in it."

To Elvira's surprise, Tibby hissed. "It's a cat cage. If you ever see Second Mom take it out of the closet, making the sounds *vet,* *checkup,* and *shots,* well, all I can say is you'd better run as fast as you can and hide where Second Mom can't find you."

Elvira was astonished. She couldn't imagine ever wanting to hide from Second Mom. "What's so bad about those words?"

"Well, for one thing, after she says them, she puts you in this cage and closes the door so that you can't get out!"

Her eyes growing round, Elvira caught her breath, horrified to even think about being trapped. Being trapped was just about the worst thing that could happen to a cat.

"Next, she puts you in that beast she keeps in the garage. So that means that you're in something else you can't get out of."

Elvira was even more horrified, so horrified that she began switching her tail back and forth in agitation. She well remembered the beast. When Second Mom put her in it to bring her home, its growls had terrified her. She had jumped into Second Mom's lap and covered her eyes with her front paws. She stayed like that the entire trip, shaking from head to tail, waiting for the beast to gobble her up. The thought of being in it again was unbearable. The next time she might not be so lucky.

Tibby wasn't through. "Even worse, the beast takes you and Second Mom to this building where you can see and smell lots of other animals. Some of them are *dogs*!" Tibby shuddered as she said that last word. So did Elvira.

Tibby continued. "Then, as if that weren't enough by itself, a stranger, a complete stranger, mind you, pokes and prods you with his fingers and then stings you with a sharp needle."

Moaning, Elvira collapsed on the floor, covering her ears with her paws. But she could still hear Tibby, who, enjoying the effect her words were having on Elvira, was determined to spare no detail. "The worst is yet to come. This stranger also pokes a little stick up your rear end!"

At this point, Elvira dissolved into a quivering, whimpering puddle of terror. Tibby stood composedly by, waiting for her friend to collect her wits. Gaining her composure at last, Elvira sat up. In a shaky voice, she asked, "What were those sounds again?"

"*Vet . . . checkup . . . shots.*"

After muttering the sounds softly to herself so as not to forget them, Elvira said, "Where's a good place to hide when Second Mom says these words?"

Tibby sighed gloomily. "I don't know. I haven't found one yet."

14

Tussles and Wussles

Within a matter of days, Elvira learned that Tibby had not exaggerated. The sight of the cat carrier and the sounds *vets, checkup,* and *shots* boded no good for a cat. And just as Tibby had claimed, there was nowhere she could hide—not under the couch or the beds or behind the freezer or refrigerator—that Second Mom couldn't find her and drag her, paws dug in, out.

Elvira was not finished with lessons, though. She had one more to learn, the most important one. This lesson Tibby saved for an afternoon when Second Mom was out on errands. As soon as Second Mom had departed, Tibby availed herself of the opportunity to sit in Hon's recliner. It was there that Elvira, strolling through the room a few minutes later, found her. Stopping in midstride, she gaped in disbelief. Hon's recliner was strictly off limits.

Tibby spied Elvira at about the same time that Elvira spied her. Yawning nonchalantly, she said, "Come on up. I need to talk to you."

Shaking her head, Elvira backed away a few steps, squeaking, "I thought we weren't supposed to sit in Hon's chair."

Tibby eyed Elvira scornfully. "Silly, the rules don't count if there's no one here to scold us or yell and smack a newspaper at us. We can do whatever we want then."

Elvira had never thought of rules from that perspective before. It did seem to make sense, though. What did disobeying a rule matter if Second Mom wasn't there to find out? Filled with admiration for Tibby's wisdom, Elvira jumped up. For a few minutes, each busied herself grooming the other's face. Finally settling down for an afternoon chat, Elvira said, "There's something I don't understand. If Second Mom belongs to us, and Hon belongs to Second Mom, why aren't we the ones making the rules?"

Tibby didn't want to think about this question, much less answer it. "I didn't invite you up to have you ask silly questions. I want to tell you about William."

"Who's William?"

"William is my brother. He lived here with me before you came. One night, when he was chasing a rabbit, he ran into a road. A big beast, like the ones that race up and down the road in front of our house, like the ones in our garage, attacked him. I haven't seen him since. So stay away from all roads. Especially at night."

Elvira solemnly promised that she would never, ever get close to a road. She didn't want to disappear like William. She loved her life at Second Mom's house too much. At that moment, Second Mom's car turned into the driveway. Hastily jumping from the recliner, Tibby made a beeline to the dining room and scuttled under the table. Elvira, who was thinking how sad it would be to lose Tibby the way Tibby had lost William, did not notice the car. Nor did she hear Second Mom open the back door.

Suddenly, she looked up to see Second Mom standing in front of the recliner, hand on hips, looking sternly down at her. Hanging her head guiltily, she hastily leaped down and sprinted toward the dining room.

Second Mom followed closely behind. As soon as she entered the room, she observed Elvira's tail sticking out beneath the bottom slat of a window blind. She strode over to the window. "Elvira, you know you aren't supposed to be in that recliner. You-know-who'll skin you alive if he finds out. Why can't you be like Tibby? She never gets into Dave's chair. She's a good cat. Aren't you, Tibby?" With these last words, Second Mom walked over to the dining table to give Tibby a pat on the head.

Recognizing the tone of praise in Second Mom's voice, Tibby twitched her tail and smiled in satisfaction. Elvira, also sensing the praise being heaped upon her friend, felt her heart swell in indignation. Why, Tibby was the one who had persuaded her to get in the recliner in the first place! Never again would she let Tibby talk her into doing something that she knew she shouldn't do.

Second Mom breathed a sigh of relief when she saw that her two cats had become friends. She thought she had the most beautiful cats in all the world. By this time, Tibby had almost reached her full size. With her long, thick gray and orange hair, she looked magnificent and formidable. Elvira, on the other hand, had short, coarse black hair with swirls of orange and tan and lightly flecked with white at the tip of her tail and around her eyes and mouth. Tiny and fine boned, she moved as fluidly and gracefully as a squirrel and as swiftly, especially if she were chasing Tibby. Tibby, by contrast, seemed cumbersome unless she was hunting or being chased by Elvira. Then she could move quickly enough.

Of course, Tibby and Elvira didn't always get along. Cats, like people, seldom do. Tibby had a bad habit of butting Elvira away from her snacks and devouring them herself when she had finished her own, especially if the snack was sardines and cream. Second Mom always made sure that she had a snack in reserve for Elvira to eat when Tibby wasn't around.

Tibby also thought that she had sole rights to Second Mom's lap, even if she never sat in it for any length of time. Sometime she sat in it barely long enough for Second Mom to stroke her once or twice and tell her what wonderful creatures cats were, especially her. Sometimes she was out of her lap before the words were out of Second Mom's mouth.

Meandering through the living room one afternoon, however, shortly after Elvira's arrival, she found Second Mom and Elvira in

Second Mom's recliner, Second Mom talking to Elvira as she brushed her fur. Tibby's eyes widened in outrage. Not only was Elvira usurping her place in Second Mom's lap, Second Mom was also bestowing upon her the same sounds and looks of adoration that properly belonged to her and only her.

"Elvira, I do believe you'd let me brush you all day long until I brushed all your hair out. Then you would be nothing but a scrawny polka-dotted kitten. Now wouldn't that be a sight? I would still love you, though." Elvira's only reply was to thump her tail contentedly against Second Mom's leg, sublimely oblivious that she was trespassing.

Tibby had seen and heard enough. Marching over to the recliner, she stared fixedly at the intruder. Elvira, who felt safe from Tibby as long as she was with Second Mom, merely stared back as she snuggled deeper into her lap. Seeing that she wasn't making a dent in Elvira's composure, Tibby turned her attention to Second Mom, staring at her just as hard as she had at Elvira, her eyes filled with displeasure. Second Mom, however, did not seem to get the message. Smiling down at Tibby, she patted her lap. "Come on up, Tibby. There's always room for you." But Tibby was not about to share Second Mom's lap with Elvira. Drawing herself up to her full stature, she turned her back and stalked huffily away.

She didn't let the matter end there, though. Lurking around corners the rest of the morning, she watched Second Mom closely. As soon as she saw her sit down, this time on the couch to do some mending, she took a running leap into her lap, landing on top of the sewing box. Needles, pins, thread, and measuring tape flew through the air.

From that day on, Second Mom's lap was burdened with cats whenever she sat down. If Elvira happened to reach her lap first, Tibby stared daggers at her and Second Mom before marching stiffly away, tail and head held high. If Tibby reached the lap first, Elvira, however, had no hesitation about inviting herself up too, squeezing in beside Second Mom, serenely unconscious that, in Tibby's eyes, she was most unwelcome.

After five or so minutes of such an arrangement, Tibby usually jumped down, feeling victorious that she had claimed Second Mom's lap first, leaving Elvira the leftovers. As soon as Tibby left, Elvira took her place, feeling victorious that she had ended up in Second Mom's lap after all.

Second Mom was aware of the struggle taking place. "To think that some people believe that cats aren't affectionate!" she said to Hon one evening as the two cats sat with her. "Why, Tibby and Elvira vie for time in my lap. And Elvira's such a loving little cat. When I pet Tibby, she accepts it as her due, as if she's a princess and I'm one of her subjects. Elvira, though, gets all squirmy and squeaky, as if she's grateful for the least attention. I believe she would let me hold her all day, every day if I wanted to. William was like that. He'd sit in my lap as long as I'd hold him. I'm glad I have Elvira for my sake as much as for Tibby's."

Hon, reading the newspaper in his recliner, merely grunted assent at these sentiments, not even bothering to look up. He had long ago learned that when Second Mom rhapsodized about her cats, no other response was necessary. Or wanted.

As he continued to read, Second Mom continued ruminating. "However, I must say that Elvira is much more polite than Tibby. She always asks to get in my lap first. She'll stand right in front of me, not making a move until I pat my lap and invite her up. And when she jumps up, she seems to float through the air. Tibby, though, just hurtles herself up. Without warning. I never know when she is coming or from what direction. The other day I was sitting at the dining table eating a bowl of cereal. All of a sudden, out of nowhere, Tibby landed with a big galumph, half in my lap and half on the table. Milk and cereal spilled everywhere."

Still absorbed by the newspaper, Hon merely grunted again at Second Mom's comments. "Elvira especially loves to take naps with me. Actually, she doesn't so much take a nap with me as she takes a nap on top of me. When I turn over, she jumps off but climbs back on me as soon as I'm settled again. She'll stay there until I'm ready to get up. Once in a while, she'll wake up long enough to yawn or give a paw a lick or two, then it's back to sleep. If I say something to her, she'll open one eye halfway, as if to let me know that she hears me but doesn't think that what I'm saying is important enough to wake completely up. Last week, when I was sick in bed all day, she stayed with me the whole time."

Having finished the article he had been reading, Hon turned to the next page, rattling the paper as he straightened and folded it for easier reading. Oblivious to the distraction, Second Mom continued the one-sided conversation. "I'm so blessed to have her and Tibby. They're my little girls. I thank God every day for them. They don't care what I look like or what kind of a house I live in or how rich I am. That's why cats are so wonderful. They love people for what they're like inside, not outside."

These last few comments caught Hon's attention. He lowered his newspaper and looked at Second Mom. "So do dogs."

Nonplused at this observance, Second Mom chewed her lip for a moment. Then her face brightened. "Maybe so. But the trouble with dogs is that they're not cats." Point scored, Second Mom left Hon to his reading as she triumphantly swept from the room in search of Tibby and Elvira. She wanted to tell them how fortunate they were to be cats and not dogs, which they already knew.

Besides thinking that she should have sole rights to Second Mom's lap, Tibby also thought she should be Elvira's boss. After all, she was bigger, and Second Mom had belonged to her first. Elvira, however, thought that she should be boss simply because she was Elvira.

At least once or twice a week, Second Mom came upon them staring hard at each other, Elvira prone on the floor or a bed as Tibby, standing with a front paw raised in warning, towered regally over her. Only when she felt that Elvira had become properly submissive did Tibby turn away, whereupon Elvira immediately sprang for her back. The battle usually ended with Elvira, close upon Tibby's tail, snagging a few tufts of hair as Tibby, fleeing, sought refuge, usually behind the freezer or the living room stove. Second Mom made it a rule to leave them alone at those moments, knowing there were some matters the two cats would have to resolve themselves.

But she told Hon, "You'd think that eventually Tibby would learn not to turn her back. But so far, she hasn't. As for Elvira, she's a sweetie pie, but she's also one determined little cat. She may not end up being boss, but neither will Tibby. They'll have to learn to share being top cat on the totem pole.

"To think that I wasn't even looking for a kitten like Elvira," continued Second Mom. "I wanted a fluffy white and yellow one. Then I noticed this scrawny black kitten, so tiny I could pick her up with one hand. With not a bit of fluff on her anywhere. And what a fierce expression she had! But when I saw her, I had to have her and no other. I think she was meant to be mine."

Elvira thought that she was meant to be Second Mom's too. As far as she was concerned, there wasn't a better Second Mom anywhere. Not that she didn't have a few shortcomings. She couldn't run up a tree or climb up a window screen or jump on top of the kitchen counter. And she didn't like mice, especially the dead ones she sometimes managed to sneak into the house.

She couldn't understand Second Mom's reaction to them when she dropped them at her feet. She just wanted to show Second Mom what a good hunter she was and to encourage Second Mom to do a little hunting of her own. She also hoped that eating a mouse or two in front of Second Mom might show her what mice were made for. But Second Mom never showed the slightest inclination toward hunting. Nor did she ever take even the tiniest nibble of a mouse, no matter how plump and juicy looking. Instead, she took it outside and dropped it in her flower beds. What a waste!

But Second Mom more than made up for her deficiencies. For one thing, she was good at opening doors, especially the ones to the cold box for their cream and to the sardine box for their sardines. If she and Tibby had only themselves to depend on for such feats, they would be in a pickle. Depending on Hon would be worse.

And how many times a day did Second Mom go to the back door to let her and Tib Wib in or out? She never fussed or complained, just stood at the door patiently until they had decided whether or not they really did want in or out. And like Tibby had said, she didn't fuss or throw shoes when they scratched and meowed at the door in the middle of the night wanting a snack. Instead, she got out of bed and fixed them one.

Even more important, she always had their meals on time and never forgot about their morning and afternoon snacks. Plus, there was nothing better than lying in her lap being rocked to sleep or jumping on her stomach when she was taking a nap and dozing off with her.

But what impressed her most about Second Mom was how brave she was. And Hon too. She had to give credit where credit was due. Neither one showed the slightest hesitation about climbing into one of the beasts in the garage. At first she had thought the beasts intended to carry them off and eat them. So she couldn't understand why they seemed so willing, even eager at times, to climb into their stomachs. They even smiled happily as the beasts roared off with them. She had marveled that the beasts always returned to disgorge them unscathed. She finally concluded that Hon and Second Mom probably put up such a fuss that the beasts thought better of eating them.

After she had made a few trips herself to the vet in one or the other of the beasts, though, she realized that the beasts weren't interested at all in eating Second Mom or Hon. Instead, they were taking them to the vet just like they took Tibby and her. She couldn't understand, though, why Second Mom and Hon had to see the vet so often. Hon went almost every morning and didn't return until late afternoon. Second Mom went only two or three times a week, seldom staying more than half a day. Sometimes, though, Second Mom and Hon went together, often staying several days. She was thankful that she didn't have to go to the vet that often and stay that long. An hour about twice a year was about all she could stand.

When Elvira shared these thoughts with Tibby, Tibby shook her head. "What a dunderhead you are, Elvira. Where do you come up with such ideas? Second Mom and Hon don't go to the vet every time they climb into one of the beasts. Sometimes Second Mom goes out to get stuff and bring it back home. Haven't you noticed the bags she usually comes back with? Where do you think they come from? The vet?"

Elvira nodded.

Tibby rolled her eyes in exasperation. "You're even more of a dunderhead than I thought. Just what do you think is in those bags? Medicine?"

Elvira nodded again.

Tibby rolled her eyes again. "Not only are you a dunderhead, you must have a brain the size of a pea. Second Mom brings home our food and our snacks and our toys in those bags. But Second Mom isn't always going to get stuff when she gets in one of the beasts. Sometimes she's gallivanting around with Hon having a good time without us." Indignation rounded out the last of her words.

Elvira took a backward step, shocked at this revelation. How could Second Mom have a good time without her and Tibby along? No, Tibby was wrong. But no sense in arguing. Tibby always thought she was right.

Once Elvira realized the beasts didn't have Second Mom and Hon or her and Tibs in mind for a snack, she lost some of her wariness around them. If one was resting in the driveway, she might jump on its head for a catnap in the sun. But if she felt it quiver even the slightest, she was down and gone in a heartbeat. No trips to the vet for her. At least not if she could help it.

15

The Saga of Tibby and Elvira

OF COURSE, ELVIRA REALIZED THAT besides trips to the vet, there were also a few other drawbacks to living in the gray house on the hill. Mainly Hon. Not that she didn't like him. But he never talked to them or invited them to jump into his lap. Nor did he walk slowly and lightly or talk softly and gently like Second Mom.

Second Mom wended her way from one room to another, humming and talking to them as she put away laundry or picked up strewn clothes (mostly Hon's), newspapers (again, mostly Hon's), and books (mostly hers) and, in general, restored order to the house. Hon, though, strode through the rooms with steps that resounded with determined purposefulness. His voice was filled with an authority not to be brooked. Just the sound of him was enough to make her and Tibby flee.

What she found hardest to bear, though, was his unpredictability. He created a stir wherever he went, bursting into rooms unexpectedly, filling them with his feet and his voice. Nor was there any telling what he was going to do next. If he were sitting in his recliner watching the box with moving pictures, he was just as likely as not to suddenly jump up, yelling and tearing at his hair while stomping about the room. Or he might unexpectedly leap up and head to the kitchen to stare into the cold box, not even looking to see if she or Tibby were lying in his path. Quite a few close calls had occurred. Now when she saw his feet approaching or heard his voice booming nearby, she fled in the opposite direction. She also made sure, just as Tibby had advised, to never jump onto the kitchen counter if he were around.

Worse than Hon were the visitors. Second Mom had lots of them. Too many in her opinion. When they arrived, what a commotion and upheaval they brought with them. Tables and chairs rearranged, unfamiliar voices laughing and talking ceaselessly, strangers walking in and out of rooms she and Tibby considered theirs.

To show their displeasure at such intrusions, she and Tibby usually disappeared into the bath cabinet that Second Mom left open for them all the time. They hoped she might eventually take the hint and banish anyone that advanced farther than her front door, but so far, she hadn't. She and Tibs often wondered how Second Mom would feel if they invited a houseful of cats to visit them, and to have a little peace, she and Hon were forced to flee to the bathroom cabinets!

Second Mom's most regular guests were two tall giants, much larger than Hon. When they were present, the whole house rang with their voices and laughter. They sounded exactly like Hon. Invariably they tried to pet Tibby and her. But she and Tibby would have none of it. Whenever they saw the two with their heavy steps and huge hands approaching them, they fled. The giants then made complaining sounds like "Mom, Tibby and Elvira are such scaredy cats. If we so much as look at them crossways, they take off running." When each started bringing a female with him, well, that was four humans too many for their small house.

As if human visitors weren't bad enough, once one of Second Mom's guests brought a dog with her—a house dog, to make bad matters worse. They stayed for days! She and Tibby were shut in Second Mom's room the entire visit. Second Mom even put their food and water saucers beside her bed and their litter boxes in her bathroom. Yet the dog was allowed to roam about the rest of the house, as if it, and not they, were the owner. To add insult to injury, it barked incessantly. Thank goodness Second Mom left a window open so they could come and go as they pleased. But even outside, they had to peer cautiously around every corner, shrub, and tree to make sure the dog wasn't on one of its frequent strolls around the yard with the person it owned.

Matters came to a head one morning when Second Mom forgot to shut the bedroom door completely after bringing them breakfast. A little later, while they were relaxing on Second Mom's bed digesting their food and thinking about possibly going outside, the dog pushed the door open with its nose and pranced into the room. Tibby immediately rose, hissing and spitting. Then they both bolted to the bath cabinets, the dog barking at their heels. At the cabinet door, Tibby, making a stand, turned and swatted it across the nose.

Yelping in surprise and drawing back, the dog wheeled around and fled, still yelping. Within moments, Second Mom appeared. Lifting them out of the cabinet, she examined them carefully, making sounds like "Oh Tibby and Elvira, I'm so sorry! How could I have forgotten to close the bedroom door? Thank goodness you're not hurt. But you must be terrified!"

For the rest of the day, Tibby harrumphed in satisfaction, meowing comments like "Harrumph, I guess I showed that dog who's boss" or "Harrumph, I bet that dog doesn't come nosing around us anymore." She, on the other hand, had quivered and quaked at the slightest sound for the rest of the day.

Thankfully, the dog and its person left two days later. But no more had she and Tibby recovered from the trauma of the dog's presence, just as the house was beginning to smell less like dog and more like cat, than something almost as bad showed up—a short, tubby human who couldn't even sit up, much less walk. But it could bang and yell and scream and kick to no end. For some unfathomable reason, whenever it showed up, Second Mom and Hon seemed to take a special delight in it. They held and rocked it and sang and cooed to it. When it began sitting up, they put a blanket on the floor where it could play with its toys. Sometimes they even sat on the blanket and played with it.

Once in a while, she sat down next to the blanket herself, just out of reach of the miniature human, studying the creature intently, trying to figure out if it were a boy or girl and why Second Mom and Hon placed such importance on it. In turn, it grinned and babbled to her or waved one of its toys at her.

Matters took a distinct turn for the worse when the tubby creature began crawling on all fours. She and Tibby were dumbfounded. Didn't it know that humans walked on their hind legs so that they could use their front paws for carrying things? Their puzzlement changed to consternation when they realized that the little human was going to spend a great deal of time crawling after them from room to room, laughing and grinning and babbling. Thereafter, they had to be on the alert when it was present, dashing under beds and tables and dodging behind sofas and chairs whenever it approached. They weren't even safe in the bath cabinets. If it found them there, it tried to crawl in with them.

Matters worsened when the human, now not so small, started walking on its hind legs. She and Tibby were relieved that the creature had finally figured out that it was supposed to walk instead of crawl, but now it could pitter patter after them, hands held out toward them, still grinning and laughing and babbling. Thankfully, they could move faster than it could. They couldn't always avoid it, though. Sometimes Second Mom held them in her arms so it could stroke them. She always made sure it did so softly and gently, but nevertheless, it was a tense situation, no two ways about it.

Many visits passed before she and Tibby realized that it wasn't going to pull their fur or their ears and tails and they didn't have to run every time they saw it approach. Unfortunately, just as they were starting to relax round it, about the time they figured out that it was a she because she looked so much like Second Mom, another small human showed up, as small and loud and as grabby and crabby as the first had once been. A short time later, two more appeared. At the same time!

Would there be no end to them? The only measure of comfort she and Tibby had was that the creatures would eventually become halfway civilized. And that sooner or later, they always went home.

In addition to the upheaval visitors introduced in the household, there were the unexplainable things Second Mom and Hon did. Like bathing in a huge tub of water. She and Tibby liked to rear up and place their front paws on the ledge of the tub to watch the elaborate efforts Second Mom took for something as simple as a bath. Didn't she know that the easiest way to take a bath was to lick yourself all over with your tongue? Even more puzzling was why sometimes she stood in the tub and let rain pour down on her. Not even Tibby, who always had an explanation about everything under the sun, could figure that one out.

Taking baths in a tub filled with water and letting rain pour down on her could be put down to Second Mom's ignorance. Other bewildering behavior couldn't. Like helping the small humans hunt for eggs in the grass, shouting with proud glee when one of them found one and put it in a basket. What was all the fuss about? They were just eggs. And not even real ones at that! She and Tib Wib found eggs all the time in the fields and on the creek bank. Moreover, theirs were real.

Even more puzzling was the pumpkin that Second Mom put on the front porch ever so often. But only after scooping out its insides and carving a scary face with wicked-looking eyes and teeth on one side of it. The face grew scarier when Second Mom put a lit candle inside the pumpkin. She did that only during the evenings. On those occasions, she and Tibby avoided the front porch entirely. They knew the face wasn't real but better to take no chances.

Of all the weird things Second Mom and Hon did, however, none was stranger than dragging a tree into the house. Even more unfathomable was that after Hon dragged the tree in and stood it up in a corner, he and Second Mom hung shiny balls and beads and strings on it. And strand after strand of lights. Afterward, Second Mom piled boxes on top of boxes under the tree.

Of course, she and Tibs had to sniff about the tree, trying to puzzle out all the intriguing smells emanating from it. There was the smell of the tree itself, as well as the smell of the birds, worms, and bugs that had once taken up residence in it. They also enjoyed making a nest for themselves among the boxes. They had to be careful about the lights, though. They would go into a trance if they stared too long at them. Tibby also liked to swat at the tree's branches or at the shiny objects and strings dangling from it but only when Second Mom wasn't in the room. Otherwise, Second Mom made sounds like "No, Tibby, no!" Tibby said such sounds were an affront to her dignity.

Nor did Second Mom allow them to play with any of the shiny strings they happened to find on the floor. She promptly took them away and hung them back on the tree, making sounds like "No, no. If you swallowed one of these icicles, you might choke or even worse. Then it would be to the vet with you." She and Tibs didn't recognize any of the sounds except *vet*. That they recognized too well. At its sound, they forgot immediately about dangling balls and strings on the floor and headed for a dark place to hide.

About the time that Second Mom and Hon put the tree in the house, she started singing and humming and spending most of her time in the kitchen, stirring pots and putting pans in the hot box. For days on end, wonderful smells filled the whole house. Sometimes Second Mom gave them a tidbit from one of the pots or pans.

One evening shortly after the tree came into the house, a whole crowd of humans would present themselves at the front door, their arms loaded with more boxes. After all these boxes had been placed under the tree, someone dressed in red with white hair on his head and face appeared with even more boxes, shouting, "Ho! Ho! Ho!" He sounded just like Hon. What a terrible melee followed! Feasting and singing and laughing and talking as boxes were opened and paper and ribbon scattered over the entire living room. There was so much excitement that she and Tibs, ever curious, forwent their usual hiding place in the bath cabinets to peek around the living room doorway and observe the commotion.

Second Mom always saved a box for them to open. After all the company had departed, she sat on the floor with the box while they sniffed and swatted it. They knew it held a present for them. One year, they received a toy mouse that ran across the room making squeaking noises. Tibby was scared to death of it. Another time, they received a ball of yarn that meowed when they batted at it. When they finally unwound the last bit of the yarn months later, there lay a tiny toy kitten. Their favorite toy, though, was the tunnel that sprang out of the box when Second Mom lifted the lid off. She and Tibby liked to crawl into it from opposite ends and meet one another in the middle.

But the absolutely best present they had ever received wasn't a toy. It was the magic disc that made birds and squirrels and chipmunks appear on the box of moving pictures. On those occasions, she and Tibs sat as close to the moving pictures as they could, head back, eyes following every movement the birds, squirrels, and chipmunks made. Once in a while, they tried to get behind the box, convinced the critters lived there. But doing so was impossible because the box was set in the wall. So they had to be content with just watching them.

Not that Second Mom allowed them to watch very often. If she saw them sitting in front of the box waiting for her to get out the magic disc, sometimes she shook her head and made noises that sounded like "No birdies or squirrels today, little girls. I don't want you becoming couch potatoes or TV junkies."

From that time on, though, she and Tibby began to pay more attention to the sights and sounds that came from the box. Most of the time, they heard or saw nothing very interesting. Sometimes, though, they saw animals unlike those they saw on the disc. If they saw dogs, they immediately headed for the bath cabinet. Once they saw some cows that looked like those in the field behind the house. Once in a while, they might sight some fish like the ones in the pond. Or maybe some frogs and lizards.

Once they saw a huge cat with lots of fur around its neck and a few moments later another huge cat with spots all over it. Their eyes grew wide at the sight. They hadn't known that cats grew that big. Or that some had fur around their necks while others were polka-dotted. They had certainly never seen any such cats. They hoped that they didn't grow that large. If they did, the beds and couches and chairs in the house, indeed, the whole house itself, would be much too small for them. They would have to move outside. That was a prospect neither of them wanted to think about.

Mostly, though, rather than dogs or cats or cows, they caught glimpses of animals that they didn't recognize. Like that tall creature with the extra long neck and a head that reached almost to the top of the trees. And another tall animal with a long nose that it could curl above its head or uncurl to reach the ground.

One time while they were drowsing in the living room in front of the wood stove, they heard the sound of a wolf howling. Until that night, they hadn't known that wolves existed, much less what they sounded like. But when they heard that howl, they knew immediately what they were hearing.

Springing up, they looked wildly around. Then they heard the sound again. It was coming from the box of moving pictures! Both scrambled for the bath cabinets, refusing to come out for the rest of the evening, even at bedtime. Second Mom let them stay there the whole night. Hon didn't even complain. For a long time afterward, before entering the living room, they looked cautiously around to make sure there were no wolves lurking in the corners.

As much as they liked the magic disc and the other presents they received at tree time, they found the paper and ribbons scattered on the floor much more intriguing. They loved the way the paper snapped and crackled at them, fighting back when they pounced on it for a tussle. And the ribbons were always good for a chase around the room. They made the most of them, for they knew that in a day or two, for no apparent reason, Second Mom would take everything off the tree, the paper and ribbons would disappear, and Hon would drag the tree out of the house to the creek bank for the birds to nest in. In her opinion, that was the only sensible thing that had happened to the tree since Hon dragged it in.

On the whole, there was no denying that humans were strange creatures. Thank goodness Second Mom and Hon had Tibs and her to keep them on the straight and narrow for most of the time. Otherwise, no telling what other tricks they might get up to. Overall, though, in spite of vets and Hon, regardless of dogs and crawling humans and pumpkins with scary faces, in spite of wolves on the moving picture box, no one and nothing could have driven her away. She loved and needed Second Mom too much. And Second Mom loved and needed her too.

Elvira was right. Second Mom did love and need Elvira. She loved her simply because she was Elvira. But she was also grateful that Elvira had helped Tibby cope with the loss of William. Whenever she happened upon the two cats asleep, front paws wrapped around each another, she realized what a good thing she had done for Tibby.

Slowly, as the days and months and years passed, Tibby's grief lessened until it was just a gentle tug on her heart. Gradually, her memories of William faded until he was only a dim presence in her mind. Occasionally, though, when she and Elvira were playing on the creek bank, she would pause, certain that another cat had once played there with her. Sometimes when she neared William's grave on the bank, she would sniff at the grass and then look around with a far off expression in her eyes. Only when she noticed Elvira nosing around in the weeds did she return to the present, hurrying over to see what her friend was up to. And once in a while in her dreams, she found herself running with a cat that looked like her at her side. She always woke from those dreams with the name "William" in her thoughts and a heaviness in her heart as if she were grieving, but for what she knew not.

Gradually, even the dreams and the name "William" ceased to haunt her. She could not remember a time when she had not lived with Elvira and Second Mom and Hon. And so the four lived in the small gray house on the hill and were happy.

16

Fate Throws a Curve

Second Mom looked at the clock—7:30. She had overslept! Bolting upright, she saw Hon in front of the dresser mirror knotting a tie. "Why didn't you wake me?"

He smiled at her in the mirror. "You looked tired last night. So I decided you needed to sleep late this morning. Don't worry about breakfast. I'll get something on the way to the office."

Groaning, Second Mom slid back down into the bedcovers and closed her eyes. "It was all those windows I washed yesterday. I think I overdid it."

Walking over to the bed, Hon bent over her and kissed her on the forehead. Second Mom smiled, eyes still closed. "Take it easy today," Hon ordered. "I'll see you this evening. And don't bother with supper. We'll go out."

"Good," said Second Mom, dozing. "I think I'll stay in bed a little longer." Suddenly, she opened her eyes. "Don't let Tibby in. She'll never let me have any peace." Too late. Before she could get the words out of her mouth, Hon had opened the bedroom door, and Tibby, followed by Elvira, had scooted inside.

Tibby proceeded to meander aimlessly around the room, waving her bushy tail as she scent marked with the side of her face the bed, the desk, the door jamb to the bathroom, and anything else she wanted to claim as hers. Meanwhile, Elvira, hopping onto the bed, curled up next to Second Mom's knees. Before she had no more than settled herself, Hon came back into the room. "Forgot my wallet." Walking over to the desk where it lay, he picked it up. As he stuffed it into a pocket inside his suit coat, he noticed Elvira staring hard at him. "Why is she staring at me like that?"

Second Mom smiled. "She's telling you to go away, that it's her turn to be with me now."

"Tell her she doesn't have to worry. I'm leaving right now." Leaning over the bed, he gave Second Mom a second good-bye kiss before departing once more. As soon as his footsteps had faded down the hall, Second Mom tensed for what she knew would follow. Almost immediately, she felt a heavy thump on her chest, followed by a demanding "Meow! Meow!"

Second Mom peeked out between barely raised eyelids at Tibby, who, standing on her chest, was regarding her with unblinking steadiness. Raising her eyelids as far as they would go, Second Mom stared unblinkingly back. After a few seconds of this impasse, Tibby put out a paw and, with claws retracted, gently touched Second Mom's face. "Meow! Meow!"

Second Mom narrowed her eyes. "Tibby, I'm not getting up. Go away." To punctuate her intentions, she shut her eyes.

"Meow! Meow!"

Refusing to respond, Second Mom lay still. After a few moments, the weight on her chest vanished, followed by a thump on the floor. Sighing in relief, she turned over on her side, nestling into Hon's pillow. She was almost asleep when Tibby landed with a thump again, this time next to her head.

"Meow! Meow!"

"Go away, Tibby! I'm sleeping."

"Meow! Meow!"

Second Mom didn't answer. After a few seconds, Tibby jumped off the bed once more. Burrowing her face into Hon's pillow a second time, Second Mom relaxed into sleep again, only to be jerked awake by a heavy weight landing on her side.

Second Mom sighed in frustration. "Okay, Tibby. You win. I'm awake." Sitting up, she threw back the bedcovers and swung her legs off the bed. Standing up, she reached for her robe while eyeing Tibby sternly. "I would put you out and close the bedroom door, but you would only scratch on it and caterwaul until I opened it." She glanced at Elvira, who having also given up trying to sleep, was sitting quietly on the side of the bed. "Why can't you be like Elvira? She never wakes me up."

Pulling on her robe, she smiled fondly at Elvira. As she did so, she noticed that Elvira was holding her left front paw slightly off the bed. "You can put your paw down, sweet pea. You have my permission." Laughing silently at her joke, she headed for the bathroom.

When she came out a few minutes later, Elvira still had her paw raised. Frowning, Second Mom walked over to the bed. Sitting down next to Elvira, she took the paw in her hands. "Is there something wrong, sweetie pie? Let Mama see."

Squeezing and pressing gently on the paw, Second Mom looked into Elvira's eyes for a flicker of pain. But Elvira's eyes remained steady. Nor did she flinch as Second Mom continued to squeeze and press. Puzzled, Second Mom stood up. "Well, I didn't notice anything. If you're still holding your paw up tomorrow, though, I'm calling the vet."

At the sound of that last word, both Elvira and Tibby scattered, Elvira limping slightly on her left paw. Frowning at Elvira's limp, Second Mom wondered what had given them such a startle. Shaking her head in bemusement, she headed for the kitchen to fix breakfast for them, the birds, and herself in that order. As she sat down at last to her cereal, she gave a happy sigh. Life was good. Except for Elvira's paw. But more than likely, that would be well by tomorrow.

Second Mom was wrong. The next day, Elvira was still holding her paw up whenever she was standing and limping slightly on it whenever she took a step. Second Mom went straight to the phone after breakfast. Within the hour, Elvira, most vexed, found herself in the carrier on the way to the vet. This trip had not been included in her plans for the morning.

After pressing and squeezing Elvira's paw, just as Second Mom had done and then pulling on huge magnifying goggles and inspecting it closely, Dr. Hood shook his head. Pushing the goggles up over his forehead, he contemplated Elvira with a puzzled look. "I can't see a thing, not a scratch or a bite or a puncture wound. Nothing. We could be backing up the wrong tree, though. Let's take a look at her leg."

Taking an electric razor, Dr. Hood shaved Elvira's leg almost up to her shoulder. Then pushing the magnifying goggles down over his eyes again, he inspected the leg as carefully as he had the paw. All this Elvira bore with uncomplaining grace. She had long ago realized that the more she cooperated with the vet, the more quickly she would return home.

Dr. Hood's inspection of Elvira's leg proved equally fruitless. Pulling off the goggles, he said to his assistant, "Tell me if she flinches." Then looking intently into Elvira's eyes, he pressed and squeezed Elvira's leg. "Aha!" he said after a few moments. At the same time, his assistant said, "She flinched."

Looking at Second Mom, Dr. Hood said, "Her paw's not the problem. It's her leg. I didn't see any sign of an infection on it from a scratch or a puncture wound, though. My guess is she probably has a bit of muscle strain. I'm going to give her some medicine for it. If she's not on the mend by this time next week, bring her back in."

Not only was Elvira not on the mend after a week, her limp had grown worse. So it was that she found herself back in Dr. Hood's examination room seven days later, hobbling across the floor as Dr. Hood and Second Mom observed her progress intently.

"You're right, Jane," Dr. Hood said before Elvira was halfway across the room. "Her limp is worse."

Second Mom nodded. "Do you think she could have a hairline fracture? I want you to x-ray that leg."

"Don't you worry. We're going to do an x-ray. And an MRI if the x-ray doesn't turn up anything." Looking at his assistant, he nodded in Elvira's direction.

Scooping Elvira off the examining table, the assistant spirited her out of the room and down the hall. Second Mom looked out the door, smiling reassuringly at Elvira, who, her head over the assistant's shoulder, was looking anxiously back at her. Only when the assistant and Elvira disappeared through another doorway did Second Mom turn back to the examination room. She began pacing the floor worriedly, looking every minute or so at her watch.

Just as she was beginning to think Elvira would never return, the assistant opened the door and entered the room, Elvira still in her arms. "She did great. She's a real sweetheart," she said, handing Elvira to Second Mom. "As soon as the x-rays are developed and Dr. Hood has had a chance to look at them, he'll be back in." Then she was out the door again.

Settling into a chair with Elvira in her lap, Second Mom began rocking her body back and forth, crooning as she stroked Elvira's back. She crooned and rocked, crooned and rocked for so long that she began to think that Dr. Hood had forgotten about them. She had almost crooned and rocked Elvira and herself to sleep when Dr. Hood, x-ray film in hand, walked in. After clipping the film to a board on a wall, he turned to Second Mom. "It's not good, Jane. Elvira has a bone tumor."

Second Mom stopped rocking as the words echoed in her mind. Her chest constricted so tightly that for a moment, she couldn't breathe. The room receded to a distant point, and she and Elvira seemed to become tiny figures alone on a vast, desolate, rapidly darkening plain. The whirr of rollers on the floor as Dr. Hood pulled up a stool and sat down in front of her jerked her back to reality.

Staring at Dr. Hood blankly, she heard him say, "Although it's rare in cats, I'm fairly sure the tumor's an osteosarcoma, the worst kind of bone cancer, very aggressive in most animals. It's not as aggressive in cats, but it's still bad news."

Clutching Elvira closely, Second Mom began to cry. "I'm going to lose my little girl, aren't I?"

"Now don't start crying or you'll make me cry," said Dr. Hood, handing her a tissue. "The sooner we jump on this, the better. I want you to leave Elvira so I can do a biopsy of the tumor today and send it off. It'll take about a week to get the results back. If they show what I think they will, chemotherapy and radiation won't help. I'll have to amputate Elvira's leg at the shoulder. That will give her about two to three years more, on the average. Otherwise, I advise putting her to sleep. Else the pain she's experiencing will quickly become unbearable."

Second Mom regarded Elvira, still stretched out in her lap, half asleep, unaware of the enemy growing inside her and the fate awaiting her. Turning her eyes to the x-ray, Second Mom stared at it as if it might reveal what was the best decision for Elvira's sake. After a long minute, she looked at Dr. Hood. "Do the biopsy. If it's what you say it is, I'll agree to the amputation."

Somehow Second Mom stumbled through the rest of the day, too numb to cry, not even when she handed Elvira back to Dr. Hood's assistant to be taken away again. Once home, she filled the seconds, minutes, and hours until Hon arrived by cleaning out and rearranging the kitchen cabinets, a chore she had been postponing for weeks and one she hoped would keep her mind off Elvira, who would be in a cage until the next morning, bereft of her comfort.

Finally, as the hands on the kitchen clock showed five o'clock, Hon's car pulled into the garage. Pulling off her apron, Second Mom rushed to the back door. Flinging it open, she burst into tears.

Concern written on his face, Hon took her in his arms and steered her by the shoulders to the couch. Sitting down, he pulled her down next to him and handed her his handkerchief. Leaning against him, Second Mom managed, between sobs, to choke out her news. "It's a terrible day," she concluded, "when the most comforting words you hear are 'This kind of tumor progresses slowly in cats' and 'Cat's do very well with amputations.'"

"I know, sweetheart, I know," Hon said, patting her shoulder. "Why didn't you call me? I would have come home."

"I needed to be alone."

For a few seconds, both were silent, Second Mom thinking of what lay ahead for Elvira and Hon thinking of what lay ahead for Second Mom. Breaking the silence at last, Second Mom blew her nose hard. "I don't understand why this had to happen. I try so hard to protect them. I take them to the vet twice a year for checkups and vaccinations. I brush their teeth and doctor them for fleas and ticks. I watch their snacks. I make sure they stay in the yard at night and make them come in before the lights go out. But I couldn't protect Elvira from this."

Holding her close, Hon said, "No, sweetheart, there are some dangers you can't protect her or Tibby from. Or us either, for that matter."

Second Mom gave a short laugh. "When Elvira's leg didn't get better, I was certain she had a hairline fracture. When I put her in the car this morning, I said, 'It's a glorious day, Elvira. You're going to start getting better as soon as Dr. Hood tapes that leg good and tight. You'll be running around in no time.' Those were my exact words: 'It's a glorious day.' It never occurred to me that she might have a bone tumor.

"But I think Dr. Hood knew as soon as I walked in with her. He got such a funny look on his face. I didn't pay it any attention, though, just assumed he was surprised that the medicine hadn't worked."

Second Mom's voice quavered as she finished her thought, and her eyes threatened to overflow once more. Taking a sobbing breath, she blew her nose on Hon's handkerchief to gain control so that she could say what she had been thinking about all afternoon.

"This afternoon, I realized that Elvira hadn't brought a mouse to the door, not a single one, for the past month, not since the last of February. Yet spring's the time when she hunts the most. If I had been paying enough attention, I would have known something was wrong with her much earlier. And she's lost two pounds. That's almost a fourth of her body weight. How could I not have noticed? She's nothing but a bag of bones."

"You pay plenty of attention to her. Blaming yourself is not going to make her better. If you start getting down, so will Elvira."

Second Mom nodded her head as if in agreement, but inwardly, she shook her head. How could she be bright and cheerful with Elvira facing who knew what? Why, even Tibby was moping around the house, disconsolate ever since she had arrived from the vet without Elvira. She was really going to be distressed when bedtime came and she had to sleep alone on their rug.

The next morning, Second Mom arrived at the vet's office before it was open. Peering through a front window, she spotted Dr. Hood's assistant talking on the phone. She waved her arms to catch the assistant's attention. Spotting her almost immediately, the assistant waved back. Walking to the front door, Second Mom waited impatiently to be let in. She did not have to wait long. Within the minute, the assistant had unlocked the door.

Laughing as she let Second Mom in, the assistant said, "I bet the doctor you'd be here bright and early. Sit here and I'll go fetch Elvira."

As soon as Second Mom had her beloved cat in her arms, her spirits lifted. Once home, she rocked her in her recliner for over an hour, Elvira thumping her tail in contentment for every rock that Second Mom made.

17

A Day of Reckoning

THE NEXT SEVEN DAYS SEEMED more like a year than a week. Second Mom's heart missed a beat every time the phone rang, even though she knew Dr. Hood couldn't be calling with the biopsy results so soon. If she did temporarily manage to forget about the call she was waiting for, seeing Elvira limp through a room or across the yard served as a stabbing reminder.

Yet when she finally picked up the phone and heard Dr. Hood's voice, she remained calm. "I'm sorry, Jane. Elvira does have a bone tumor, an osteosarcoma, just as I feared. If you haven't changed your mind about the amputation, I'll need to operate as soon as possible. Tomorrow, if you can bring her in. Say in the morning around eight?"

Second Mom stared into space, unable for a moment to think. Hearing Dr. Hood clear his throat on the other end of the line, she managed to gather her wits. "Tomorrow's fine. We'll be there at eight."

For the rest of the day, Second Mom felt strangely detached, unable to summon any feeling regarding the coming morrow. To distract herself, she busied herself in her flower beds, pulling up weeds, deadheading flowers, and pruning any errant branches she found on her shrubs. Occasionally she looked up to speculate on what Elvira's life would be like with only three legs. Would she be able to tussle with the kitchen rug or swat a ball across the room? Would she be able to pounce on a mouse or climb a tree? Doing all those things took two front legs.

Late that afternoon, she walked down to the creek bank, calling her two cats, who by that time had awakened from their afternoon siestas. As she watched them crest the hill and race down it toward her, she realized that this was the last time Elvira would run on four legs, the last time she would prowl among the grass and brush on the creek bank unimpeded. Would she even be able to run after tomorrow? Would she want to come down to the creek bank again if she couldn't keep up with Tibby?

That evening at supper, she voiced her concerns to Hon. "What if she can't hunt? She lives to hunt. Her heart would break if she could no longer catch a mouse. And mine would too."

Putting his fork down, Hon looked at her. "You have to have faith in Elvira. She'll figure out how to do what she wants to do. Maybe not at first but sooner or later."

Second Mom sighed. "You're right. I do know one thing, though. I thought deciding on the operation was the hardest thing I've ever done. But handing her over for it tomorrow will be harder."

At bedtime, Second Mom put away the cats' food and water saucers so that Elvira's stomach would be empty the following day. Thus it was that early the next morning, a hungry and thirsty Elvira found herself again in the cat carrier on the way to the vet, feeling most vexed a second time. She was sure she had made this trip not long before. Twice, in fact. Worse, Second Mom had forgotten to feed her breakfast. Going to the vet with a full stomach was bad enough. Going with an empty one was more that any cat ought to have to bear. The only thing that made the situation bearable was the sweater she was lying on. It smelled like Second Mom. Nestling in it, she waited out the trip.

At the vet's, Second Mom took Elvira, her front paws clinging to the sweater, from the carrier and, after disentangling her claws from the sweater, gave her one last hug before handing her to the assistant. Once the assistant had Elvira firmly in her arms, Second Mom handed her the sweater. "I want Elvira to have this. I've slept with it for the past week, so it smells like me. It will be a comfort to her."

"How thoughtful! I'll make sure she has it the whole time she's here."

Second Mom smiled her thanks. Then leaning over, she kissed the leg that would soon be gone. The assistant smiled reassuringly. "Don't you worry. Elvira will be fine. Except for her leg, she's a healthy cat. You take good care of her."

Second Mom gave the assistant a small smile. "Thanks. I try to."

"I'm going to take her on back now. Dr. Hood's waiting for you in his office to answer any last-minute questions."

Second Mom didn't have any questions for Dr. Hood about the operation itself. "But I would like to see her sometime this afternoon after she wakes up."

Dr. Hood nodded. "I don't see any reason why you can't do that. Say around four."

"That will be fine. You'll call me if there are any problems? I'm only fifteen minutes away. And let me know when she's out of surgery?"

Dr. Hood assured her he would keep her informed of Elvira's progress throughout the day. "Anything else?"

Second Mom hesitated slightly before saying, "I know this is going to sound like I'm trying to tell you how to run your operating room, but I've heard that patients often wake up from surgery extremely cold. I don't want Elvira to wake up chilled. So I went on the Internet and found some information about a warm-air blanket. Some doctors use them to keep their patients warm after an operation. Do you have anything like that?"

Dr. Hood assured her that he had something similar and that Elvira would not be cold when she woke up. Second Mom drew a deep breath. "Well, I guess that's it." She made a move to rise from her chair but stopped midway and sat back down. "I almost forgot. I would like to have her leg."

Dr. Hood stared at her for a moment before looking away, blinking his eyes and swallowing hard. Turning to face her once more, he said, "I think that can be arranged."

Opening her handbag, Second Mom took out a plastic bag with a hand towel in it and handed it to the doctor. "You can put the leg in this. I'll pick it up when I come back this afternoon."

For Second Mom, the rest of the morning passed in a blur. She busied herself in the house, stopping occasionally to look at the clock, wondering what stage of the operation Elvira might be undergoing. Every once in a while, she looked at the phone. True to his word, Dr. Hood called her around noon, reporting that the surgery had gone well and that Elvira was doing fine. Unable to settle down to any task after that, Second Mom put on some of her favorite music and, leaning back in her recliner, closed her eyes. There she stayed until four, not even rising to fix herself lunch.

For Elvira, the rest of her day sped by for the most part in unawareness. The first time she awoke, a soothing warmth enveloped her. She sensed lights and voices as if from a long distance away. She made a small movement to stand up, but the room started whirling around her and her left shoulder began throbbing. Settling back down, she closed her eyes. Darkness immediately engulfed her.

When she awoke again, she found herself in a large cage. Second Mom was standing at its open door, stroking her back and talking softly to her. Lifting her head, she tried to look at her left shoulder, which still throbbed. It also felt as if something tight was binding it. But the room began whirling again, so she lay her head back down. Closing her eyes, she listened to Second Mom's voice until darkness descended again.

Second Mom stayed a little while longer, continuing to stroke Elvira's back and talk to her. When she turned to leave, Dr. Hood appeared at her side, handing her the plastic bag she had given him that morning.

So light did the bag feel that for a moment Second Mom thought Dr. Hood must have forgotten to put Elvira's leg in it. As she slipped it into her tote, a tear slid down her face. Turning to Dr. Hood, she shook his hand. "Thank you for everything you've done."

Dr. Hood smiled. "All in a day's work. I guess you know you have some little cat there. She's a real sweetie. Never made one squeak or gesture of complaint."

Second Mom nodded. "I know. Tibby and I are so blessed to have her in our lives."

When Second Mom reached home, Hon was in his recliner, reading the newspaper. "I have Elvira's leg," she told him. "I want to bury it now."

Looking up, Hon put the paper aside. "I already have the hole dug. But don't you want to rest first? You've had a hard day."

"No, I can rest later."

Casting the newspaper aside, Hon rose. "Let's go then."

The two walked down together to the creek bank, with Tibby following. At the bank, Second Mom knelt in front of a small grave, which had been dug a few feet from William's. Taking the leg, still wrapped in its towel, from the plastic bag, she placed it in the grave. Swallowing hard to stop her tears, she spoke. "One day the rest of Elvira's body will be with you. Until then, make some beautiful flowers and green grass." Standing back up, she looked at the small bundle in the grave until it had been covered with dirt.

On the way back to the house, she said, "I hope I've done the right thing . . . that I decided on the operation for her sake, not for mine."

Hon hugged her. "You had it done for both your sakes. And for Tibby's too."

Second Mom smiled. "Thank you. Tomorrow the hard part starts. I'll need to remember those words."

When Elvira woke again, the sun was shining through the window next to her cage. Feeling an urge to stir, she struggled to stand up. No matter how hard she tried, though, she couldn't make her left front leg cooperate. She had no feeling at all below her left shoulder, which was throbbing worse than it had the day before.

But she didn't give up. Shifting all her front weight to her right leg, she finally managed to rise, staggering a bit. As soon as she gained her balance, she looked down. Shock surged through her. Her left front leg up to her shoulder was gone! What had happened to it? More important, how was she going to walk? What if she weren't able to? She dismissed that thought immediately. Pain or no pain, leg or no leg, she was going to walk.

Gathering all the resolve she could muster, she gave a short lurching hop on her remaining front leg, followed by a wobbly step with each of her back legs. Exhilaration mixed with relief filled her heart. She had done it; she had walked! Bowing to exhaustion and pain, she sat down. But only for a moment. She had taken only one step. Could she take another? Ignoring the dizziness that threatened to overwhelm her and the pain in her shoulder that was rapidly becoming excruciating, she stood back up. Struggling to keep her balance, she took another lurching hop-step-step and then another and another.

Stopping to rest for a few seconds, she spotted Second Mom's sweater at the back of the cage. Pausing frequently, she slowly hop-stepped toward it. Upon reaching it, she dropped down, exhausted. Resting her head on her one front paw, she waited for Second Mom.

When the door to the room opened a few minutes later, her ears twitched. She lifted her head expectantly only to lay it back down when the vet's assistant, carrying a tray, entered the room. Putting the tray on a table, the assistant walked over to her. "Why, look at you, Elvira! How did you get to the back of that cage? I bet you've been walking, haven't you?" Reaching into the cage, the assistant gently slid the sweater with Elvira still on it toward her. "I know you must be hurting, baby. I have something for that. But let's try to eat and drink a little bit first."

Elvira turned her face away from the proffered food and water. Yesterday morning, she had been ravenous, but today, the mere thought of food and water nauseated her. Abandoning her efforts, the assistant gave her an injection for pain. Then after patting her on the head, she closed the cage door, leaving her patient to doze.

When Elvira next awoke, she found herself, wrapped in the sweater, being put into the cat carrier. She heard a voice close by. It was Second Mom's! Peering through the carrier's side screen, she found Second Mom peering back.

Second Mom smiled. "Oh, Elvira, I'm so glad to see you. Let's go home." She turned to Dr. Hood. "Does she know yet that she's lost a leg?"

Dr. Hood nodded. "Yes, she knows."

Tears welled up in Second Mom's eyes. "I wanted so much to spare her that knowledge. But, of course, there was no way."

Dr. Hood patted her shoulder. "Remember, Jane, with animals, there's no emotional adjustment to the loss of a limb. There's only a physical one. Elvira is not grieving. She's accepted the loss of her leg, and she's already walked. She's won half her battle right there. You're the one who's going to have a tough time. Hang in there. Give Elvira room to do what she can when she can. Let her find her own way. At her own pace."

Second Mom smiled through her tears. "I will. Thanks again." Then, picking up the cat carrier, she and Elvira headed home.

Round One to Elvira

ELVIRA SLEPT ALL THE WAY to the small gray house on the hill. She slept so soundly that Second Mom glanced at her through the carrier's side screen every minute or two, worried that she might have stopped breathing. Only the occasional twitching of an ear or tail assuaged her fears.

In the house, Second Mom set the carrier on the living room floor. Opening its top, she carefully lifted Elvira out, putting her next to the hearth on a pet bed she had bought especially for her homecoming. Her food and water saucers, as well as a litter box, had been placed nearby. When she was satisfied that Elvira was comfortable, Second Mom sat on the floor next to her and looked around for Tibby. Not spotting her in the room, she called out, "Tibby, Elvira's home. Come and see."

At that moment, the phone rang. Springing up, Elvira looked around wildly before fleeing across the room, through the foyer, and into the guest room, where she dived under the bed. Her heart wrenching at seeing Elvira's lurching hop-step for the first time, Second Mom dashed after her, trying to reassure her. "It's okay, baby, it's okay. It's only the phone." Seeing Elvira dive under the bed, she knelt next to it and peered under it. Elvira was lying on the floor on her right side, eyes huge with alarm. Afraid that she might hurt Elvira if she tried to pull her from under the bed, Second Mom patted the floor. "Come on out, sweetie. I can't reach you under the bed." But Elvira was adamant. She was under the bed, and she wasn't moving.

Reluctantly acceding to Elvira's refusal, Second Mom moved the pet bed, saucers, and litter box to the guest room. Leaving the litter box next to one side of the bed, she pushed the pet bed and the saucers as close to Elvira as she could. "At least I know she can move fast if she needs to," she muttered as she stood back up.

"I thought you were going to put Elvira in the living room," Hon commented when he arrived home that evening.

"I was, but Elvira had other ideas. I think she feels vulnerable right now. Even the ring of a phone frightens her. So she's hiding out under the bed in the guest room. She probably feels more secure under something low. And with the shades drawn, the room's dark. It's also quieter than any other room in the house."

"I tried to tell you she wouldn't like the living room," said Hon. "But you wouldn't listen. I bet she doesn't like that pet bed either. Too difficult to get up from it."

After Second Mom left Elvira to her own devices, she slept the rest of the day. Her food and water saucers remained untouched, her litter box unused, much to Second Mom's dismay. The next day, however, she managed a few nibbles of food and a few laps of water. As Hon had predicted, she ignored the pet bed, finding it easier to rise from a hard surface. Not that she was doing much moving. When she wasn't sleeping, she lay still, listening to the familiar sounds of home—the clatter of Second Mom's shoes on the floors, the far-off roar of the vacuum, the deep song of the wind chimes on the front porch.

Once in a while, Tibby meandered in to sniff at her. If Elvira were awake, she lifted her head to sniff at Tibby in return. Every hour or two, Second Mom wriggled under the bed to pet and talk to her. Sometimes Elvira was sleeping so deeply that Second Mom touched her chest to make sure that it was rising and falling.

"She never moves, except to drink and eat, and that very little, and to use the litter box," she complained after Elvira had been home a week. "Shouldn't she be a little more active by now? Do you think I should call the vet?"

Hon lowered the paper he was reading. "No, I don't. What's Dr. Hood going to do? Stand her up and tell her to walk?"

Second Mom sighed despondently. "I guess I'm expecting too much too soon. When I brought her and Tibby home from the vet after being spayed, Tibby limped around for a week as if she had been mortally wounded. Elvira, though, hit the floor running and never looked back. I guess I thought she would be up and around that quickly after this operation."

"Being spayed, Jane, hardly compares to having an amputation. Elvira's been through major surgery. She needs time, more than the seven days you've allotted her, to recuperate. Remember what you said Dr. Hood told you about letting her get better on her own. As long as she's eating and drinking and she's not in any pain, she's all right. She'll start moving about more when she's ready. Until then, let her be."

Second Mom nodded. Hon was right, as usual. She would have to be patient. Elvira would improve, *was* improving daily. If only she would do so a little faster. She decided to check on her one more time before turning in for the night. Going to the guest room, she peeked under the bed. As she had expected, Elvira was lying quietly, head on her front paw, eyes closed. Second Mom checked her food and water saucers and, rubbing her behind her ears, softly bid her good night. Elvira's ears twitched, but she did not open her eyes.

The next morning, upon arising, Second Mom returned to the guest room, as she had every morning since Elvira's surgery. Looking under the bed, she felt her heart lurch. Elvira was gone! Dumfounded, Second Mom kept staring at the spot where Elvira should have been as if Elvira might materialize if she stared long and hard enough. Only after she had completely absorbed the fact that Elvira wasn't there was she able to stand up. Reassuring herself that Elvira could not have gone far, she began searching the room, peering under the arm chair and the bedside table and behind the vanity and chest of drawers, as she tried to coax Elvira to come out. "Elvira . . . Elvira, where are you? It's time for breakfast. I can't bring it to you unless I know where you are."

But Elvira did not appear. Growing more concerned by the minute, Second Mom undertook a systematic search of the rest of the house, beginning in the living room, proceeding to the dining room, and ending in her and Hon's bedroom. She looked under, on, and behind all the furniture. She raised all the blinds. She peered into every cabinet and closet, even though they had been closed all night. All her efforts, however, failed to produce Elvira. With nowhere else to look, she sought out Hon, who was in the bathroom, shaving. "I can't find Elvira anywhere in the house. I don't know what to think."

Eyeing her in the bathroom mirror, Hon paused his razor. "What do you mean you can't find her in the house? Where else could she be?"

"I don't know where else she could be. All I know is that she isn't in the house. She wasn't under the bed in the guest room when I went in to check on her this morning. So I searched the house from top to bottom. I can't find her anywhere."

"She has to be in the house somewhere," Hon reassured her as he resumed shaving. "Even if you didn't find her. She'll show up sooner or later."

"Where? And why would she be hiding? Do you think she might be depressed? Animals *can* get depressed, you know. Remember Tibby when William died? What if Elvira's decided she doesn't want to live with only three legs? She may have crept off somewhere to die. Animals do that, you know, when they're sick . . . or . . . or dying." Second Mom's voice ended on a quaver.

Halting his razor in midstroke, Hon caught and held Second Mom's gaze in the mirror. "You're overreacting, Jane. If she hasn't shown up by tomorrow morning, then you have grounds to worry."

"Tomorrow morning! I can't wait that long to find her!"

"What else can you do? Mount a search party?"

Hon was right. There was nothing to do but wait. Suddenly she had an inspiration. She called Tibby, who was lying on Second Mom's bedroom floor waiting for Second Mom to come out of the bathroom and feed her. Hearing Second Mom's summons, she immediately rose and hopefully trotted into the bathroom. But Second Mom had something other than breakfast in mind. "Tibby, where's Elvira? Elvira," she said, looking at Tibby intently. "Go find Elvira."

Tibby stared back, unmoving. Second Mom tried again, speaking slowly and enunciating each word emphatically. "Elvira, Tibby, go find Elvira." Tibby sat down and meowed faintly. Second Mom sighed in frustration. She should have known that wouldn't work. Suddenly, she snapped her fingers. The living room stove—she had forgotten to look behind the living room stove. She hurried to the living room, Tibby following, meowing insistently. Squeezing beside the stove, she called Elvira's name as she bent down to stare into the dark space behind it. But there were no yellow eyes staring back.

Defeated, Second Mom bowed to Tibby's plaintive meows and gave up the hunt for the time being. Instead, she headed to the kitchen to fix breakfast for Hon and Tibby. Then she filled two clean saucers with food and fresh water and took them to the guest room, just in case. Before quitting the room, she glanced quickly around it, hoping against hope that Elvira had reappeared. She hadn't. Dispiritedly, Second Mom returned to the kitchen.

She spent the rest of the day busy with her usual household chores, stopping every hour on the hour to recheck the guest room, to no avail. She also made occasional dashes to other rooms, convinced that she had heard a tiny squeak of a meow coming from them or telling herself that she might have overlooked a corner or a piece of furniture in her first search. Alas, the tiny squeaks turned out to be nothing but fancies of her imagination, and the empty corners and spaces behind and under the furniture remained just that—empty.

By bedtime, even Hon was worried. Maybe Jane was right. Maybe Elvira had hidden somewhere in the house to die. If so, where? "If she doesn't show up by breakfast, I'll help you search for her until we find her," he told Second Mom as they crawled into bed. "And look at her disappearance this way. You wanted her to start moving about. Now she has. Wherever she's hiding, she had to walk to get there."

There was little consolation in Hon's last words and his offer to help find Elvira in the morning was small comfort, but Second Mom smiled thanks as best she could before turning off the bedside light. Needless to say, neither got a good-night's sleep, with Second Mom worrying about Elvira and Hon worrying about both.

As soon as the room began to lighten in the faintest of excuses for morning, Second Mom threw back the covers. Tiptoeing across the room, she quietly opened and shut the door so as not to disturb Hon. Tibby, surprised by Second Mom's appearance at such an early hour, rose from her rug and followed Second Mom down the hall, expecting breakfast. But Second Mom didn't go to the kitchen. Instead, crossing the living room, she headed for the guest room. On the threshold of the foyer, she stopped. There, in the doorway to the guest room, sat Elvira.

Tears welled up in Second Mom's eyes. "Elvira, where have you been? Why didn't you come out when I called?" Snatching Elvira up, she scolded, "Do you know you've given me fifty gray hairs in the last twenty-four hours?"

Elvira showed not the slightest remorse. Instead she struggled to get down. Once on the floor again, she hop-stepped laboriously across the room to the bed and disappeared under it. Watching her progress, Second Mom felt as if a knife were stabbing her heart. The first time she had seen Elvira's hop-step had been devastating enough. Would she feel that way every time she saw Elvira walk?

Blinking back more tears, she looked under the bed at Elvira. Trying to be lighthearted, she said, "I'm going to bring you some food and fresh water. While I'm gone, whatever you do, don't disappear again. I'm not a spring chicken, you know. I don't need any more worry wrinkles on my face."

Elvira, regarding Second Mom unblinkingly, didn't making any promises. The rest of the day, Second Mom kept a close watch on her, returning to the guest room every thirty minutes or so to make sure she hadn't disappeared a second time. To her delight, Elvira wasn't always under the bed. Once, Second Mom found her lying in front of the window, soaking up the sun. Another time, she discovered her under the bedside table giving herself a bath. Twice she found her underneath the armchair, asleep, legs twitching from a dream.

"Elvira's turned the corner," she told Hon jubilantly at supper. "She's moving around, not staying under the bed all the time. Maybe she's feeling stronger, more like her old self."

"I hope so," said Hon. "I couldn't take many days like yesterday."

"Me either. I wonder where she was hiding all that time. And why? Such a mystery."

A few days later, Second Mom solved the where of the mystery. As she was dusting the guest room for cat hairs, Elvira hop-stepped a few paces from under the bed before lying down. Licking her front paw, she wiped it over the right side of her face. Second Mom paused dusting, suddenly struck by a disquieting realization. Elvira didn't have a left front paw. How would she wash the left side of her face? Would she be able to reach that side with her right front paw? And how would she manage to sharpen the claws on her right paw? She wouldn't be able to sharpen them on a tree or post, as she usually did, because she didn't have a left leg to stand on. As Second Mom mused on these questions, Elvira rose and slowly hop-stepped to the vanity. Putting aside her concerns, Second Mom watched Elvira's progress. Seeing her walk still filled her with pain, but if Elvira could accustom herself to her plight, so could she.

After rubbing her face against the vanity until she had satisfactorily marked it as hers, Elvira hop-stepped to the back of it, and without further ado, squeezed behind it. Second Mom, still watching, waited for her to materialize from the other side. When she failed to do so after a few moments, Second Mom frowned. What was Elvira doing? There couldn't possibly be enough space between the vanity and the wall for her to comfortably sit or lie down. Tucking her feather duster under her arm, she marched to the vanity and peeked behind it. Her mouth dropped open in astonishment. Elvira was nowhere to be seen.

Second Mom chewed her lip in thought. If Elvira wasn't behind the vanity, she had to be under it. But how? There was probably less than half an inch between the bottom drawer on each side of the vanity and the floor. Elvira couldn't possibly fit into a space that small. Could she? To find out, Second Mom pulled out the left bottom drawer. No Elvira. She pulled out the bottom drawer on the other side. There lay Elvira, yellow eyes staring up.

"The vanity has a crawl space of a few inches beneath the bottom drawer on each side," Second Mom told Hon at supper that evening. "I had never noticed it. There's just enough room for Elvira to squeeze under a drawer and lie down. That's probably where she was hiding the other day. But why was she hiding and why didn't she come out when I called her?"

Hon looked at her, a twinkle in his eyes, and intoned dramatically, "Cats! Never shall man ken their mysterious and enigmatic ways."

Giving him a long, level glance, Second Mom ignored his comment. "All that worry about her, and she was in the guest room the whole time. So I've made up my mind. I'm not going to worry about her anymore. If she disappears, I'm not going to try to find her. She'll come out of hiding when she's ready. And I'm not going to worry about her being depressed. Or sleeping more than usual."

"About time," observed Hon.

Second Mom bridled. "Don't sound so superior. If I disappeared somewhere in the house, you'd tear the house down, if you had to, to find me, and you know it."

Hon grinned. "I wouldn't have to. You'd come out when you got hungry."

True to her word, from that day on, if Second Mom couldn't find Elvira anywhere in the guest room when she went in to check on her, she didn't panic. She simply surmised that Elvira was under the vanity. If she weren't, she didn't want to know.

Shortly after solving the mystery of Elvira's hiding place, Second Mom opened her bedroom door one morning to find both Elvira and Tibby waiting for her on the other side. Second Mom's eyes brimmed with tears of joy. "Elvira, I'm so glad you've joined us again. Have you decided to move out of the guest room?"

Apparently, Elvira had, for from that morning forward, she spent more and more of her time with Tibby and Second Mom, eventually venturing outside occasionally to lie on the sundeck or to prowl around the shrubs with her lurching hop-steps. Second Mom would have much preferred keeping Elvira inside, but she knew she must let Elvira resume as much of her old life as possible. So she let her go outside whenever she wanted. But she kept a strict watch over her. If she didn't see her when she glanced out a window, she immediately headed out the door to find her.

She knew that she had promised Hon not to worry, but out of doors, danger—mainly in the guise of dogs, foxes, and coyotes—lurked everywhere. With only three legs, how would Elvira defend herself from them? She wouldn't be able to use her front claws because she needed her only front foot to stand on. She would either have to outrun the danger or climb a tree. But would she be able to run fast enough? And with only one front foot, would she be able to a climb a tree? If she did manage to, how would she get down?

What if she fell into the creek when the water was high? Would she be able to paddle to safety with only one front leg? And if she did make it to the bank, how would she drag herself up? Second Mom could think up no end of worries like these, none of which she voiced to Hon.

19

Round Two to Elvira

W<small>HEN NONE OF HER FEARS</small> came to fruition over the next week or two, Second Mom began to relax. Then one morning, trouble came calling, swooping low over the backyard. Startled, Second Mom looked up from the pan she had been fiercely scrubbing at the kitchen sink. She frowned. Had a vulture just flown past her window? Surely not. The only vultures she had ever seen were either circling high in the sky, scouting for a dead animal to feast on, or gathered at the side of a road devouring a possum or a raccoon that had been run over. Since there were no dead animals in her backyard, she couldn't possibly have seen a vulture. Relieved, she resumed her scrubbing.

Suddenly, she gasped and flung down the scrub brush. Elvira! Elvira was outside! Hadn't she read somewhere that vultures sometimes attacked weakened or injured animals? Had one seen Elvira lurching around the yard and, thinking she was injured, swooped in for the kill? Yanking off her rubber gloves, she dashed out the back door.

Calling Elvira's name repeatedly, she scanned the backyard. No Elvira. Heart thumping hard in her chest, she ran to the front yard, still calling Elvira's name. She sagged in relief as she spotted Elvira hop-stepping along the sidewalk fronting the flower bed outside the living room window. "Oh, Elvira, thank goodness you're okay."

Hearing her name, Elvira stopped and turned toward Second Mom. At that moment, the vulture zoomed over the spot where Elvira had been moments before. Panicked, Second Mom streaked to her side. Scooping her up, she sprinted to the front door, jerked it open, and fled inside. Still clutching Elvira, she ran to the living room window and scanned the sky. The vulture had disappeared. Trembling, she sank down on the couch, still clutching Elvira, who by this time was struggling to get down.

As soon as Second Mom released her, she hop-stepped to the front door. Second Mom shook her head. "Elvira, there's no way that you're going back outside without me. In fact, there's no way you're going outside the rest of the day, with or without me. Now I'm going to fix some tea to calm me down. I'll give you a snack too—some sardines. How would you like that?"

Astonished, Elvira stared at Second Mom as she left the room. Never before had Second Mom ignored her request to go outside. She continued standing at the door, certain that Second Mom would be returning shortly to open it for her. Only when she smelled sardines did she abandon her post.

At supper that evening, Second Mom related Elvira's narrow escape to Hon. Chewing steadily, he listened to her tale without comment. When she was finished, he burst out laughing. Affronted, Second Mom drew herself up in her chair as imposingly as she could. "What's so funny? I was scared to death."

Reaching over to her, he patted her shoulder contritely. "I'm sorry, sweetheart. But I can see you clutching Elvira as if she were a bag of gold that the vulture was trying to steal. I bet you didn't let her outside the rest of the day."

"For your information, to me she's worth more than all the bags of gold in the world. And no, I didn't let her outside the rest of the day."

Hon couldn't help the twinkle in his eye as he said, "I hope no one makes me an offer like that for her."

Second Mom stared icily at him. "I am trying to have a serious conversation about Elvira. You're not helping."

Hon patted her shoulder again. "I know. I'll be serious. Go on."

"What I'm trying to say is I don't know whether or not to let Elvira outside anymore. Today was just too close a call."

"Honey, I really don't think you have to worry about vultures attacking Elvira. They're only interested in dead cats, not live ones. This one was just probably scouting her out to see how injured she was. To see if she might be dying anytime soon. I doubt it will be back."

Second Mom was not impressed by his reassurance. "Well, I remember reading in a novel last year about vultures swooping down and carrying off a mamma cat and her kittens. If one could carry off a mamma cat, one could carry off Elvira. She weighs next to nothing."

Hon shook his head. "You're worried about something you read in a novel? Jane, a novel is not an encyclopedia. If you want to know about vultures, get the encyclopedia down. Or look on the Internet."

"I already have. This afternoon."

Hon leaned toward her. "And what did you find out? Do vultures eat live animals?"

Second Mom compromised. "The article didn't say they did. But it didn't say they didn't either."

Putting down his napkin, Hon stood up. "I give up. There is never any winning with you. You have way too much imagination. Keep Elvira inside if doing so makes you feel more secure. I just don't want you distraught about something that can't happen." Leaning over, he gave Second Mom a peck on the cheek and then headed for his recliner and the newspaper.

Second Mom let the issue drop. Supper over, she cleared the table, put the leftovers in the refrigerator, and filled the dishwasher with the dirty dishes. The entire time, however, she was deep in thought. Hon glanced up at her once or twice from the paper but said nothing.

Finally, as Second Mom began wiping the kitchen counters, she spoke. "I don't think Tibby would mind too much about not being allowed outside. She's inside most of the time anyway. But Elvira's different. Except in the winter, she spends most of her time outside. Keeping her in the house would be like putting her in a cage. I can't do that to her. I had rather her have a short, joyous life than a long, miserable one.

"Besides, keeping her inside doesn't guarantee her safety. If she had been an inside cat, she would have still gotten cancer. I should be worrying about it recurring in her instead of what I have been fretting about."

Throwing his newspaper aside and rising from his chair, Hon walked over to Second Mom. Standing behind her, he put his arms around her. Second Mom looked up at him and smiled. "I think you made the right decision, sweetheart. You're a good mother."

Second Mom nodded. "I think I made the right decision too. God made cats to come and go as they please. And that's what I'm going to let mine do."

And so Elvira continued to come and go as she pleased, increasing in strength and stamina daily. One morning, she wandered into Second Mom's bedroom as Second Mom was making the bed. After butting her head a time or two against Second Mom's legs, she sat down to watch her straighten and smooth the sheets and blankets and pound and plump the pillows. Second Mom smiled. "Are you waiting for me to finish making the bed so you can jump up for a nap?" She no sooner had the words out of her mouth than her smile changed to a frown. How could Elvira jump onto her bed, or onto anything else very high for that matter, with only one front leg to land on? She could easily lose her balance and fall.

Pondering this dilemma, she gave a few final tugs and pats to the bedcovers. In the midst of a tug, inspiration struck. She began throwing all the pillows, one by one, onto the floor. Elvira stared intently, head moving up and down, up and down, eyes following every throw. Next, Second Mom stacked the pillows on top of one another, making a semblance of stair steps up to the bed. Elvira's head moved back and forth, back and forth, eyes following each pillow from floor to stairway.

When Second Mom was finished, she turned around proudly, sweeping an arm toward the pillows. "Look, Elvira. Now you won't have to struggle trying to jump on the bed. Instead, you can walk up the pillows. And go back down too. Why don't you give it a try?" To underline her meaning, Second Mom swept her arm again, this time from the pillows up to the bed.

Elvira continued to regard Second Mom's gestures with interest. "Go on," urged Second Mom. "It's easy. Look, I'll show you." Leaning down, Second Mom walked her hands up the pillows to the bed and then back down. Straightening up, she smiled at Elvira encouragingly. Elvira, in turn, waited to see what Second Mom would do next. Second Mom just stood there, though, looking at her. Elvira stared back. Then losing interest as Second Mom continued to look at her, she leaped onto the bed.

Openmouthed, Second Mom stared at her. Finally, she broke into laughter. "Well, Elvira, I see you don't need my help at all. Like Dr. Hood said, you'll figure everything out. I should have more faith in you. From now on, I will. I can't wait to tell Hon how you jumped on the bed with no help." Needless to say, when she told him, she didn't mention the part she had played.

Within a month, Elvira could do almost anything she had done before her operation. It never occurred to her that she couldn't. She kept her claws sharp and the left side of her face clean. She jumped onto whatever she wanted—beds, chairs, even the back of a couch.

She still had regular spats with Tibby about being top cat on the totem pole. Nor did she hesitate to show any tomcat who happened to turn up exactly where on the totem pole he belonged. "Tibby and Elvira usually ignore the toms if they aren't too pushy," explained Second Mom to Hon one morning after Elvira had had a brush-up with one the evening before. "When they first started coming around, though, my two cats didn't know what to do. If one appeared while they were outside, they would rush to the back door, tails quivering in agitation, meowing to come inside. A couple of minutes later, they'd be at the back door again, wanting out. But as soon as the tom showed himself again, back in they wanted to come."

"Sounds like a couple of old maids getting all flustered the first time a man pays them any attention," Hon observed.

Giving him a severe look, Second Mom ignored his comment. "Now, though, they're rather blasé about the toms. The one last night, however, made the mistake of putting a paw on the bottom step of the sundeck, where Elvira and Tibby were sitting. Tibby just sat there, looking at him. Elvira, though, tore across the deck, fur raised, hissing and spitting.

"Believe you me, that tomcat didn't waste any time in backing down. A wise decision on his part. I have no doubt that Elvira, missing leg and all, could have licked him out of sheer determination, even if he did have four legs and outweigh her by at least five pounds. She hasn't lost any of her moxie, that's for sure." A frown appeared on Second Mom's face. "I hope she doesn't bite off more than she can chew."

"Now don't start worrying again," cautioned Hon.

"I can't help it. She and Tibby are my little girls."

Faith Restored

OVER THE NEXT FEW WEEKS, Elvira's hop-step became smoother and less halting, more practiced and sure, as if Elvira no longer had to think about how to walk with only three legs. She could do so automatically. The afternoon she raced down the hill to the creek bank at Tibby's side to prowl among the weeds and grass skirting the creek, Second Mom's eyes welled with tears and her heart swelled with pride.

The only activity that Elvira didn't resume was hunting. The only place that she didn't venture to was the field in back of the house. "I can't understand why she doesn't hunt anymore," Second Mom worried aloud to Hon, blinking back tears. "Maybe she's too tired. She wasn't too tired, though, to run down to the creek bank the other day with Tibby and me. But she does sleep more that she used to, almost as much as Tibby. And you know how much Tibby sleeps—sixteen hours a day at the very least."

Thus Second Mom, glancing out the kitchen window a few days later, was overjoyed to spot Elvira sitting in the field, her back to the house. Fighting back tears once more, she said softly, "Please, God, please help Elvira catch a mouse. She has such courage, and she's been through so much."

In spite of Second Mom's prayers, Elvira failed to produce a mouse that morning or that evening. About a week later, however, Second Mom found her at the back door one morning, a dead mouse in her mouth. Second Mom had never allowed her cats to bring mice into the house. That morning, however, Second Mom let her in, mouse and all.

"She's sneaked mice past me before," she told Hon that evening. "Sometimes she brings a live one in. So I have to get the mouse away from her before she kills it. I know killing mice is one of the things that God intended cats to do when he created them. But I don't have to watch. Poor Elvira! She'll spend fifteen minutes searching for her mouse after I manage to catch it in a jar and put it outside.

"This morning's the first time that I've ever knowingly let her bring one in. Now that I've let her, she'll probably think she can bring in all the mice she kills."

"Yep," concurred Hon, nodding his head. "You've probably started something you're going to regret."

"Well, I simply didn't have the heart to turn her away today. She looked so proud of herself, as if she knew that with only three legs, she shouldn't have been able to pounce on a mouse but had managed to do so anyway."

In the end, the only lasting effect Elvira suffered from her amputation was a tendency to be overly skittish at any unexpected sound or movement, no matter how familiar. A sudden burst of laughter, the clatter of a lid on a pan, the rattle of a newspaper—any such sound sent her in the opposite direction. Outside, Second Mom's sudden appearance around a corner, an unexpected flurry of leaves on the ground, or the growl of wind around the corner of a house was enough to set her in flight.

As Dr. Hood had foreseen, healing from the amputation took far longer for Second Mom than it did for Elvira. For weeks, her hearts wrenched at seeing Elvira make her way through the house or across the yard in her lurching hop-step. Remembering how graceful and fluid Elvira had once been, but would never be again, could make her burst into tears.

"Why are you crying?" Hon asked her when he found her cooking breakfast one morning, tears running down her face. "Be glad you still have her. Be grateful she's alive. Be proud of how well she's adjusted."

"I am glad I still have her. I am grateful," said Second Mom, trying to stop her tears. "I am proud. She deserves a medal; she truly does. But I need time to get used to her with only three legs. I need time to adjust. It's my loss too. I need time to grieve for both of us."

Sometimes, Second Mom expressed her grief not with tears but with anger. One evening as she was folding laundry on the couch, Elvira, stumbling from a misstep as she crossed the living room, fell to the floor, landing on her left shoulder. Second Mom exploded. "I don't understand why Elvira has to endure this!" she cried out, flinging down the dish towel in her hand. "She didn't do anything to deserve getting cancer."

Tossing aside the paper he was reading, Hon rose from his recliner and walked over to the couch. Pushing aside the laundry Second Mom had stacked by her side, he sat down beside her and gave her a small hug. They sat quietly for a few moments before he spoke. "I don't know why Elvira has to suffer either. But she's not crying over what life has handed her. When she fell down, did she complain or feel sorry for herself? No, she just got back up and kept on going. Just like she did when she found out she had a missing leg. She accepted the fact and learned to manage with the three she still had. Follow her example. Accept the situation. Be glad you still have her and get on with life."

"Unfortunately, I'm not a cat," Second Mom said, sniffing back tears. "I'm just a human."

Second Mom knew Hon was right. But knowing didn't lessen her grief. She continued to break down in tears at least once a day and suffered outbursts of anger almost as often. As the weeks became months, however, her tears flowed less and less often, her anger gradually wore down to acceptance. The sharp pang in her heart at seeing Elvira lurch through her life lost its edge, subsiding eventually to a dull ache.

Yet no matter how well Elvira seemed to adjust to her loss, no matter how much her own pain lessened, Second Mom never for a second forgot that Elvira had been given a death sentence of less than three years. That first year, she choked down dread every time Elvira coughed. Her heart missed a beat every time Elvira turned her face away from a meal. Her stomach tied itself in knots every time Elvira slept overly long. Religiously, chest constricted in anxiety, she took Elvira for a chest x-ray every three months. Each time the x-ray revealed no spot. And each time, Second Mom sagged in relief.

Then one morning, about a year after Elvira's amputation, while she was scattering birdseed on the ground, Second Mom heard a sudden *woosh*. Looking up, she saw Elvira shoot halfway up a nearby tree, her eyes on a blue jay perched on the topmost branch. Angrily squawking, the jay flew away. Elvira stared hard at the bird for a few seconds before slowly backing down the tree.

Second Mom watched the scene play itself out, transfixed. She had not been sure Elvira could climb a tree, much less back down one. She felt as if she had witnessed a miracle. From that moment on, she knew that no matter what happened to Elvira, no matter whether or not her cancer returned, she would be all right. Her body might die, but her spirit would always remain invincible. The ache in Second Mom's heart was no more.

Almost before Second Mom knew it, the second year had rolled by, then the third. Elvira's lungs developed no spots. Her body remained cancer-free. "Beats me," said Dr. Hood, shaking his head as he looked at Elvira's x-ray at the end of that third year. "Still no sign of cancer. She's overcome the odds so far. But the cancer could recur at any time."

Second Mom nodded. "I know that. But life's uncertain from one moment to another for us all. So I count every second I have with her and Tibby as a blessing and keep on praying. And no matter God's answer, Elvira and I both will be all right."

Thus did Elvira hop-step her way through life on her own terms. She never missed a trip to the creek bank with Tibby and Second Mom; she hunted almost every day; she made all tomcats toe the line. And in her dreams, she ran on four legs.

*****

Years passed. Tibby and Elvira became fierce, skilled hunters, keeping Second Mom's yard and the fields free of mice, moles, and snakes. Although she was smaller, Elvira was the more dedicated, going out in even the worst weather. Often on the hottest days of July and August, Second Mom would glance out her kitchen window to see Elvira's head sticking up above the tall grass of summer, waiting for a mouse to scurry by. Or she might see her waiting for a shrew to scamper across her path as the driving rains of November or the falling snows of January fell on her head.

All the while, Tibby could be found asleep in the middle of Second Mom's bed, taking refuge from the weather. Second Mom told Hon, "Elvira loves hunting more than any cat I've ever had. It's what she does for a living. Can she jump! And with only three legs! I saw her leap ten feet through the air the other day to pounce on something. Probably a mouse."

By the time the two cats were eight years old, middle-aged for a cat, they were almost inseparable. Where one saw Tibby, one saw Elvira. And where one saw Elvira, one saw Tibby. Sometimes when Second Mom looked at them, her heart missed a beat as she realized that, like herself, her two cats were growing older and there was nothing she could do to make time slow down.

More years passed. Before Second Mom knew it, her two cats were fourteen, well into old age. They moved more slowly, played less, and slept more. Their bones ached, and they chilled easily. They stayed inside more and more and hunted less and less. The mice, moles, and snakes gradually crept back into the yard and fields. But Second Mom didn't complain.

One morning, Tibby woke feeling unusually tired and achy. When Second Mom opened her bedroom door, she rose from her rug with a groan and hobbled slowly to the kitchen for breakfast. However, she could manage only a few bites. Feeling cold, she limped to the hearth in the living room and lay down on the rug in front of it. Gradually, the stove's warmth filled her body, taking away her chill and soothing her aching bones. She closed her eyes.

When Elvira finished her breakfast, she curled up next to Tibby as closely as she could. She, too, closed her eyes. Second Mom let them sleep undisturbed all morning. But at noon, she decided that Tibby needed to eat, as she had only nibbled at her food that morning. Pouring some cream in two saucers and opening a can of sardines, she called the two cats to lunch. Waking up to the smell of sardines, Elvira lurched as fast as she could to the kitchen.

But Tibby did not wake. Walking over to the hearth and bending down, Second Mom touched her lightly, saying, "Wake up, Tibby! It's time to eat! You're having sardines and cream!"

Tibby still did not wake. Bending closer, Second Mom put her hand on Tibby's chest. After a moment, she slowly withdrew it. Sitting down, she cradled Tibby in her arms, saying softly, "Oh, Tibby, my little Tibby Wibby." Then she wept for the days that had been but would never be again.

After Elvira finished her lunch, she sat with Second Mom and Tibby on the hearth rug. She knew nothing of death, but she knew, sniffing at Tibby's still figure, that she would never play or hunt with her friend again. She knew that she would sleep no more with her on the rug outside Second Mom's bedroom.

That evening, Hon found the three of them rocking in Second Mom's recliner, Second Mom holding Tibby's body with Elvira curled up next to her. Bending down, he hugged Second Mom, patted Elvira, and stroked Tibby's head gently. Then he went out to dig Tibby's grave along the creek bank, next to William's.

By the time Hon returned to the house, Second Mom had brushed Tibby's fur one last time and wrapped her body in a soft blanket. Holding the bundle close, she walked down to the creek bank, Hon and Elvira following behind. At the grave, she knelt and placed it gently and carefully in the dirt at the bottom, just as so many years ago Hon had placed William's. Wiping her tears away, she said, "You run now, Tibby, in fields much larger and greener. You run now with William. Be happy."

After Second Mom stood back up, Hon filled in the grave. When he was finished, he put his arms around Second Mom, holding her close. Then he and Second Mom, with Elvira in her arms, walked back to the house.

21

A Grumpy Morning

WILLIAM WOKE UP THAT MORNING on the outside of Sweetie Pie, next to the edge of the bed. He hated sleeping on the edge because he had to cling tightly to the blankets all night to keep from falling onto the floor. He preferred sleeping in the middle, in the narrow valley between Third Mom and Sweetie Pie. Their blanketed forms were like huge bulwarks, keeping him safe from any predators. Of course, no predators lurked anywhere in heaven, much less in the vicinity of Third Mom and Sweetie Pie's bed. All the same, William slept better with the bulwarks looming on each side of him.

But he had reached the bedroom late the night before, engrossed in a conversation with one of the two Toms about halos. The conversation had run along the lines of how heavy they were, how did God decide who had earned one, what happened if its wearer did or said or thought something that wasn't perfect in goodness, and other weighty questions of that sort. By the time he had reached the bedroom and jumped on the bed to claim his usual space, he found it already taken by Suki, Sweet William, and the two Dorcas.

While he was treading the bedcovers trying to decide where else to settle, the rest of the cats had claimed the head and foot of the bed. So he had been forced to settle for sleeping on the outside of Sweetie

Pie, next to the edge. Of course, he had not been alone. Neiki, ever inseparable from him, had scrunched up next to him as closely as possible. And, as usual, she had ended up on top of him.

When he opened his eyes that morning, still groggy from sleep, he thought he was in his usual place, between the bulwarks. He promptly rolled over to dislodge Neiki from her usual sleeping place on his back. Unfortunately, he rolled over onto, not bed, but air. Before he could gather his wits, he hit the floor. Neiki followed, landing with a thud on top of him. Too late, he remembered where he had gone to sleep the night before.

As soon as Neiki landed, she righted herself and hopped back onto bed. "That was fun!" she whispered, looking over the edge of the bed at William, still on the floor gathering his wits. "Let's do it again."

Jumping up next to her, William lay down, squeezing as close to Sweetie Pie as he could. Closing his eyes, he whispered, "Falling onto the floor is not fun, Neiki, particularly if you're the one on the bottom. Next time, you go first, and I'll fall on top of you."

Giggling, Neiki curled up next to him. "You say the funniest things, William."

A whispered warning sounded from under the blankets. "Shhh, you two. It's not even daylight yet. Any more talking and it's out to the barn for the both of you. With the cows and chickens."

Neiki, irrepressible as ever, whispered, "See what you did, William. You almost got me thrown out with the cows and chickens!"

"Me?" William whispered indignantly. "You were the one making all the noise."

"Was not!" declared Neiki.

"Was too!" rebutted William.

"Was not!"

"Was too!"

Just as Neiki was about to commence the third round of denials and accusations, a figure rose from the bed, grabbed the two errant cats, deposited them outside the bedroom, and closed the door.

Neiki promptly burst into meows of sobs. Scratching on the door, she wailed, "Let me in please. I won't talk anymore. I want Third Mom."

William, reminded of the first time he and Tibby had been put outside Second Mom's bedroom for the night, also burst into meows of sobs. He wasn't sure whether he was crying for Third Mom or for Second Mom and Tibby. He only knew he had to cry. Just as he was about to add his scratches to those of Neiki, the door opened.

"Don't cry, kitties. Come back in," Third Mom said consolingly, kneeling down to give each a pat. Standing back up, she headed to the bathroom where she grabbed her robe off the door hook and slipped into her house shoes. "Might as well start breakfast," she yawned. "Everybody's awake."

Peeking in the door, William saw the rest of the cats sitting up in bed glaring at the two miscreants for spoiling their last hour of sleep. Sweetie Pie was in the midst of them, glaring the hardest. Flinching at the sight of twenty-six accusing eyes turned in his direction, William slunk to the kitchen, followed by Neiki and, shortly after, by the remaining cats, complaining loudly about the early hour.

Their complaints lessened considerably when Third Mom took a box of Heavenly Delight from the kitchen cabinet. The cats lined up, their meows of protest turning into purrs of anticipation. William's heart sank, though, when he realized it was his turn to be at the end of the line. Being at the end meant that he had to wait for Third Mom to pour thirteen other bowls of food and set them on the floor, one bowl at a time. Twitching his tail nervously while treading the floor, he meowed plaintively until, finally, Third Mom, reaching the end of the line, set his bowl down.

It had no more touched the floor than he crouched over it. Opening his mouth for the first gobble, though, a nauseating smell assailed his nose. Liver-flavored Heavenly Delight, yuk! His least favorite, especially in the morning when his stomach, at its emptiest, demanded something extra delicious to fill it up.

Briefly, he considered asking for another flavor. But he knew better. When Third Mom had begun keeping cats, she had given each one whatever flavor of Heavenly Delight it wanted at every meal. But by the time cat seven put in its appearance, she felt like both a waitress and a short-order cook, trying to prepare and serve seven different meals for seven cats three times a day. That wasn't even counting snacks. She had to write their orders on a tablet just to keep them straight.

And what a cat gulped down for breakfast one morning, it was likely to turn up its nose at the next time, acting as if Third Mom had offered it a bowl of chicken tongues or cow ears. Third Mom found herself having to stock as many as twenty different flavors of Heavenly Delight and an equal number of differently flavored snacks. Her kitchen cabinets were crammed with so many boxes and bags of cat food and cat snacks that there was no room for the boxes and bags that belonged to her and Sweetie Pie. After an especially trying breakfast spent trying to fill the orders of seven finicky and persnickety cats, some of whom changed their minds before she could put in front of them what they had originally requested, she put her foot down. "No more catering to every cat's taste buds. As of today, you eat what's set before you. Like Sweetie Pie does. Or go hungry. And no complaining." From that day own, her cabinets held only three flavors of Heavenly Delight— one for each meal of the day—and three flavors of cat snacks. The cats ate them until they were gone. Then they started on three other flavors.

So William knew there was no sense in asking for something more appetizing. He thought momentarily about not eating breakfast at all. Third Mom was strict, though, about the cats eating at least three bites of what was put before them. Plus no snacks for any cat who didn't eat at least half his food. Glumly, William addressed his bowl. He managed three bites, swallowing them half-chewed to get them down as fast as possible, holding his breath to avoid the smell. After the third mouthful, he eyed the remainder, shuddering.

He couldn't manage another bite, much less half his meal. Maybe a morning snack wasn't that important after all.

As he had eaten only three bites of breakfast, he gave himself only the most cursory of an after-breakfast face scrubbing before wandering outside to the back porch. Restless and irritable, he lay down for an after-breakfast snooze. But sleep wouldn't come. Just as it was about to descend, his tail would twitch, a leg jerk, or an ear perk up at an unexpected sound. After a few minutes of tail twitching, leg jerking, and ear perking, he sat up, trying to think of something to do that would take away his low spirits. His forehead was deeply wrinkled from the effort of his thoughts when Big Tig and Black Bart rounded the corner of the house.

"Hey, William," meowed Black Bart, "what are you thinking so hard about? Come and play hide-and-pounce. You can be it and hide first." William shook his head. Any other time he would have eagerly joined in the game. Right now, though, he couldn't summon any enthusiasm for hide-and-pounce or for anything else.

Suddenly, he realized what was wrong. He was having a grumpy day. Waking up on the edge of the bed—that's what had done it. He sighed despondently. Grumpy or not, he would have to act pleasantly all day. Third Mom frowned mightily on grumpiness that lasted for more than ten minutes. She said that every day was what you made of it and in heaven, there was no reason not to make every day a happy one. She believed in going for the joy. Going for the joy, though, was the last thing he felt up to that morning.

At that moment, the skies opened, and a cold rain began to pour. Clouds had been darkening while he had been on the back porch, but so sunk in his own gloom had he been that he had failed to notice the gathering downpour. Forgetting about his low spirits, he sprang up and raced for the cat door, as did the other cats caught outside in the unexpected shower. They met at the cat door. There followed a desperate attempt by ten cats to go through the door all at the same time. Legs and tails tangled and voices rose. The confusion ended with Callie and Miss Paws getting stuck in the door, desperately trying to wriggle themselves either in or out. They didn't care which as long as they got unstuck. Waiting for the two stuck cats to free themselves, the rest of the cats milled miserably around the door, getting wetter by the second and complaining bitterly.

Just as they were about to give up ever escaping the rain, Third Mom saved the day. Hearing their caterwauling from the kitchen, she ran to the back door and flung it open. Having learned nothing from Callie and Miss Paw's dilemma, the rest of the cats swarmed for the door at the same time, falling over one another in their frantic efforts to get inside. Shaking her head at their behavior, Third Mom hurried to the cat door where she gently pried Callie and Miss Paws free and brought them inside with her.

The drenched cats headed for the living room, where they began drying themselves off, pausing between licks every minute or two to exclaim in exasperation about their soaking wet fur. William spent fifteen minutes licking dry every square inch of himself that he could reach.

Meanwhile, his spirits sank lower and lower. How much worse could his day get? He had rolled off the bed and been ignominiously put outside the bedroom. Through no fault of his own, he would like to add. Then he had to wait forever for his breakfast, which turned out to be liver flavored. Now this. Even worse, he wouldn't be getting a midmorning snack as he had eaten only three bites of breakfast. His stomach was already growling for lunch.

Gloomily, he decided to go to the cat room and climb into one of the nooks. Nothing could go wrong there. Nor would he have to watch the other cats eat their snacks. He wouldn't come out until he felt better. Or until lunchtime. Whichever came first.

22

A Light at the End of the Tunnel

Alas, the solitude William sought was not to be. As he plodded into the cat room, a voice startled him from above with a softly
drawling "Hello, there." Glancing up in dismay, he spied Suki sitting on the topmost ledge. Wouldn't you know it? Wouldn't you just
know it? Feeling his tongue become tied as it always did around her,
he jumped on the ledge farthest from her. He hoped that she would
get the message that he was not in the mood for conversation.

No such luck. Again Suki's voice drawled from above. "What's
the matter? Cat got your tongue?"

Ignoring her comment, William lay down, head on his front paws.
Closing his eyes, he resolved to pay her no mind. Just as he was on the
verge of dozing off, the sound of singing drifted from Suki's direction:

> Three little kittens
> Lost their mittens
> And they began to cry.
> "Oh, Mother dear,
> We very much fear
> That we have lost
> Our mittens."

Suki sang the entire song, all eight stanzas, much to William's irritation, which increased with every verse. His only hope was that she would cease and desist after she finished the last stanza. But as soon as she soon as finished the last one, she began again:

> One little kitten
> Lost his tongue,
> And he began to cry.
> "Oh, Mother dear,
> I very much fear
> That I have lost
> My tongue."

The song made no sense when sung that way, and the rhyme was atrocious, but Suki seemed to take delight in it, nonetheless. As for William, he felt like crying. He was determined, however, to show Suki that he was not upset in the slightest. As soon as he felt a tear well up in an eye and threaten to run down his face, he clenched his jaws until the urge to cry passed. His knew one thing. He might not be completely good yet, but he was way ahead of Suki. He had better earn a halo before she did! That's all he could say!

In the midst of these thoughts, Suki grew quiet. William wondered what she was up to. But he was determined not to look around to find out. He didn't intend to give her the satisfaction of knowing he was interested in anything she did. However, as the silence lengthened, his curiosity grew until he could fight it no longer. As inconspicuously as possible, he craned his neck around. He need not have worried. Suki was engrossed in one of her numerous daily baths, completely oblivious to his presence.

She was famous for the number of baths she took, at least five or six a day, and on muddy or rainy ones, more than that. "I don't know why she takes so many," Callie or Miss Paws liked to sniff on occasion. "What does she ever do to get dirty? All she does all day long is sit and admire herself. You'd think she was Cleopatra's cat."

"Well, you know what they say about cats having nine lives," the other always rejoined. Then both would shriek with laughter.

William always felt sorry for Suki when the other cats made fun of her, even if most of what they said was true. But at the moment, his sympathy was in short supply. Turning back around and laying his head back down, he closed his eyes and covered them with his front paws. He was almost asleep when he heard Third Mom open a cabinet door in the kitchen. One ear perked up slightly. Next he heard the rattle of a bag of cat snacks being shaken. Snack time!

He sighed despondently. Might as well go back to sleep so he wouldn't have to hear the other cats, who were having a much better day than he was, munching and purring in the kitchen. He was sure they wouldn't miss him at all. Why, Third Mom might even give them his share. Which would be totally unfair. Just because he wasn't allowed a snack didn't mean that the other cats should have it. He closed his eyes for the umpteenth time that day.

And for the umpteenth time that morning, his attempt to sleep was interrupted, this time by Suki's voice. "Aren't you going to have a snack?"

William opened one eye to see her standing at the door, looking up at him as her tail twitched in her impatience to get to the kitchen. "Can't," he said gruffly. "I didn't eat half my breakfast this morning."

After contemplating him a moment, Suki said, "That's too bad. Well, see you later." Flashing him a look of sympathy, she disappeared through the doorway and sashayed down the hall, humming the tune to "Three Little Kittens."

Left to his own devices, William tried not to think about the most wonderfully delicious, extraordinarily tempting snack he was sure Third Mom was handing out at that very moment, one the cats had never had before and would probably never have again. Much better than the usual fare. Just his luck to miss out on it. One thing was for sure. He wouldn't ask Suki how delicious it had been. He would act as if missing out on it bothered him not at all.

Bogged down in a morass of self-pity, he failed to notice Suki's return to the cat room. Only when she meowed softly, "Hey, little boy, I have a treat for you," did he realize she was back. Snapping momentarily out of his doldrums, he looked warily at her, wondering what other taunts and tricks she had in mind. To this surprise, she had a treat in the shape of a fish between her front feet.

"For you," she said. "No, really," she added, observing the doubtful expression in his eyes. "And there's more." Leaving the treat on the floor, she turned and bounded from the room. William didn't budge. He didn't trust Suki. She was up to some trick.

Within less than half a minute, she was back, swatting another fish shape in front of her. "Here's another. One more to go." Then she turned and bounded from the room a second time, to return shortly, swatting the third fish ahead of her.

"See, I saved half of my fish for you. Why don't you come down? Don't you want them?"

William still didn't budge. Why was Suki being nice? That wasn't like her. More than likely, as soon as he opened his mouth for the first fish, she would gobble it as well as the other two. Then laugh. Well, he wasn't going to give her the satisfaction.

"Why do you care whether I have a snack or not?" he asked. "Especially after making fun of me with that mean song."

Suki looked puzzled. "Mean song? Oh, you're talking about 'Three Little Kittens.' I was just trying to make you laugh. You looked so grumpy when you came into the room. And you looked so disappointed about missing your treat. I thought you might cheer up if I brought you half of mine."

William couldn't believe what his ears had heard. Suki concerned about another cat's feelings? That wasn't like her. He decided to test her. Jumping down, he walked over to the treats. Looking at her out of the corner of one eye, he bent his head over one of the treats and opened his mouth, expecting Suki to make her move at any second. But she sat there quietly as he hungrily consumed all three. As soon as he had finished the last one, guilt coursed through him.

After wiping his mouth with his tongue, he said, "I'm sorry I seemed ungrateful. Thanks for the treats. I really did enjoy them. As I told you, I didn't have much breakfast."

Suki grimaced. "I know. Liver-flavored Heavenly Delight is not my favorite either. It's all I can do to eat enough to earn my snack."

Now William really didn't know what to think. This was the first serious conversation he had ever had with Suki. And as far as he knew, it was the only real conversation she had ever had with any cat. He hated to admit it, but she wasn't half as bad as he had thought. Oh, rats and snakes, what if she earned her halo before he did? Such an idea didn't bear thinking about.

Suki interrupted his thoughts a second time. "For some reason, I put you and the others off. There's something about me all of you don't like, but I don't know what it is or how to fix it."

For a moment, William thought Suki was going to cry. In fact, he was sure he saw a tear teeter on the tip of a lash and slide down her face. If there was one thing that might make him more jittery than Suki, it would be her tears.

To forestall any further ones, he spoke up hastily. "W . . . e . . . l . . . l . . ., you are a very elegant, refined-looking cat. So we naturally expect you to be a little snooty . . . to think that you're better than we are. That's okay. We can live with that. But you never play with us. You stay to yourself. What's more, you never talk to us. Instead you yawn and look totally uninterested. And . . . and . . ." William tried to think of something else, certain that he had not covered the litany of complaints that the other cats had against Suki. Inspiration struck. "Plus, you do take an awful lot of baths. When you're not even dirty. And sometimes you say mean things."

Overwhelmed with William's list, Suki sat down with a thump. With bated breath, William waited for her to speak. After several tense moments, she did. "Oh." A few more tense moments followed. Then, without warning, she burst out caterwauling.

William's heart sank. He pranced in dismay around her. "Please don't cry, Suki. Please. I'm sorry! I'm sorry! I take it all back."

Suki bawled even harder. Within seconds, Third Mom was at the door. Hands on hips, she surveyed the room but could find nothing amiss. She looked at William questioningly. He hung his head. Walking over to Suki, she picked her up and patted her consolingly. "Sakes alive, Suki, tell Third Mom what's wrong, little girl. I'll fix it for you."

Suki struggled to stop sobbing. "William said some bad things about me. He told me that"—sob, sob—"that none of the other cats"—sob, sob, sob—"that none of the other cats like me." Sob. "And after I shared my treats with him."

Third Mom looked reproachfully at William. "Is this true, William? Did you say bad things about Suki? Did you tell her that none of the other cats like her?"

William was flabbergasted. How could Suki have told such a big fib? And after being so nice to him! Well, he wasn't going to let her get away with it. "No," he said stoutly. "She asked me why none of the other cats liked her, so I told her why. But I tried to be nice about it."

Third Mom looked reproachfully at Suki this time. "Is this true, Suki?"

Suki hung her head. "Yes," she muttered softly.

Third Mom looked sternly at her. "If you asked William why none of the other cats liked you and he told you, then what were you crying about?"

"Because none of the others like me."

"But you knew that already. So why are you crying now?"

"Because I want to make the other cats like me, and I don't know how," Suki wailed. Then she started crying again.

Third Mom sighed. "I think we've had a talk about this several times, Suki. You can't make another cat like you. But you can make yourself more likeable. Like you did with William when you shared your treat with him. Try playing with the other cats once in a while. You might find you like hide-and-pounce and chase-the-mouse. Come on. Let's go to the kitchen and have another big talk."

As they left the room, Suki still in Third Mom's arms, he heard her say, "But I don't want to play. I don't like my fur to get dusty. And I can't stand muddy paws. Besides . . ." Her voice gradually faded away as she and Third Mom made their way down the hall.

William breathed a sigh of relief. Now he would have some peace and quiet. But how unpredictable Suki was—considerate and generous one minute and tattling and telling fibs the next. He need not worry. He was bound to earn his halo first. Paws down.

As he leaped back onto a ledge, an unpleasant realization hit him. From now on, he would have to come to Suki's defense when the others started talking about her. He would have to tell them about her efforts to cheer him up, no matter how misplaced they had been, and about her sharing her morning snack with him. No one would believe him. They might even make fun of him. But no matter. He would have to tell. Or else he wouldn't be able to face himself in the mirror when he checked out his reflection to see how his halo was coming along.

Not that he had seen any evidence of one so far. But just in case it was so small he couldn't see it yet, he didn't want to do anything that might cause it to start shrinking. Getting this far had been hard enough. He didn't want to start backsliding. He sighed in discouragement. Life in heaven sure was a complicated business. When would it begin to get easier?

Happily, William's lunch went much better than had his breakfast. Third Mom must have taken pity on him and the other cats who detested liver-flavored Heavenly Delight, for the bowls were filled with sardine-flavored Heavenly Delight, his favorite. Had Third Mom poured a bit extra in his bowl? He could have sworn his portion looked a little larger than usual. Even better, Neiki saved part of her meal for him also. He gratefully gobbled it down, not mentioning that he suspected that Third Mom had already given him a little extra. He wasn't that perfect yet!

After lunch and the requisite face cleaning, nap time loomed. This meant a mad scramble for one of the cat hammocks in the living room, there being fourteen cats and only five hammocks. Third Mom's rule was first come, first served. Nor was any cat allowed to push another cat off a hammock and claim it for itself.

William was determined to have a hammock that day. He certainly deserved one after the unsettling morning he had endured. Hopefully, his grumpiness would disappear after taking a nap in a hammock. Surreptitiously, he inched closer and closer to the hammocks.

The moment finally came that all the cats had been anticipating since finishing lunch. The last cat gave the last scrub of a paw to its face. At that point, the cats eyed one another in silence for a few seconds. Suddenly, without any discernible signal, they all made a dash for the hammocks. William rushed to the one nearest him. Just as he was about to put a paw on it, one of the Dorcas slid in front of him and jumped onto the hammock. The other Dorca followed suit.

William was outraged. He had been gypped! He had practically had his paw on that hammock and the two Dorcas knew it! They weren't playing by the rules. If there was one thing he hated, it was a cat who didn't play by the rules. He opened his mouth to complain but, upon second thought, shut it. The last time two cats had made a fuss over a hammock, neither one ended up with it. Third Mom put it away in a closet, and the two cats had to find another place to take a nap.

William drooped. He knew when he was defeated. He should have stayed in bed this morning. Then everything that had gone wrong with his day wouldn't have. Feeling himself on the verge of tears for a second time that day, he trudged to the couch and hopped onto it, Neiki following closely behind. Turning around several times before he found a comfortable position, he finally curled himself into a ball, tucked his head into his chest, and closed his eyes. He felt Neiki curl up next to him. Sleep quickly descended.

He was in the midst of a dream about being the proud possessor of the largest halo ever seen on a cat when he felt something shaking him. He opened his eyes in annoyance. Neiki had better not be playing tumble cat on him. He was not in the mood for one of her games.

But the something shaking him was not Neiki. It was Third Mom. Seeing she had his attention, she put a finger to her lips. "Shhh. Don't wake Neiki. I want you to come with me. Tibby's here."

William and Tibby Forever

Upon awakening from her nap, Tibby rose, stretching and yawning until she felt wide awake. Next she glanced around, expecting to find herself by the wood stove in Second Mom's living room, with Elvira close by. To her amazement, she found herself in a large field, one she immediately knew she had never been in before. How on earth had she gotten here? She certainly had no memory of waking up and going outside, much less of wandering into an unfamiliar field and lying down for another nap. But evidently she had, for here she was.

At that moment, a mouse scampered by. And what a mouse it was—the plumpest, juiciest-looking mouse she had ever seen. Without thinking, she gave chase. Through the grass, the mouse darted, first one way and then another, with Tibby in close pursuit. At last, with a prodigious pounce, Tibby captured it between her paws. She couldn't wait to have a bite. To her surprise, the mouse did not squeak or try to escape as mice usually did when they found themselves within her grasp. Instead, it looked up at her and grinned. Astonished, Tibby found herself staring into a pair of impudent eyes. Shaking her head as if to clear it, she firmly reminded herself that she was a cat and the creature between her paws a mere mouse. Closing her eyes, she opened her mouth wide.

At that moment, she heard a voice calling her name. Opening her eyes and closing her mouth, she looked around. In the distance behind her, she spotted a woman holding a gray and orange cat with black stripes. Both woman and cat were looking in her direction. Something about the cat caught her attention. A name long unbidden stirred in her memory. *William.* Her heart quickened. *William! The cat was William!* Forgetting the mouse, she raced toward her brother. "William! William!" she meowed loudly as she ran. "It's me, Tibby."

At the sight of Tibby running toward him, William struggled to get free. Laughing, Third Mom put him down. As soon as his paws felt the grass, he galloped toward his sister. In an explosive leap, the two cats embraced in midair, landing in a caterwauling of happy meows and tangled legs. For the next few minutes, bodies entwined, they lost themselves in an ecstasy of nose kissing and head butting.

At last, catching her breath, Tibby said, "William, you've come back! You've come back! I can't believe it!" Suddenly in the midst of her exultation, an angry look replaced the joyous one that had been on her face a moment before. "Why did you leave me? I thought I would never see you again. Do you know how sad I felt? And lost? Why didn't you love me and Second Mom enough to stay? Or at least tell us where you were going and when you were coming back?"

"Oh Tibby! I didn't want to leave you," said William. "Remember the night we chased the rabbit. Well, I was hit by a beast when I ran into the road. Actually, it's not really a beast. It's a car. But you'll learn all that later."

Tibby nodded. Now that William had mentioned it, the memory of that night came flooding back.

"When the car hit me, I was killed. That means my body was so damaged that it couldn't live any longer. But the part of me that was still alive, my soul, came here, to heaven, to get a better body, one that could never be killed."

Tibby stared at William. Then she looked around the field. "Is this field heaven? Am I in heaven too?"

William laughed. "Yes, Tibby. You're in heaven too. But heaven is much larger than this field. Heaven goes on forever and ever. No cat can ever get to the edge of heaven."

Tibby still looked puzzled. "Why am I here? I didn't chase a rabbit into a road and get killed. The last thing I remember is lying down by the stove this morning."

William looked tenderly at Tibby. "When you lay down this morning, your body was so tired and worn out that it died. So you're—"

Tibby interrupted. "What does *died* mean?"

"It's just another word that means your body stopped working. As I was saying, when you died, your soul came to heaven to get a new one."

Upon hearing William's words, Tibby looked down at her chest and front legs. Next she twisted her neck around to look at her sides and back. William smiled, remembering that he had done the same thing once.

"I'm beautiful again!" Tibby exclaimed in wonder after she had finished inspecting her new body.

William smiled indulgently. "Don't you feel younger too? I saw you chasing something a while ago. Weren't you able to chase it without getting tired or hurting? Weren't you able to run as fast as you once could? Maybe even faster. That's because of your new body."

Tibby nodded thoughtfully. Deciding to try out her new body, she sprinted away in a streak of pumping legs and thrusting chest, running and leaping and twisting. Only when she was at the far end of the field did she turn around and head back at a sedate pace.

"Oh William," she said when she reached his side, joy once more written on her face, "you're right. I'm not tired or achy or cold anymore. I can run faster than I've ever run in my life. I can't wait to show Elvira and Second Mom."

Suddenly, a puzzled look crossed her face. She glanced at William, then down at herself, and then at William again. Finally she said, "Why am I so much bigger than you? You used to be the big one."

"That's because you were full grown when you died. But when I died, I was just a five-month-old cat with more growing to do. So when I arrived in heaven, I received a five-month-old body. It's stayed that age so that when Second Mom sees me again, she'll see me as she remembers me. She can watch me grow up just like she watched you grow up."

Tibby's eyes shone. "Can we go home right now? I know she's missing me. And Elvira too." She looked at her new body again, swelling with pride at her long hair, fuller and shinier and softer than it had ever been.

William had been dreading this question. Hoping for the best, he said, "We can't go back home, Tibby. Heaven is our home now."

Abruptly, Tibby quit admiring herself and stared at William, her eyes slowly widening. "Not go home? Never see Second Mom or Elvira Wira again?" Her voice quavered as she spoke. Then she burst out in loud howls, "I want to go home right now! I want my Second Mom and my Elvira Wira!"

Agitated by Tibby's howls, William began howling too. For several moments, the air was filled with their heartrending sounds. Gradually, however, Tibby's howls abated to sobs and hiccups. Noting that Tibby was calming down, William gained control of himself. Touching his nose to hers for a long moment, he said, "Don't be sad, little Tibby Wibby. You'll like heaven, I promise. You're going to live with me and all the other cats that Second Mom has ever had. Plus you'll have a Third Mom and a Sweetie Pie to love and take care of you. Best of all, one day Second Mom and Elvira Wira—whoever that is—will come live with us."

Tibby stopped sobbing and hiccupping, looking hopefully at William. "Really? They're going to come too?"

"Yes, Tibby, they're going to come too."

"Today?"

"Probably not today. But soon. And until Second Mom comes, Third Mom is going to be your mom. She's the woman that you saw holding me. Let me take you to meet her now."

As William led Tibby to the woman, who had been waiting all this time in the same spot Tibby had first seen her, he asked, "By the way, who's Elvira Wira?"

For a moment, Tibby didn't answer, so filled was she with longing at the sound of Elvira's name that she couldn't speak. Only after swallowing down an impending sob was she able to speak. "She's a kitten Second Mom brought home to cheer me up after you disappeared. Only now she's a cat. An old one. She calls herself Elvira Wira of Tyra Lyra. She thinks the name makes her sound important. But I call her plain old Elvira. She's my best friend."

"Don't worry," she added as William stopped in his tracks and looked at her with a hurt expression in his eyes. "You're my brother, and no one can ever take your place. We belong together."

Again William touched his nose to Tibby's. Then they made their way to Third Mom.

*****

Tibby, with William at her side, settled easily into Third Mom's house, although at first she was jealous of Neiki. She soon realized, though, that just as she had enough love in her heart for both William and Elvira, William had enough love in his for both Neiki and her. By the end of the week, all three were inseparable. If Neiki slept on one side of William, Tibby slept on the other. If Neiki wanted to play hide-and-pounce with William, Tibby played too. If one spied a rabbit to chase, the other two were close behind.

Like all the cats at Third Mom's, Tibby spent her days doing the three things that cats do best—playing, eating, and sleeping. Of course, she had to learn the same lessons and rules that all the cats had to learn when they first arrived at Third Mom's. But with William there to guide her and give her advice, she did not suffer the cuffings and withering stares that he had endured. Moreover, he was a great help in filling her in on the other cats' idiosyncrasies.

"There's Neiki, of course. You've probably already figured out she's harum-scarum and flibberty-gibetty. Hopefully when she grows up, she'll be a little more settled. But that's not going to happen until Second Mom arrives. We'll just have to put up with her craziness until then.

"You've already made friends with Prissy and Little Cat. Little Cat was Prissy's only kitten. She died when she was barely two months old. When Prissy first opened her eyes in heaven, there sat Little Cat in front of her. They both burst into tears of joy. Prissy immediately set about making up for lost time in being her mother. Or so I've been told. I wasn't here to see it myself. I hadn't even been born yet. Anyway, you've probably already figured out that Prissy acts as the mother cat to the rest of us too."

Tibby nodded. Prissy had been invaluable, especially in the not-eating-the-mice-you-catch department. "It's like this," Prissy had explained. "It's not enough to not eat the mice you catch because God won't let you. You have to want not to eat them because you realize what exquisite creatures they are, with velvety fur and tiny feet and fan-shaped ears and gentle eyes. Only then can you start earning your halo. Don't get too impatient, though. You can't unlearn fourteen years of eating mice in two months. It might take years."

Tibby sighed, thinking about how far away she was from a halo. William interrupted her thoughts, continuing his description of the cats. "Then there's Suki. You can't help having noticed she's standoffish and unsociable. She's not as bad as everyone says she is, though. She did take Sweet William under her wings, so to speak. She tries to be a good mother to him. Makes sure he eats all his meals and gives himself a bath every day. She licks him dry when he gets wet. Snuggles with him if he's cold."

"Okay, okay, I get the idea," said Tibby. "What about the others?"

"Let me see . . . whom have I left out? Oh yeah, the two Toms. They don't like to be woken from their morning nap until ten or eleven. Better wait until lunch to be on the safe side, like I do. Then there's Dorca One and Dorca Two. Whatever you do, don't mix them up. They become miffed if you do."

Tibby frowned. "But Third Mom confuses their names all the time. How can I be expected not to? I've only been here a week."

"I know, I know," William consoled. "Just don't, though. Otherwise, they stalk away and ignore you for hours. Callie and Miss Paws also hang out together. They're the ones always talking about Suki behind her back. Third Mom says they're far from their halos and not getting any closer. Whatever you do, don't play hide-and-pounce with them."

"Why not?" Tibby couldn't imagine a cat not wanting to play hide-and-pounce. Jumping out from the shrubs at some unsuspecting victim and meowing "Boo" in her loudest voice was her favorite game.

"Just take my advice and don't. Now let's see, what cats have I left out? Oh, yeah, Black Bart and Big Tig. They look like ruffians, but they're real sweethearts. They love to tussle, and they're always ready for a chase.

"How many is that?" William began counting the names on his toes. "Prissy, Little Cat, Suki, and Sweet William . . ."

"It's thirteen," said Tibby. "You mentioned thirteen cats. I counted them on my toes while you were talking about them. How many are there supposed to be? I can only keep up with so many at one time, you know. I have the brain of a cat, not of an elephant."

Soon the days passed in a seamless flow for Tibby as they had long done for the other occupants of the square white house. Some were filled with sunshine, singing birds, and gentle breezes. Others were filled with rain, gusts of wind, and swirling leaves. But all were filled with peace and happiness.

There was, though, one fly in the honey for Tibby. Try as she would, she simply could not leave Third Mom's pet chickens alone. She had no problem ignoring Third Mom's two pet frogs, for they were lumpy, uninspiring creatures, sitting for hours in the sun without moving so much as an eyelid. Nor was she tempted to bother the pet rabbits. The field in back of Third Mom's house was filled with rabbits just daring her to chase them. But Third Mom's pet chickens were a different matter.

It wasn't that she meant to chase them when she saw them walking around in the barnyard pecking at the corn Sweetie Pie threw them every morning. But the brilliant red and orange of their feathers excited her unbearably. On top of that, she found their attitude most insulting. Chickens were supposed to squawk and flap their wings in terror when a cat appeared. Yet Henrietta and Mr. Combs, knowing that the cats were under strict orders not to chase them, strutted around the barnyard with their heads held high, faces smirking.

After a few minutes of watching such behavior, Tibby would find herself bounding over the barnyard fence in all-out pursuit of the forbidden prey. Of course, she didn't intend to eat the chickens. She merely wanted to show them a thing or two about proper chicken behavior.

Up and down the barnyard the three would go, Henrietta and Mr. Combs flapping their wings and shrieking in outrage, Tibby close on their tail feathers. By this time, all the other cats were usually lined up outside the barnyard fence watching the chase. Some urged Tibby on, yelling, "Come on, Tib Wib, show those chickens who's boss." Others, especially William, begged her to stop.

"How are you going to earn your halo if you keep on chasing Third Mom's chickens?" they pleaded.

Tibby, encouraged by the attention the other cats were giving her, doubled her efforts. Not that she ever caught one of the chickens. Long before that happened, Third Mom, hearing the ruckus, invariably yelled out the back door, "Tibby, get back in the yard this second and leave those poor creatures alone! You know better than that! You're going to get them all tuckered out before it's even lunchtime! And the rest of you, quit egging her on. Shame on you."

Reluctantly, Tibby would quit the barnyard with a longing backward look at the once-again smirking birds, followed by the rest of the cats, some disappointed that the excitement had ended, the others relieved that it had. Retiring to the back porch, Tibby would lay her head on her paws, her eyes following every move the two fowls made, longing to give chase again, her tail swishing back and forth in frustration. Only with the greatest of efforts was she able to restrain herself.

She explained to William, "I try to be good, William. I really do. But those two chickens bring out the worst in me."

William tried to be encouraging. "I know you want to be good. But like Third Mom says, 'Even though heaven is a perfect place, none of us are perfect when we get here. We have to work our way to complete goodness.' That's what you're doing, Tibby, working your way to complete goodness. Hopefully, by the time Second Mom arrives, you'll be completely good. You just have to keep on trying hard not to let Henrietta and Mr. Combs rile you so much."

Tibby had her doubts that she would ever be able to reach perfection by the time Second Mom arrived. But she never failed to brighten at the prospect of her arrival. She thought about her every day. And about Elvira. Often in the middle of whatever she was doing, be it eating Heavenly Delight and lapping cream, swatting a plastic ball, or chasing a mouse, she would stop to go find Third Mom and ask, "Are they coming today?"

Third Mom always stopped whatever chore she was engrossed in to give Tibby a hug before telling her, "No, Tibby, I don't think today's the day. But one day soon."

Tibby had been in heaven less than three months, when late one evening, just before bedtime, Third Mom took her aside. "Tibby," she said, "God told me that Elvira will be coming tonight. After all the other cats are in bed, we'll go wait for her in the yard."

Tibby was beside herself with joy. Elvira Wira was coming! She was so excited that she could hardly stand still on the kitchen counter while Third Mom and Sweetie Pie brushed her fur and teeth. After all the cats had been readied for bed, William observed, "Goodness mice and moles, Tibby! You act like you have fleas tickling your paws."

Tibby could contain herself no longer. "Oh, William, guess what! Elvira's coming tonight. After all of you are in bed, Third Mom and I are going out in the field to wait for her."

All the other cats crowded around Tibby, also excited to know that another cat was expected shortly. "What is she like?" asked Neiki. "Is she like me?" The last question was asked with a note of wistfulness in her voice. She so wished one cat would show up that was as rambunctious and worrisome as the other cats declared she was.

Tibby looked at Neiki thoughtfully for a moment. "Well, a little bit," she finally said. "She's mostly black like you. And when she was young, she was always up to something, like you. Used to worry me to death. She's slowed down some since she got old. She's tiny like you too. But she's full grown, and you're just a kitten. So when Second Mom comes and you start growing again, you'll probably end up bigger than she is."

Neiki sighed happily. How wonderful it was going to be to have another cat even a little like her in the family. Almost like having a sister. And with Elvira to play with, she wouldn't have to bother William so much. Even though he had kept his world and never complained about her.

While Neiki was lost in these thoughts, Tibby continued to describe her friend. "Her name's Elvira, but she calls herself Elvira Wira of Tyra Lyra, as if she were well-born. I found out differently, though, from one of her brothers. I ran into him one day while I was hunting. According to him, she was born in a cornfield and raised in the dirt under a sundeck. Not like William and me who were born on a blanket in a box inside a shed, like proper kittens. So I just call her Elvira or sometimes Elvira Wira. But never Elvira Wira of Tyra Lyra. No sense encouraging her in that direction.

"Be warned right now. She has an awful fierce-looking face. But she's a real sweetie pie." Tibby made this last remark with an apologetic look at their own Sweetie Pie, who at the moment was taking the cat treats out of the kitchen cabinet.

While the cats were busy crunching and munching their imitation mice, Tibby, too excited to eat, continued her description. "She's an excellent mouser. Of course, I taught her all she knows." Tibby paused at that last remark, as if deliberating. Then completely ignoring the fact that she was still giving trouble over the chickens, she added, "She's headstrong, though. I don't know how she's going to take not being able to eat the mice she catches. She could give trouble over that."

"I'm sure she'll be fine," said Third Mom, coming into the living room at that moment. "Now off to bed, little kitties, while Tibby and I wait for Elvira."

"We want to wait too!" some of the cats clamored.

A few other joined in. "It's not fair. Tibby gets to wait. We never get to wait? Why can't we go too?"

The rest chimed, "Yeah, why can't we wait, like Tibby?"

Third Mom sighed patiently. "You know why. We go through this every time another cat arrives. Elvira knows Tibby. She doesn't know the rest of you. If she saw a swarm of cats running toward her as soon as she opened her eyes, she might become frightened and run away. Finding her might take days. No, it's best that only Tibby and I wait for Elvira. Now off to bed with you."

Realizing that Third Mom was right, the cats gave up and followed Sweetie Pie to bed, talking excitedly among themselves on the way. As soon as they had settled down for the night, Tibby and Third Mom, flashlight in hand, went outside to wait for Elvira. They had not been waiting long before they heard a tiny, squeaky voice far out in the field. "Second Mom, where are you? I'm lost! Come find me!"

Tibby immediately recognized the voice. With a joyous leap of her heart, she bounded in its direction. Within seconds, she was rolling and tumbling with her old friend as if they were in the backyard at Second Mom's. In the morning, when the other cats woke, they beheld a tiny, small-boned cat with a fierce-looking face and black fur swirled with tan and orange, just as Tibby had described. She was curled up asleep next to Tibby, who was curled up asleep next to William, who was curled up asleep next to Neiki, who, wide awake, was swatting gently at William's whiskers.

24

Unexpected Company

IMMEDIATELY AFTER BREAKFAST THAT MORNING, all the cats gathered around Elvira, wanting to hear about Second Mom. Most of them asked questions like "Does Second Mom still live in the gray house on the hill?" "Does she still bring cat treats home every time she goes to town?" "Does Hon still live with her?" But Tibby had a more important question. "Did Second Mom get a kitten to take my place?"

At first, Elvira felt overwhelmed by the cats surrounding her and the questions they were rapidly firing at her. But being a creature of no small determination, she managed in her squeaky voice to answer the questions, a little hesitantly at first but with more and more assurance as she proceeded. She discovered that she enjoyed being the center of attention. At Second Mom's, she had always had to share the spotlight with Tibby. Not too many of Second Mom's visitors had been impressed by a scrawny, three-legged black, tan, and orange cat with piercing yellow eyes and a frowning brow. Tibby, imposing and magnificent with her long, soft hair, tawny eyes, and large frame, had received the lion's share of attention.

Now that Elvira had the spotlight, she was determined to make the most of it by answering any and all questions put to her by the other cats. She assured them that Second Mom still lived in the same house and that, yes, Hon, unfortunately, still lived with her. Yes, Second Mom brought home cat treats every time she returned from town. Smiling at Tibby, she said, "No, Second Mom didn't bring home a kitten after you died, Tibby. I think she knew I was too old to put up with one and teach it the ropes. I could barely make it from bed to food saucer to litter box.

"I missed you so much. And I was cold at night without you. So Second Mom let me sleep next to her and covered me with a blanket. I didn't get cold anymore, and I didn't get so lonesome for you at night. Hon didn't even seem to mind. I guess he figured I was too old and tired to bother him.

"And I was. I finally became almost too weak to move. So Second Mom put a rug in front of the fireplace for me to lie on during the day. She put my food and water saucers and the litter box close by, like she did after my amputation. Every morning, she carried me from her bed to the rug. She was always thinking of me. Sometimes she lay down next to me, talking to me while she rubbed my face and ears and belly. I loved it when she did that."

Elvira's voice started quivering. Tibby touched her nose to Elvira's in commiseration. The other cats were silent, remembering what a wonderful mother Second Mom had been to them. They also wondered if she would get another cat to replace Elvira. After all, Second Mom had to be getting a little old herself. Look at how many cats she had already had. Their lives added up to a great many years.

But as to just how many they were unsure. "Why don't we add the number of years we all lived," suggested Callie. "That should give us a good idea of how old she is." Miss Paws nodded in agreement.

Impressed with the logic of this suggestion, the cats immediately began counting on their toes. Even Little Cat and Sweet William, neither of whom knew what a number was, much less how to add them, started totaling. But mathematics not being a cat's strong suite, none of the cats came up with the same total. The top number was three hundred forty years, the bottom one eight.

The cats were stumped as how to further proceed. After a few moments of silent rumination, Suki broke the impasse. "Adding up the total number of years we lived is not going to work. Don't forget that Second Mom sometimes had as many as three or four cats at a time. Plus, she didn't get those at the same time, and they didn't die at the same time. And what about the times she didn't have any cats?"

The other cats murmured, "Not have any cats?" They couldn't imagine Second Mom without at least one cat. But Suki was right. Adding up the total number of years each cat had lived wasn't going to give the correct age. They looked at Suki admiringly. She might be snooty, but she was smart. No arguing about that.

Big Tig spoke up. "Seems like there's no way to know how old she is. Not until she comes to heaven anyway."

A collective sigh of acknowledgment arose. Big Tig was right. For the time being, Second Mom's age was unknowable. That was what Third Mom always said when they asked her what was God's favorite creature and why had He made dogs. "Don't ponder such questions. God's unknowable."

At that point in the discussion, the cats always wanted to know how they could be sure He existed if He were unknowable. "Look around," she would say. "Do you know of any creature that could have made all you see and hear and feel and smell? Could a fox or a lion or a bear have done that? Or a cat? Could I?"

At that question, the cats looked at one another and shook their heads. "Well, there you are then. Only something with unimaginable power and intelligence could have done so. That's God. If you listen carefully, you can hear Him. His is that small, still voice you hear when you're tempted to do something wrong, like wanting to eat another of God's creatures or chasing Petunia and Pettigrew Pinks or Henrietta and Mr. Combs. It's called your conscience."

The cats tiptoed around the house and yard for at least an hour after such a reminder, shushing one another to better listen to God's small, still voice. If one thought that it might have heard even the tiniest of whispers from inside itself, the others rushed over to put their ears to its chest to see if they could hear it too. Of course, they never did.

Today, though, there were more pressing matters than trying to hear one another's consciences. Remembering that he had a question he wanted to ask Elvira, one of the Toms meowed, "What's an ampu . . . ampula . . . ampulation?"

"Amputation," corrected Elvira. "It's where a vet cuts your leg off."

All the other cats but Tibby drew back in horror. Elvira smiled. "That's how I felt when I found out one of my legs had been cut off. Why the vet did it, I don't know. I guess he had a good reason, though. He had kind eyes and a kind smile. He didn't look to be someone who would whack a cat's leg off just because he wanted to. Anyway, I learned to manage without it. And now I have my leg back. Isn't God good?"

The others nodded. God had indeed been good to them. He had given them three moms who loved and pampered them and who treated them as if they were the most important creatures in the universe. Which they were.

While they were still mulling over their good fortune, Elvira turned to Tibby. "I forgot to tell you something last night, Tibs. Second Mom was rocking me in the recliner when I died. I heard her say, 'Now she runs on four legs.' I could understand what she was saying, Tibs, I really could. Then the room grew black. The next thing I remember was waking up in a field in the dark. And I had four legs! How did Second Mom know I was going to have four legs again?"

The cats solemnly considered this new perplexity. Tibby finally came up with the only logical answer. "Silly, Second Mom knows everything."

"Third Mom says only God knows everything," Suki said. The other cats nodded. Suki was right again. Tibby grudgingly conceded the point. "Well, Second Mom knows next to everything, especially about cats." The cats nodded again. Elvira's first morning in heaven ended with the cats feeling impressed with their own collective wisdom, even if they couldn't figure out how old Second Mom was.

Three more cats eventually showed up at Third Mom's. Their arrivals put an end to the cats' speculation about whether Second Mom would get any more cats. First came Shala, a blue-eyed cat with long, curly ginger and white hair. She was the most beautiful cat the others had ever seen, so dainty looking that they were hesitant to play with her. Only when they discovered that she could tumble and tussle with the best of them and could chase mice and rabbits even better than Black Bart or Big Tig did they treat her as the rough-and-tumble cat she was.

Rufus, a clumsy-pawed, big-boned silver cat with a huge smile on his face arrived next. All the cats loved him immediately. Shala was especially glad to see him, for they had lived together at Second Mom's. A few years later, Pretty Polly, a small, plump tan and white cat, appeared on the back door steps after supper. With her sweet smile and shy, quiet demeanor, she had made friends with the other cats by bedtime, all of whom clamored for her to sleep next to them.

After Pretty Polly, no more cats appeared for a long while. Early one morning, however, someone completely unexpected showed up. The cats had barely finished their breakfast when a knock sounded at the front door. Although they were not quite through with their morning face scrubbings, they rushed to the door, Third Mom trailing behind. "Mercy, who can be visiting this early?" she asked as she opened the door, the cats peering out from behind her in wide-eyed wonder.

To her surprise, a man wearing khaki work pants and shirt, brown work boots, and a straw hat was standing on the porch. When he saw Third Mom, he took his hat off and smiled. "Good morning, ma'am. My name's Mr. Halloran. Dave Halloran. Sorry to disturb you this early in the morning, but I believe you're keeping my wife's cats. I've come to see how they're doing."

The other cats looked at one another. It was Hon! All the cats in the household felt as if they knew Hon, even though many of them had lived and died before Second Mom ever met him. But the cats who had lived with him had told the others about the dreadful man who lived with Second Mom.

So all the cats knew that Hon didn't like cats pouncing on his head or leaping onto the kitchen counter. They knew that he became violent if a cat, faint from hunger, jumped into his lap to wake him up while he was asleep. Nor would he allow any cats in Second Mom's bed at night! He made them sleep on a rug on the hard floor outside Second Mom's bedroom.

In fact, there was nothing better that the cats liked to do on a rainy day than compare notes about the atrocious Hon. Yet after reflecting on all the bad things about Hon, William always had to give him credit for saving Tibby's life when she slipped into the crack between the mattress board and the bedstead. Nor did he ever fail to add, "Remember the time you disappeared, Tibby. That night, Hon took a flashlight and looked for you up and down the road and in the field behind the house. Then the next morning, he got up before Second Mom and I were even awake and walked up and down the creek bank calling for you. I heard him when I woke up. He came back muddy and wet and cold."

Prissy always defended Hon too, remembering aloud how he had always made sure she was safely in for the night if Second Mom were away. After hearing William and Prissy speak up in his behalf, Neiki always felt honor bound to say with tears in her eyes, "He always laughed when I hid in my sack and peeked out at him or climbed into one of his shoes."

At that point, Elvira always recalled that Hon had opened the door to Second Mom's bedroom early every morning so that she and Tibby could jump on the bed and say "Good morning" to her. Then the other cats who had lived with Hon recalled the good things he had done for them. He never complained about being fed last. He let them keep their toys in the living room, right under his feet. If they ripped his newspaper before he had a chance to hide behind it after dinner, he never made a fuss.

Even Tibby had to give him his due, recollecting that one time when she had the chills from a cold, he allowed her to sleep with Second Mom and him two nights in a row. "Hon let her put me right between them. He even let Elvira sleep at the foot of the bed so she wouldn't have to sleep by herself. I stayed so warm and toasty that after the second night I woke up completely cured." The other cats always started sobbing at this last recollection, each thinking that perhaps Hon hadn't been so dreadful after all.

25

Two Houses Are Better Than One

T HAT MORNING ON THE PORCH, however, all the good memories about Hon vanished completely. Remembering only the bad things, the cats grew wide eyed when they heard Third Mom invite him in for a cup of coffee. As he entered the house, they scattered in every direction, tripping over one another in their haste.

Only after Third Mom and Hon were conversing quietly over coffee at the kitchen table did the cats dare stick their head around the doorway to eavesdrop. They heard Hon say, "I'm sorry I waited a while to visit you. I found out from a neighbor right after I arrived in heaven that my wife's cats were living here. I had to visit all my relatives first, though. Then, of course, my wife's relatives wanted me to visit them.

"My job takes a lot of my time too. I'm a carpenter—no need for lawyers in heaven. But carpenters are in demand. Lots of houses to build. People just keep coming. I've been so busy that I've had to work on my own house at night and on weekends. It's pretty well finished by now, though.

"I hate to admit it, but I never cared for Second Mom's cats all that much. I didn't realize until I got to heaven that all of God's creatures, not just humans, are important to Him. I wish I could do everything all over again. I sure would treat those cats differently.

"I know my wife is going to want them with her when she gets here. She was always saying, 'Dave, you're going to look up one day in heaven and see me coming, with all my cats following behind.' I just laughed when she talked like that, but now I see that I *am* going to be living with her cats one day. So I thought I might as well come over and make my peace with them. And get to know them better."

Just at that moment, Third Mom spotted the cats. "Here they are right now, Mr. Halloran. Kitties, Mr. Halloran—that's Hon to you—wants to say hello. He's built a house down the road to live in. And for Second Mom and all of you to live in when she comes to heaven."

The cats edged cautiously into the kitchen, milling around the doorway in case the need to flee arose. Ignoring their hesitancy, Third Mom continued. "Since he's so lonely without Second Mom, I thought that you might take turns spending nights with him. You could get to know one another better. After all, when Second Mom comes, you're all going to be living in the same house. No better time to get started on learning to live happily together than now. Who would like to spend tonight at his house?"

At this request, the cats, forgetting their skittishness in the presence of Hon, sat down in a tight group. They glanced at one another and then at Third Mom, following which they gave their entire attention to the floor, as if they had never noticed it before. Not one raised a paw. For a long moment, an uncomfortable silence reigned. Third Mom finally broke it. "He also wants to let you know he's sorry for how he treated you. He wants you to forgive him."

The cats looked at one another again and then at Hon. None except Prissy looked very forgiving. Third Mom prompted them again. "Learning how to forgive is just as important as learning how to ask for forgiveness. It's a big step in growing in goodness."

Hon interceded. "Perhaps I need to ask the cats for forgiveness myself." Looking squarely at them, he said, "Will you forgive me for not loving you and for not taking care of you like Second Mom did?"

For a long moment, none of the cats made a sound. At last, one of the Toms broke the silence. "I forgive you. Just don't let it happen again."

With the ice broken, all the other cats chimed in with their declarations of forgiveness, each one determined not to be outdone by the others in its readiness to forgive and forget. Third Mom smiled proudly. Then she said, "Now, do I have any volunteers to spend the night with Mr. Halloran?"

Again the cats eyed each other. Again there were no volunteers. Forgiving Hon was one thing. Spending the night with him was another.

Third Mom sighed. "I know that you want to stay here with me until Second Mom comes. But think how happy she'll be when she finds out that all of you have made friends with Hon and are even staying part of the time with him. I'll show him how to brush you and get you ready for bed. And tomorrow morning, you'll come back over here."

After a moment's silence, Prissy spoke up. "I'll spend the night." Looking at Hon, she added, "You always made sure I was in for the night if Second Mom was away."

Little Cat, who never let her mother get too far from her side, declared, "I'll go too."

Hon looked at Prissy and Little Cat in gratitude. "Thank you, Prissy. Thank you, Little Cat. I promise I'll take extra good care of you. I'll even let you sleep on the bed with me. Might as well get used to doing so now rather than later." The cats' mouths dropped open in amazement. Sleep on Hon's bed with him? Did he really mean it? Had he grown that much in goodness already?

William decided that if Prissy and Little Cat were going, he should also go in order to keep an eye on them and to report back to the other cats in the morning. After he had volunteered, Neiki and

Tibby and Elvira all spoke up, declaring that if William went, they were going too since they always slept together and couldn't bear to be parted for even one night.

That evening, the departing cats bid nose good-byes to the other cats before jumping one at a time into Third Mom's lap for a farewell hug. Afterward, with reluctant steps, they made their way to the door with Hon. On the way out, as if thinking better of her decision, Tibby held back, looking at Hon unwaveringly in the eye. "You're really going to let us sleep on your bed?"

Hon met her eyes without blinking. "Yes, Tibby. All of you can sleep with me."

Tibby persisted. "And jump on the kitchen counter?"

"And jump on the kitchen counter."

"You won't yell at me and smack a newspaper and scare me to death?"

"No, I won't yell at you if you get on the counter. Or scare you to death with my newspaper."

William broke in. "Can we sit in your recliner?"

Hon hesitated before sighing in resignation. "Yes, you can sit in my recliner."

"You won't forget the snacks before bedtime?" Elvira asked.

"No, I won't forget the snacks before bedtime. I bought some today when I stopped at the grocery for cat food. If I go to sleep in the recliner before I hand them out, you can jump on me to wake me up and remind me."

Satisfied, the six volunteers walked out the door. In spite of his assurances, however, trepidation seized their hearts when Hon opened the door to his house. They crossed the threshold with bated breath. Once he had them alone, he could do anything. But Hon was true to his word. He brushed their fur and teeth and inspected them for fleas and ticks. He even talked softly to them while he was getting them ready for bed and hugged each one when he was finished. He gave them a snack without being reminded. He let them sit in his recliner with him while he read the paper. And when he turned out the lights and went to bed, the six cats were there with him, snuggled up against him in snoozy delight.

After the cats reported back to the others the next day, they set up an immediate clamor for a chance to spend the night at Hon's too. Before the week was out, all the cats were going back and forth between Third Mom's house and Hon's as they chose. After Hon bought some toys for them to keep at his house and stocked his refrigerator with cream and his kitchen cabinets with sardine-flavored Heavenly Delight for Cats and imitation mice, fish, and birds for snacks, they felt that both houses were their home.

Third Mom and Sweetie Pie quickly became friends with Hon too. Hon began eating breakfast and supper with them after Third Mom said that she might as well cook for three as for two. One evening, Third Mom noticed that Hon's blue pants had faded onto his white shirt and that neither shirt nor pants had been ironed. So she began washing, drying, and ironing his clothes. In return, Hon offered to mow their yard and do whatever odd jobs needing doing around the house whenever Sweetie Pie was too busy with his farming to attend to them.

One day, Hon invited the cats over for advice on how to make the house he had built for Second Mom a perfect house for cats also. "Feel free to make suggestions," he encouraged. "If you don't ask, you won't receive."

The cats were silent for a moment, not wanting to seem too critical of the house that Hon was so proud of. Finally Big Tig and Black Bart spoke up. "Well, a cat door like the one Third Mom has would be handy," proffered Black Bart hesitantly.

"Yeah, or else Second Mom is going to spend all day at the back door, letting nineteen cats in and out a hundred times a day," Big Tig pointed out.

Hon had to agree. Nineteen cats to let in and out on demand all day, every day might be a bit much, even for a cat lover like Second Mom. "I'll get to it first thing tomorrow. Anything else?"

The cats looked up and down and all around the room, considering how to make Hon's perfect house more perfect. After a few moments, nudged on by the paw jabs of the other cats, Prissy hesitantly broke the silence, looking apologetically at Hon. "Now I'm not complaining, you understand, but a cat room with ledges and walkways to climb and walk and sprawl on and nooks to hide in might be appreciated. Like at Third Mom's. Not that your house isn't perfect just the way it is."

All the other cats nodded and meowed in agreement. Hon swallowed hard at the thought of having to add another room to a house he had thought pretty well finished. But some of the cats looked so beseeching and the others so stern that he nodded. "Yes, I see what you mean. Cats need a room of their own. That doesn't seem too much to ask since all the other rooms are for humans."

The ice broken, Tibby lost no time in meowing her wish. "Well, I, for one, want a couch and chair that I can claw and rip to shreds without anyone frowning or scolding. And some curtains." She looked gleeful just thinking about the prospect.

The other cats wondered why they hadn't thought of the idea. They wrinkled their foreheads to spur their brains to work harder. Soon ideas began to come fast and furiously. Elvira wanted a cat hammock for each cat. "Third Mom just has five. That's not nearly enough. I have to wait a week sometimes before I find one empty for my morning nap. And I never get one for my nap after lunch."

"How about a big patch of catnip at the back door?" asked Neiki. Nothing delighted her more than a good roll in a catnip patch in the morning. "It gets my blood flowing proper to my brain. Otherwise, I tend to be crazy the whole day."

The other cats turned to stare at her in disbelief. Neiki was never more crazy than when she had just thrashed around in Third Mom's catnip patch. They had quickly learned to avoid her for at least an hour afterward. However, they refrained from pointing this out, not wanting to discourage Hon from planting any catnip at all. Catnip was something they all enjoyed. Just not as much as Neiki.

William spoke last, an anxious look on his face. What if Hon thought his idea ridiculous? Or too expensive or persnickety? But Hon had said to speak up. So he did. "I think a bigger bed would be nice. The one you have barely holds you and four or five cats. And Second Mom isn't even here yet. Where are she and the rest of us cats going to sleep? Not to mention the cats that haven't arrived yet."

To William's surprise, Hon said, "You're right, William. A bigger bed is in order. We're much too crowded in the one I have now. And, Tibby, I promise a couch and chair and curtains you can claw and rip to shreds to your heart's content." Tibby smiled in satisfaction, looking as pleased as if she had just swallowed a canary.

Hon continued. "Nor do I see any reason why each of you can't have your own hammock. How about that, eh, Elvira?" Elvira squirmed and squeaked in appreciation, pleased as much by Hon's attention as by his promise. Hon wasn't finished. "Neiki, I don't see why we can't have two patches of catnip by the back steps, one on each side. How does that suit you?"

Neiki's eyes grew large at the dizzying thought of having two patches to roll in. When she tired of one, there would be the other inviting her. Her brain was sure to work right with two catnip patches to get her blood flowing. The rest of the cats, however, groaned inwardly. There would be no end to Neiki's craziness once she had two patches of catnip. However would they stand her then?

So the days passed, with the cats coming and going between Third Mom's house and Hon's until they could barely remember a time when Hon had not been a part of their lives in heaven. Or that once they had regarded him with trepidation.

For quite a few years after Hon came, no other cats showed up at Third Mom's. Then one morning, Hon arrived for breakfast with a small orange cat in his arms. "His name is Louis Little, the Sleeping Cat, because he sleeps so much. He's the cat Second Mom had when I died. He was waiting by the front door when I opened it this morning."

"My stars," said Third Mom, "I bet he's starving. Here, let me give him some cream and sardine-flavored Heavenly Delight. And don't bother him while he's eating," she told the other cats who had surrounded Hon and Louis Little, clamoring for news of Second Mom.

True to his name, as soon as Louis had gobbled his breakfast and cleaned his face, he hopped upon the living room couch, closed his eyes, and went to sleep. The other cats sighed in disappointment. News of Second Mom would have to wait. But after supper that night, Louis answered their questions.

What he had to say saddened everyone. Second Mom had grown too old to take care of herself any longer. "I was pretty old too, almost twelve. So we had to leave our home. Second Mom moved to a place where she had just one room to herself. Lots of other old people also lived there. But I couldn't stay there. Second Mom gave me to someone she called Susan. I called her Substitute Mom."

Hon interrupted. "That's our granddaughter. I'm sure some of the cats remember her." Elvira and Tibby and Second Mom's cats that had followed them nodded that they remembered Susan.

Louis resumed his story. "At first I didn't like living with her. I missed Second Mom and our home. But she looked after me and loved me just like Second Mom had. I couldn't help but love her back after a while. Mostly because she took me to see Second Mom whenever she went to visit. Second Mom was always glad to see me. She held me in her lap and talked to me and gave me treats. When it was time to leave, we always touched noses. Then she would give me a hug."

At this point, all the cats burst into sobs. Hon had tears in his eyes too, thinking of his beloved having to give up her home and her cat. Their sorrow did not leave them all evening, not even by bedtime. It was there the next morning too. And the next evening. And all the mornings and evenings after. It became a part of their lives. They fell asleep with it and woke up with it. But it was a bearable sadness, for they knew that Second Mom was being taken care of and that soon she would be with them. And so they waited.

26

The Wandering Cat

SHE AWOKE COLD, HUNGRY, AND wet. Most of all, though, she was tired. She felt as if she had been cold, hungry, and wet all her life. But never this tired. Too tired to get up from the pile of old leaves and twigs on which she had slept all night to hunt for a mouse or a shrew or any other small creature that might scurry by. But she would have to were she to eat. So summoning all her strength, she sat up and looked out across the dew-drenched newly green field.

She had been many places in her time, seen many sights, and raised many kittens. But she felt as if she were finished with all that. She had a foreboding that something momentous was about to happen to her, something that would direct her life in another direction. She wasted no time in hoping that it would be to her liking. Her life had been a hard one, and she expected nothing different in the future. In the way of most creatures, she would face whatever happened without complaint and deal with it. All she wanted now was to stay in one place so she could regain her strength. But she knew that when she had stayed long enough to catch and eat most of the mice, moles, and other small creatures in the field, she would have to move on to another field or woods or creek bank. Wherever she happened to find enough prey to feed her for a while. That is if a dog or a fox or a stronger cat didn't drive her away first. She was worn out with moving on, would have liked to have a place to call her own. But she didn't, so that was that.

Dimly she remembered a time when her life had been easier, a time when she had owned a human family. The man and a woman of the family, for the most part, ignored her. There had also been a boy who fed and petted her and a little girl who tried to pull her tail. She quickly learned to avoid her paws. The four lived in a large sagging house in the middle of a dusty yard surrounded on three sides by fields and a gravel road in front. With the house came a huge barn, also sagging, where she could take refuge from the rain, the cold, and the heat. She claimed the yard and surrounding field and everything in them as hers. It was a place where she felt safe, a place where no dog or other cat would drive her away. It was a place she called home.

One morning, after she had been there about a year, a great commotion erupted. She was giving her face its after-breakfast cleaning when a gigantic beast with enormous eyes and rolling feet roared up the driveway. Stopping in front of the house, it disgorged two big, burly men who entered the house. Before long, they came out carting a large box between them. After storing it in the back of the beast, they went back inside and shortly came out with another big box. This one also went in the back of the beast. Before long, there was a constant stream of large boxes and equally large, bulky objects being hauled from the house to the back of the beast. With great interest, the cat parked herself under a nearby bush, safely out of the way of feet, to watch all the comings and goings.

Then, as suddenly as they had arrived, the two men slammed shut the doors of the beast's back, opened the doors on its sides, and hopped in. Within seconds, the beast roared back down the drive and turned onto the road. Soon it disappeared in a cloud of dust.

A few minutes later, the family emerged from the house. Everyone, even the little girl who liked to pull her tail and ears, was lugging a box. As they stored these boxes in the back of their beast, which resided in the barn, her ears perked up at their conversation.

The rising and falling of their voices as they talked to one another entranced her.

"Hey, Sid, what are we going to do with the cat? Reckon she'll git in the car?"

"It don't matter none whether she will or not, Mary. The apartment house don't allow no pets. She'll have to stay here."

"But, Dad," interjected a third voice, "who's going to feed her?"

She recognized this voice as the one belonging to the boy who petted her and made sure her food bowl was full at mealtime.

"Now don't you worry yourself none, Jerry. Cats can take care of theirselves. If something gits after them, why, they just climb a tree. And they're real good hunters. Kitty won't have no trouble keeping her stomach full. But I left her a couple a days of food, just in case she has trouble finding a mouse or something for the first day or two. So come on now, get in the car. She'll be just fine."

Breaking away from the others, Jerry ran out of the barn. Looking around the yard, he began calling, "Here, kitty, kitty. Here, kitty."

Recognizing her name, she twitched her ears slightly. Ordinarily she would have come running at the sound, but just as she started to stand up, Sid came out of the barn. She immediately lay back down, instinctively realizing that now was not the time to make an appearance.

Instead she continued watching as Sid walked over to Jerry. The two looked at each another steadily. Suddenly Jerry, stomping a foot, shouted, "No, I'm not leaving without my kitty."

Sid sighed. "Son, git in the car. Or I'm going to put you in myself. I ain't wasting no time arguing about a durned cat."

Jerry stomped his food again. "No."

Sid glared hard at Jerry, then, without warning, lunged at him. Wrapping his arms around him, he dragged him, kicking and screaming, to the beast. Opening one of its back doors, Sid shoved him inside and slammed the door. Then he climbed in the front door on the same side. Within seconds, the beast roared to life, backed out of the shed, and turned around. As it sped down the drive, Jerry, leaning out an open back window, waved and tearfully called, "I love you, kitty. I'll come back for you. I promise."

The cat watched the beast until it had faded from sight in a cloud of dust. When the last speck of dust had settled, she walked expectantly to the back porch to take a nibble from her food bowl. To her surprise, it had been replaced by a larger bowl, which was heaped unusually high with food, far more than she could possibly eat at one meal, more than she could eat in a whole day.

After she had eaten her fill, she sought the shade underneath the porch where she knew she could nap, secure from disturbance by any stray dog or wandering cat. By the time she awoke, the sun had almost disappeared from the sky. Rising and stretching, she strolled out from under the porch and sought her food bowl once more. Only after her hunger had abated did she notice the absence of light in the house. Glancing into the barn, she saw that the beast had not returned.

She was not alarmed. The beast, as well as the humans, often stayed away until late in the evening. Her food bowl was still comfortingly full. Sniffing the air, she felt her blood stir in excitement at the thought of the small scurrying creatures in the fields beyond the yard. She set her nose in the direction of the field behind the house and headed out.

That night, she caught three mice. She could have caught more, but her stomach was uncomfortably full from the unusually large amount of food she had eaten that evening. When the moon reached its highest point in the sky, she headed to the barn, where she slept the rest of the night snuggled deep in a pile of straw.

When she awoke the next morning, she rose slowly, stretched luxuriously, then headed to the back porch of the house. Her food bowl was still fairly full. Last night's meal, as well as the three mice she had caught later that evening, had worn off. She began eating ravenously. When she was finished, she lay down on the porch to wait for the back door to open and the humans to commence their daily goings and comings. But this morning, much to her surprise, no one appeared. Glancing into the dimness of the barn, she saw that the beast still had not returned. That meant the humans hadn't returned either.

She waited all day for the beast stuffed full of her family to return. Several beasts roared by the house enveloped in clouds of dust. But none slowed down and turned up the driveway. She did not worry, though. Her food bowl was still half-full. And she had always had food provided for her. First there had been her mother's milk, then food provided by the family her mother owned and then by the family she claimed as her own. That ever there could come a time when there might be no food in the bowl never occurred to her.

Until the fourth day, that is. On that morning, all she found in the bowl were three or four nibbles of food. After devouring them, she sat down to wait for more. But no more came. Not that day, nor the next. By then, she was growing seriously hungry. She went hunting every night, but the few rodents she caught were not enough to sustain her until the next night. When was her family returning to feed her? Suddenly, a thought almost too terrible to contemplate struck her. Her family wasn't coming back. Staggered by the realization, she sought refuge in the barn, where she lay down on the straw. As she licked the pads on the bottom of her paws, she mulled over her options.

She couldn't stay there. There would be no more food. She could try catching her meals, but that would be a wearying and unending endeavor. No, her best course was to leave the barn, the house, and the yard behind her and find another place to live, a place with some warm, dry barn like this one to sleep in and another family who would feed her. When she was finished grooming her paws, she walked out of the barn. She looked at the house for a long moment before heading for the fields. She did not look back.

She wandered for years. Not that she did not try at first to find another place. But the first one she found came with a long, lanky dog that made it plain before she even sat a paw in the yard that it regarded her as something to chase and chew. Barking ferociously, it barreled off the back porch as soon as it saw her approaching the house. It tore across the yard, slavering in anticipation of a thrilling chase and an invigorating cat mauling.

Nothing runs much faster than a cat from a dog. So she was long gone before the dog reached the edge of the yard. By the time it had wriggled under the backyard fence, she was even further away. Nevertheless, the dog might have caught her had it not been for a tree in the middle of a field. Without thinking, looking back, or slowing down, she dashed up the trunk, not stopping until she was midway to the top.

There she stayed, arching her back and hissing as the dog loped around the tree, first one way and then the other, still frenziedly barking, a savage gleam in its eyes. Fortunately, dogs are fashioned to behave in such an intemperate manner for only so long, after which they begin to lose energy, eventually sagging with fatigue. So it was with this dog. Its strides became shorter and shorter; its barking grew less and less vociferous; its eyes lost more and more of their savage gleam. Finally, the dog lay down, still eying its enemy. There it remained the rest of the day. Only as night began to fall and the dog's stomach to rumble did it stand up. Tongue hanging out, it looked up at the cat and then back toward the house from which it had come. Back and forth the dog looked until its stomach won out over its hatred of the cat. Off it trotted.

But she was taking no chances. Hungry as she was, she remained in the tree for the rest of the night, her mouth watering at the sound of scurrying in the grass beneath the tree. She allowed herself to climb down only when she saw the sun's rays tint the horizon. Once on the ground, she walked a few feet away from the tree and sat down in the tall grass. She waited patiently for any slight movement in the grass that might spell a small creature scampering by. Unfortunately, most of those that she had heard scurrying underneath the tree the evening before had retired to their burrows and nests to sleep the day away.

Thus did her first search for a place to call home begin and end. The second place she found was no better. She managed to make it halfway across the yard to the back steps before a huge yellow tabby tore around the side of the house, hissing and growling. She turned and fled.

At the next house, she made it all the way to the back door. But not before she had cautiously scouted for any sight, scent, or sound of a dog or another cat. She saw none. Feeling a spark of hope leap into flame in her chest, she sat down on the steps and began to meow. And meow. And meow. Finally someone wearing an apron and a cross face opened the door. She was holding a broom, which she immediately began to swipe at the cat, making unfriendly noises that sounded like "Go away, you flea-bitten, ugly bag of bones. I don't need any mangy cats to take care of. And don't come back." Wits scattered, the cat bolted in fright, stopping and looking back only when she reached the edge of the yard. The woman raised the broom and shook it at her. She did not have to shake it twice.

So it went from one place to another. There was either another dog or cat or too many teasing, yelling children or someone wielding a broom or delivering a well-placed kick. Once she happened upon a house whose back door was standing wide open in invitation. She walked in. She had never been in a house before, and she wasn't planning on remaining in this one. She merely hoped to find a tidbit or two to eat, something that she didn't have to catch. She was getting tired of mice and moles, baby rabbits, and the occasional bird.

But no food was to be had. She did notice, however, a couch on which to lie down. Jumping up, she made herself comfortable, intending to stay only a short while. She promptly fell asleep. Suddenly, she was jerked awake by a loud-pitched screech. Opening her eyes in fear and confusion, she beheld a woman bending over her. Before she could spring up, she felt hands reach down, pick her up by the scruff of her neck, and, holding her at arm's length, carry her, squirming and struggling in protest, to the back door.

Without warning, she felt herself sailing through the air as the woman said, "Out with you, you worthless furball. And good riddance." Landing on her side with a thump, she lay still, the breath knocked out of her. Collecting herself at last, her chest heaving in an effort to breathe, she struggled up and staggered from the yard.

So went her first attempts to find a home. Her later ones fared no better. Finally, she gave up the effort entirely, assiduously avoiding all yards and houses from that point on, living off the prey she caught. In a very short time, she became a proficient hunter, able to catch enough in one day to feed herself.

Her life was hard and unforgiving. Any miscalculation or misjudgment while hunting meant going without a meal. Encounters with other wandering cats usually ended in fights over territory and hunting rights. After a few of these fights, her face bore the scars of razor-sharp claws, and her ears were ragged and torn from the teeth of other cats. But she inflicted an equal measure of scars and ragged, torn ears herself.

Almost as daunting as the fights she found herself embroiled in were the extremes of weather she had to bear. The winters were cold and prey often hard to come by, the summers hot and unremitting, the wind cutting and relentless. But she endured, making her beds in piles of leaves in the woods, in the tall grasses of the pastures, and under the brushy growth along creek banks and ditches.

Her only comfort were the kittens she bore and raised. These she loved and cared for with all her heart. She watched over them protectively. She taught them to be excellent hunters, for she knew they would have to fend for themselves once they left her. The one thing she did not do was to introduce them to humans. She was through with that part of her life forever.

The years passed. She grew older and slower. Her bones began to ache, and she chilled easily. Tiredness nagged at her in increasing measure. She no longer had all the energy she needed to hunt. Much of the time, her stomach went empty. She was thankful that she no longer bore kittens, for she would have been hard-pressed to feed them. She could not have borne seeing them go hungry.

In such a way did she come to the morning she opened her eyes on a sparkling-wet green field. She did not know that before her lay a day that would change her life. She only knew that she was exhausted, hungry, and discouraged. Her spirits lower than they had ever been, she put her head on her paws and slept. She did not awaken until midafternoon. By then she was ravenous. But most of the prey in the field wouldn't begin to stir from their burrows and holes in the ground for at least a couple of hours. Nonetheless, stiff and aching, she rose and headed for the middle of the field on the chance that she might find some small bit of life, be it only a bug crawling about.

The Last Cat

SECOND MOM STARED AT THE field in front of her, lost in memories that drifted aimlessly through her mind. For the most part, they were good ones. Some were about her childhood, some about her husband and children, some about her cats. Occasionally, she smiled or laughed aloud. Sometimes she spoke aloud a name from long ago. "Dave . . . William . . . Elvira . . ." Occasionally, she wiped a tear from an eye.

Suddenly, she roused herself from her musings, her attention caught by a small animal a few yards away in the field. Good heavens, was that a cat? Lifting a hand to shade her eyes from the lowering sun, she scanned the field. Yes, it was definitely a cat. But what a scroungy cat, so scroungy it had to be a stray. Probably a hungry stray. On an impulse, she called as loudly as her weak voice would allow, "Here, kitty, kitty, here kitty."

The cat stopped short and looked around. Someone was calling her name, the one a boy had given her long ago. She had not heard it for so long that she was surprised she remembered it or the boy. Could he be calling her? She decided to go toward the voice just close enough to get a good look at the person calling her. If it wasn't the boy, she would turn around and head back in the direction she had come from. The closer she drew to the calls, however, the more doubtful she became that the voice belonged to the boy. It was too high and too soft.

When she reached the edge of the field, she stopped. A few feet away under a large tree sat a gray-haired, frail woman in a chair with round legs. The cat frowned in puzzlement. She had never seen this woman before, so how did the woman know her name? Had the boy told her? Did she know where he was?

As the cat's brain whirled with these questions, Second Mom watched her closely, not wanting to startle her with any sudden movement. After a few moments of unmoving silence from both, Second Mom slowly leaned forward in her chair and smiled warmly at her. "Hello, little cat. Where did you come from? You must be a stray. You look too thin and scruffy and battle scarred to be anything else."

Beguiled by the warmth of the woman's voice and its welcoming tone, the cat took a few steps forward. Slowly, Second Mom held out a hand to her, inviting her to sniff it. Cautiously, the cat stared at it before taking a few more steps forward, ready to flee at the slightest untoward motion. But the hand remained still. So she took a few more steps forward, close enough to crane her neck and quickly sniff the outstretched hand before drawing her neck back. Second Mom continued to hold her hand out.

The cat wavered, tail vibrating in excited uncertainty. Go forward or run away? Past experience told her to flee; thousands of years of domesticated instinct told her to stay. The cat made the bravest decision she had ever made. She decided to give humans one more chance. Slowly, she took a step forward, and then another and another until she was in touching distance of the hand. After standing still a moment, she butted the top of her head against it. As if startled by its touch, she hastily retreated a step, expecting the woman at any moment to shoo her away.

But the hand stayed motionless. After a few moments, the cat stepped forward again, butting her head against the hand a second time. This time, the hand cupped the top of her head and stroked downward between her ears in a motion the cat found most soothing. She butted her head a third time against the hand, and the hand responded as before. The cat quickly became lost in a rhythm of head butting and hand stroking, purring loudly in contentment.

Her trance was broken by the slam of a door. Wheeling around, she streaked toward the field. She did not go far, though, before turning to catch one last glimpse of the woman. She was no longer there. Instead, another woman, short and stout, was pushing the woman's chair toward a long, low building. The cat watched for a long minute before turning toward the middle of the field, a meal on her mind.

The next morning, as the cat hunted for breakfast, she wondered if the woman would return to the tree. If she did show up, would she be as friendly as she had been the day before? Probably not. After all, she was a human. How would she know, though, if she didn't show up herself? All morning, the cat was torn between her curiosity and her fear. Should she go or should she stay away? Only when she found herself heading toward the fence did she know her decision.

To her surprise, the woman had returned. When she saw the cat, she smiled. "Here, kitty, here, kitty, kitty." Then bending over, she placed a saucer on the ground.

The cat sniffed. What was that delicious smell coming from the saucer? From years of ingrained wariness, she approached the saucer as cautiously as she had approached Second Mom the day before, her mouth watering at every step. Second Mom laughed as the cat reached her side and bent her head over the saucer. "Well, I can see you're not going to say hello first. Go on, eat it."

The cat did, polishing off every tidbit in the saucer and then licking it clean as she listened to Second Mom's voice. "I knew you would like those sardines. I've never met a cat who didn't. Sorry I don't have any cream. Maybe the next time."

When the cat was finished with the saucer, she sat down close to Second Mom's leg to wash her face as Second Mom continued to speak. "I guess our next order of business is to give you a name. You're such a funny-looking cat—short legged and square. And such a blunt head. No style at all. Very plain and ordinary. Rather like a cat from a fairy tale, a cat a peasant or a miller might have to keep the mice away. You need a name that fits a cat like that. Let me see if I can think of one. Hmm . . . Tabitha? Bertha? Ludmilla? Noooo, none of those quite fit. What about Gretel? Or Gundrun? No, those aren't right either. Oh, wait, I've got it. Griselda. That's what I'll call you—Griselda. How do you like your name?"

The cat looked up at the question in Second Mom's voice, as if to say yes. Second Mom smiled and patted her lap. For a moment there flashed through Griselda's mind a memory of the boy patting his lap, inviting her to sit in it. Nor had she forgotten the contentment and ecstasy of purring that had followed as she settled herself in his lap and began kneading his legs.

She looked at the woman questioningly for a long moment as the woman continued to pat her lap, looking down at her and making welcoming sounds as she did so. "Come on, Griselda. Jump up and make yourself at home."

Griselda hesitated, and then making the second bravest decision of her life, put one front paw on Second Mom's leg, followed by the other. Next came a heave, and she was up. As she settled herself into a tight curl on the woman's lap, Second Mom said, "When Louis Little died, I thought I would never have another cat. Now here you are. Life's full of happy surprises."

The two sat thus for a long while, soaking up the warmth of the sun, listening to the trilling of birds, and smelling the fragrance of grass, weeds, and flowers. But again as yesterday, another unexpected slam of a door jerked them out of their mutual spell of enchantment. At the sound, Griselda, catapulting herself from the woman's lap, streaked again to the field. And as she had done yesterday, she stopped a few feet into the field, this time to watch the woman she had seen the night before approach Second Mom.

"Miz Jane, time to come in. It's growing colder. Can't have you catching a chill. Besides, supper's soon. By the way, was that a cat I saw running for the field?"

Second Mom smiled up at the woman. "Yes, Ruby, that was definitely a cat. We're friends. I've named her Griselda. You frightened her away when you slammed the door. If you don't slam it tomorrow, maybe she'll stick around to meet you. I'm going to ask Susan—you remember Susan, don't you? My granddaughter? She used to bring Louis Little to see me. I'm going to ask her to bring some cat food and flea medicine for Griselda."

The next afternoon when Griselda appeared, Second Mom had a big saucer of cat food waiting for her. After eating hungrily, Griselda leaped into Second Mom's lap. They sat together for over an hour, Second Mom talking quietly as she stroked Griselda's back, Griselda purring in response.

Suddenly, Griselda noticed the same woman she had seen before quietly approaching the chair. She made a movement to spring out of her lap, but Second Mom kept stroking her back. "You don't have to leave just yet. It's only Ruby. She's one of the nurse's aides that take care of me. I want you to meet her. You need to learn that you can trust all the people you see here. Soon, when the weather becomes warmer, there'll be other residents out with me enjoying the sun."

Soothed by the calmness of Second Mom's voice and the firmness of her touch, Griselda crouched back down into her lap, ready to flee at the slightest alarm, not taking her eyes from the aide. Drawing a few feet from the chair, the aide stopped and exchanged a steady look with Griselda. Reassured by the kindness in the aide's eyes and her unthreatening manner, Griselda relaxed a little more as Second Mom spoke.

"Griselda, this is Ruby. Ruby, this is Griselda. Griselda, will you let Ruby give you a pat?" Second Mom nodded at Ruby. "Hold your hand out slowly, Ruby, and let Griselda sniff it before trying to pet her."

Ruby slowly extended her hand for Griselda to sniff. After Griselda had sniffed it, the aide slowly put her hand to Griselda's head and stroked it as Second Mom continued to reassure the cat. "That's not so bad, is it, Griselda? Oh, look, Ruby, the way she's arching her head against your hand. I believe she likes you."

"Yes, Miz Jane, I believe you're right. We need to be going in now, though. Say good-bye to Miz Jane, Griselda. We'll see you tomorrow."

Second Mom lifted Griselda from her lap onto the ground. Griselda bounded into the field before turning as she had the last two times to watch the women make their way to the nursing home. She waited until they had disappeared through a doorway before continuing on.

And so in her last days, Griselda found another home. She visited Second Mom every day. On sunny days, they sat under the tree. If it rained, they sat under the awning of a nearby shed. Second Mom always had a saucer of cat food next to her chair. Sometimes, especially on the days that were sunny, other people sat outside with her. Griselda allowed them to stroke her but would lie in no one's lap but Second Mom's.

In such manner did the two spend the spring and summer. Griselda slowly grew plump. Her fur became less ragged, her eyes brighter, her step stronger. Her fatigue, while it did not disappear, receded to a bearable level. As for Second Mom, knowing that Griselda would be expecting her by the tree that afternoon gave her once more a reason for getting out of bed and beginning her day.

One morning, Griselda woke up to leaves falling from the trees in the woods where she slept every night. The next morning, she woke to the honking of geese flying south. The morning after, she awoke to a light dusting of frost on the grass. Fall had arrived.

"Griselda," said Second Mom, "I shall have to get you a small house, rather like a dog house—but not really a dog house, you understand—a house for you to sleep in when the weather grows cold. I'll put a soft blanket in it for you to lie on. Would you like a little house all your own? Would you sleep in it?" She sighed. "Probably not. You're used to sleeping out of doors. But I'm going to get you one anyway."

Griselda, sitting in Second Mom's lap, thumped her tail against Second Mom's leg as if in agreement. She was not worried at all about the rapidly approaching winter. She would weather it as she always had, growing extra fur and staying as warm and as dry as she could by taking shelter in tall grass and weeds, beneath brush, or in hollow logs.

A few days later, Griselda woke to a rainy, cold, blustery day. The wind was whipping leaves from the trees, swirling them round and round before allowing them to settle in peace to the ground. A good many of those leaves had landed on Griselda. Standing up, she shook them off as she considered whether it was worth her while to venture forth to hunt for breakfast. For the last few days, she had noticed her tiredness increasing. As most of the mice and shrews would sensibly choose to stay home and sleep on such a stormy morning, she might as well go back to sleep too.

First, though, she would have to move deeper into the underbrush to stay out of the wind and rain. When she woke up, maybe they would have lessened.

At the nursing home, Second Mom waited on the sun porch for Griselda to make her usual appearance. She planned to entice her onto the porch for their visit. If not, she would put on her heavy coat, as well as her cap, scarf, and gloves, and go outside. Knowing how cats hated change, that's probably what she would end up doing. She must remember to ask Susan to buy Griselda a do . . . no, a cat house. She would call her tonight.

To her disappointment, Griselda did not come bounding from the field at her accustomed time. Nor had she appeared an hour later. Second Mom waited the rest of the afternoon, but Griselda did not appear. Dark had begun to fall when Second Mom finally rang a bell for Ruby to wheel her from the porch.

"Have you been waiting for that cat all afternoon?" Ruby demanded when she answered Second Mom's summons.

Second Mom bridled. "Her name is not 'that cat.' It's Griselda. And yes, I've been waiting for her all afternoon. I can't imagine what could have happened. She's never been late, much less not shown up at all before today. I do hope nothing's happened."

Second Mom looked up anxiously at the aide as she made the last statement, seeking reassurance. Ruby patted Second Mom's shoulder. "Now, don't you worry none. No sense borrowing trouble. This is the first really bad weather we've had. Griselda probably decided to stay put until the rain stopped. She'll be here as soon as the weather clears. Just you wait and see."

"I suppose you're right. Oh, I do hope tomorrow's clear and sunny. She'll show up for sure then."

Griselda did not rouse from her sleep all day. The falling leaves gradually made their way through the underbrush where she lay to land on her still figure. They continued to fall on her all night. By morning, she was completely buried under them. And though the day dawned sunny and clear, and the mice, who had not so much as peeked out from their burrows the day before, began stirring from their holes, Griselda remained still. The falling leaves buried her more and more deeply

Second Mom waited on the sun porch for her all afternoon again, staring at the fence post where she usually made her appearance. She waited that afternoon and the next. On the fourth afternoon, though, she did not go to the sun porch. Instead, she stayed in her room, shades down so that she could not look out onto the backyard.

She stayed there alone until Ruby appeared to take her to supper. Smiling wanly, she said, "Thanks, Ruby, but I'm not hungry. I think I'll just stay here, if you don't mind."

"Griselda didn't show up, huh?"

Second Mom didn't answer at first. Instead, she wheeled her chair to the shades and raised them. Staring outside at the darkness, she said quietly, "No, she didn't show up. I think she's died." Her voice broke on a sob before she could continue. "I thought Louis Little was my last cat. But I was wrong. Griselda was my last cat." Turning from the window, she put her head in her hands and wept.

28

The Wonder of a Wanderer

THE OCCUPANTS OF THE SQUARE white house were taken by surprise early one morning when they were awakened by an insistent, loud meowing. Befuddled with sleep, humans and cats alike ignored the summons, turned over, and tried to go back to sleep. The meowing became louder. Suddenly, all the occupants of the bed sat up straight and looked at one another. A cat—another cat from Second Mom! How could that be?

Scrambling out of bed, the cats raced to the utility room, tripping as usual over one another's feet in their eagerness. Sweetie Pie and Third Mom, pulling on their robes, followed at a more sedate pace. Reaching the back door ahead of them, the cats milled around in a confusion of quivering tails as they treaded impatiently from one foot to another, curious as to what manner of feline was awaiting them on the other side. Arriving a few seconds later, Sweetie Pie had to clear twenty tails and eighty feet out of his path before he could make his way to the door. Finally managing to reach it without stepping on any cat toes, he opened it slowly so as not to frighten the newcomer meowing on the other side. Filled with suspense, the other cats peeked between and around Sweetie Pie's legs for their first glimpse of the latest addition to their family.

What met their eyes was a short, boxy, snub-faced cat with fur of such nondescript color and markings that there was no way to tell if it were gray, tan, black, orange, or what. Silence reigned as their brains digested what their eyes saw. At last, Miss Paws whispered what they were all thinking. "What a plain-looking cat!"

"It's so bunched up," whispered Callie.

"Look at that snub face, will you?" added Miss Paws.

"Shhhh. It might hear you," cautioned Prissy. "Anyway, what it looks like doesn't matter. What counts is its heart."

"Prissy's right," admonished Third Mom who had arrived at the back door by this time. "Look into its eyes and you'll see that it has a brave heart. Besides, God didn't make any ugly creatures. Not even spiders or bugs."

Elvira looked askance. "What about rhinoceroses? Or wart hogs? I saw them on TV the other day. I didn't think they were beautiful."

The other cats nodded. Then Rufus added, "And how can anyone think a hippopotamus is beautiful? Or a moose? Or a . . . a . . ."

"Or a dinosaur?" interrupted Shala. "Especially tyrannosaurus rex?"

All the cats shuddered and fell silent thinking about how truly frightening and fiendish looking those creatures were with their huge feet and bodies, their spikes and claws. Thank goodness God had had enough sense to separate them from the rest of heaven by a vast, unbridgeable gulf. If they had been allowed to roam wherever they wished, no telling how many cats they might have stepped on by accident. Something told them that being squashed by a dinosaur tromping carelessly around, not watching where it was putting its feet every second—well, such an experience didn't bear thinking about.

Third Mom had an answer to their questions and doubts about rhinos, dinosaurs, and wart hogs. "God thinks they're beautiful too. All of God's handiwork is beautiful. It's up to us to find in His creation the beauty that He sees." The cats nodded again. Third Mom was right. As usual.

William, tired of waiting to welcome the cat at the bottom of the back steps, made a movement toward the doorway. Third Mom said, "Let me go first, William. To reassure it."

The cats wailed, "Why can't we go first? We never get to go first. We won't scare it. We promise."

Third Mom hesitated before bowing to their wistful-faced pleas. "Well, all right. But don't swarm out. We don't want to overwhelm it."

Of course, out the cats swarmed. Griselda *was* overwhelmed. Turning, she streaked for the fence. Startled, the other cats shouted, "Don't run away. Come back. This is your new home."

Griselda stopped in her tracks. *Home!* Not since leaving her mother had she heard that word. Now twenty cats were meowing it at her. Should she go back? She was tired of wandering. Yet most of her experiences with other cats had ended in hisses and slaps on their part and retreat on hers. How did she know these would behave differently? On the other hand, they had said *home*.

Stepping from one foot to the other and back again, the end of her tail twitching violently from one side to the other, she was torn between leaving or staying, leaving or staying. Past experience urged her to flee. A voice inside her, the same voice that had compelled her toward the house in the first place, urged her to return. Finally she decided. Turning around, she warily retraced her steps until she was a few feet from the other cats.

Standing still but ready to bound away again at a moment's notice, she regarded them silently, as they did her. The moment stretched to two and then three. At last, Prissy took matters in hand, stepping forward and touching her nose to Griselda's. "Hello. My name's Prissy. What's yours?"

Griselda breathed a sigh of relief. So far no hisses or slaps. She decided to answer Prissy's question and take matters from there. "Griselda," she said. "At least that's what the woman in the chair with legs that rolled said to me every time she saw me. So I think that's my name. I used to have another one. It was a long name, something like here-kitty-kitty-here-kitty. But that was so long ago that I could be wrong."

The other cats looked at each other. Should they tell her that *here kitty, kitty, here, kitty* was not a name, only sounds that a person used to catch the attention of a cat? They didn't want to embarrass her at their first meeting.

To smooth over the awkwardness, another cat stepped up to touch Griselda's nose. "My name's Rufus. Did you live at the nursing home with Second Mom?"

Griselda opened her mouth to speak, but Callie cut her short. "Of course not, silly. Cat's don't live at nursing homes. Only old people do. Remember what Louis Little said."

"That's right," Miss Paws seconded. "Only old people."

Griselda looked at the two cats, as if taking her measure of them, before turning to Rufus. "No, I've never lived in a house. Most of my life I've been a wanderer."

The other cats drew in their breaths. A wanderer! Occasionally, they had seen wandering cats passing through the field behind Second Mom's house. These wayfarers almost never came close. If they did, the moment one of the cats or Second Mom or Hon appeared, they streaked away.

Griselda interrupted their thoughts. "Who's Second Mom?"

The other cats looked at each other again, this time in astonishment. Who's Second Mom? What was Griselda doing here if she didn't know who Second Mom was? Had God made a mistake in sending her here? If so, were they supposed to send her back? But back where? And how? Stumped, the cats stepped from one foot to the other, twitching their tails in perplexity. At last, William had an idea. "Come inside and have breakfast while we tell you all about Second Mom."

Griselda's eyes grew big. She shook her head. She had never forgotten the time she had been thrown out of a house. Since then, she had never so much as set a paw over a doorway. The other cats were nonplused. Griselda had to come in. Otherwise, how could they get to know her? How could they tell her about Second Mom? And heaven? How could Third Mom take care of her? The situation had all the marks of a forehead wrinkler. Cats hate forehead wrinklers. Time for reinforcements. Prissy called out, "Third Mom, you have to come out and talk to Griselda. She won't go into the house."

Third Mom, who had been standing in the doorway listening to the conversation, didn't need asking twice. It did not take her long to figure out that the woman in the rolling chair that Griselda kept referring to was Second Mom. Upon finding this out, the other cats breathed a sigh of relief. God hadn't made a mistake after all. They wouldn't have to send her back.

But all of Third Mom's powers of persuasion could not convince Griselda to go inside. She simply would not cross the threshold. Third Mom ended up bringing breakfast out to her. She gobbled it down as fast as she could lest some other creature come along and gobble it in her stead. The meal tasted so good and she was so hungry that she licked the bowls clean. She didn't know it, but she had had her first taste of cream and of sardine-flavored Heavenly Delight.

Licking the last bits of her meal from her mouth, she made herself at home under one of the trees and waited to see what else this place had in store for her. By day two, she knew. The humans hadn't yelled at her or tried to kick her. None of the other cats had hissed at her or tried to cuff her face. The food was delicious. More important, it was always served on time. She decided she liked owning these humans and having the company of the other cats. She would stay.

The other cats, by this time, had given up trying to persuade Griselda to enter the house. Instead, she made herself at home on the back and front porches. She sat at the back door at meal times, waiting to be fed. But put one foot inside a door, she would not.

Third Mom said, "When Griselda gets ready to come inside, she'll come inside. You can lead a horse to water, but you can't lead a cat anywhere. I should know. I've kept enough of them." The cats weren't quite sure what Third Mom meant by that last part, but they knew she was right. They would have to be patient.

In the meantime, the cats wasted no time in getting to know Griselda outside, introducing themselves to her all over again, informing her of Third Mom's rules, and explaining, with Third Mom's help, all about heaven and growing in goodness and halos. She, in turn, regaled them with stories of the danger, excitement, and adventure that living the life of a wanderer had entailed. In their eyes, she rose in esteem with every story she spun.

She also gave them, as well as Hon, Third Mom, and Sweetie Pie, the latest news about Second Mom. Hon was devastated to hear that she used a wheel chair. "Probably too weak and unsteady to walk outside," he surmised. The other cats were intrigued by the idea of a rolling chair, imagining what fun it would to ride in such a contraption. They couldn't believe that Griselda had never availed herself of the opportunity. If they had been there, they would have gone for a ride every day!

29

Gotcha!

It was, of all cats, Suki who finally escorted Griselda through the cat door. One morning, about two weeks after her arrival, Griselda plopped down beside her as she lay sunning, eyes half-closed, on the back porch steps and proceeded to say, "I just heard Miss Paws call me ugly as I passed by her and Callie in the yard. She said, 'Here comes Miss Ugly Cat.' Then they both laughed. What does *ugly* mean?"

Suki opened one eye wide and then half-closed it again, hoping Griselda would take the hint and quit disturbing her cat nap. Griselda remained oblivious. "Whenever they see me, they always burst out laughing. What's so funny about me? Do you know?"

Suki sighed and sat up. Evidently, Griselda was not going to take the hint. She might as well answer her question. Otherwise, she would never get rid of her. Looking Griselda up and down, she spoke slowly, choosing her words carefully. She didn't want a weepy cat on her paws the rest of the morning. "*Ugly* means you don't have a pleasing appearance. Your nose is too long or your eyes are too wide apart or your fur is scraggly or your tail is too short. Or maybe all four. *Ugly* is the opposite of *beautiful*, which means pleasing to look at, like I am." She sat up as straight and regally as she could, to give Griselda the full effect of her beauty.

Griselda was impressed. "You're the most beautiful cat I've ever seen. I thought so the first time I saw you. I wish I looked like you." Suki accepted the compliment as her due. It was about time one of the cats around here voiced some appreciation of her looks. This pleasing train of thought was broken by Griselda's next comment. "Do you think I'm ugly?"

Suki was silent, trying to think of a halfway tactful answer. Then she noticed Griselda's wistful eyes, full of hope that she would hear the answer she wanted to hear. To her astonishment, she found herself saying, "Why, no, you're not ugly. You have beautiful yellow eyes, round and big. Your fur is soft and thick. And . . . and . . . you have a very intriguing looking face. I've never seen another like it."

By this time, Suki was desperately casting about for compliments, but Griselda didn't seem to notice. Her eyes filled with increasing delight at every word Suki spoke. When Suki was finished, she said, "I am? I'm truly a beautiful cat, like you?"

"Yes, Griselda, you're truly beautiful." Surprisingly, she meant every word.

"You're just saying that to make me feel better."

"No, I'm not. Go into the house and look in a mirror. You'll see you're not ugly."

Griselda shook her head violently. "The first and only time I was ever in a house, someone threw me out the back door. I've never gone into another one since."

"Well, that's not going to happen here. Have you seen Third Mom or Sweetie Pie throw any of us out the back door? Well, have you?"

Griselda admitted that she hadn't.

"There you are. So come on in. After all, unless you see for yourself, you're going to forever think that you're ugly. And forever is a long time . . . a *very* long time," said Suki, emphasizing the *very* for good measure. Other than being ugly, she couldn't think of anything worse than forever thinking she was ugly.

Griselda looked a long time at the house. Then she looked at Suki. "Okay, but promise that you'll stay right by my side."

"I promise."

"You go first."

Suki narrowed her eyes. "No tricks. No backing out after I've gone inside."

"I promise."

Hopping off the back porch steps, Suki headed to the cat door, Griselda close behind. At the door, Suki looked at Griselda in encouragement before pushing her head against the flap and stepping through the door. Griselda paused a moment; then, taking the deepest breath she had ever taken, she pushed her head against the flap and stepped cautiously, one paw at a time, through the door.

Once inside, she stood still, sniffing and listening intently, half-expecting Third Mom or Sweetie Pie to come roaring down on her with a broom and throw her outside. Of course, nothing of the sort happened. Sweetie Pie was cutting corn in the back field. Third Mom, who was in her bedroom, didn't even know that Griselda had ventured inside. And if she had been aware of her presence, she certainly wouldn't have chased her with a broom or thrown her outside. Catching Griselda's attention, Suki jerked her head toward an open door and headed in that direction. Griselda wavered. She could either stay where she was, follow Suki, or hightail it back outside. But going back outside would be cowardly. She couldn't bear for Suki to think she was a coward. If she wasn't going to turn back, though, keeping close to Suki seemed to be the safest bet. Without further deliberation, she hurried after her newfound friend.

With a few halts and many words of assurance and persuasion, Suki managed to lead Griselda to Third Mom and Sweetie Pie's bedroom. When Third Mom, who was in the bedroom dusting her favorite ceramic cat, spied the two traipsing through it, she almost dropped the cat. She couldn't decide which was more astonishing, seeing Griselda in the bedroom or seeing Suki leading her through it to the bath.

Placing the figurine carefully back on her dresser, Third Mom tiptoed to the bathroom door and peeked in. She could hardly contain her laughter at what she heard and saw. Both Suki and Griselda had jumped on the bath counter and were critically examining Griselda's reflection in the mirror, Griselda turning head this way and that.

After a long moment of close inspection, Griselda said, "Callie and Miss Paws are right. I am ugly. My face looks pushed in, like a dog's I saw once. My legs are too short. The rest of me is stubby looking too. I look like a box on legs. No wonder the first humans I owned moved away without taking me. No wonder no one else ever wanted me."

"You weren't too ugly for Second Mom to like," Suki pointed out. "You said that the others at the nursing home liked you too. They must have seen something in you. And what about that boy you told me about that fed and petted you and held you in his lap?"

Still regarding her reflection in the mirror, Griselda sighed. "I wish I could see what they saw."

"How can you not see it? Notice how big and round and yellow your eyes are. Just like I told you."

Griselda looked into her own eyes.

"And your paws, how exquisitely perfect they are. Not a thing in the world wrong with them."

Lifting up a front paw, Griselda examined it in the mirror.

"And what sharp teeth! Any cat would be proud of them, even me."

Griselda opened her mouth wide and inspected her teeth.

"And your cute, little snub nose. Bound to make any tomcat's heart melt."

Griselda stared at her nose in the mirror, wrinkling and unwrinkling it for the best effect. Convinced finally that Suki was telling the truth, she sighed happily and looked gratefully at Suki. "You're right. I'm not ugly at all. Not beautiful like you are but not hopeless either. Callie and Miss Paws can laugh at me and call me all the names they want. I won't pay any attention to them."

Third Mom interrupted from the doorway. "What names did they call you?"

Turning in surprise, the two cats looked at Third Mom and then at each other. They didn't want to ignore the question, but neither did they want to be tattletales. But Third Mom was relentless. "Why did you think you were ugly? Did Callie and Miss Paws say you were ugly?" Lowering their eyes to the counter, Griselda and Suki said nothing.

Third Mom narrowed her eyes. "Well, did they?" Griselda and Suki continued looking at the counter without replying. "I see," Third Mom said. "They're getting farther from their halos every day. They're supposed to be working toward them, not moving in the other direction. I'm going to find them right now and have them apologize. You stay here till I get back."

Anxiously, Griselda and Suki looked at each other again as Third Mom disappeared round the doorway. What was she going to say to Callie and Miss Paws? What was going to happen when she came back with them? Tails twitching agitatedly, they milled around on the counter, waiting anxiously for her return. When Third Mom stepped outside, she immediately spotted the two miscreants playing chase-the-tail-around-the-tree. Callie was doing the chasing, with Miss Paws providing the tail.

Third Mom called out, "Callie! Miss Paws! Please come here. I want to talk to you."

Giving a backward glance in Third Mom's direction, the two cats continued their game. They were halfway around the tree a second time before they noticed Third Mom bearing down on them, face grim and forehead frowning. Exchanging guilty looks, the two felines stopped in their tracks. Reaching the tree, Third Mom stood over them, hands on her hips. This was a stance the two cats were familiar with, one that boded ill for a cat. Apprehensively, the two stared at the ground, wondering which one of their wrongdoings Third Mom had found out about this time.

When Third Mom spoke, though, she did so gently. "Callie . . . Miss Paws . . . did you call Griselda, that sweet little cat who would never deliberately hurt another creature, did you call her ugly?"

Still staring at the ground, the cats glanced at each other out of the corner of their eyes.

"Well, did you?"

Miss Callie spoke first. "Yes," she said, so softly as to be almost inaudible.

"Speak more loudly. I didn't hear you. And please look at me when you talk to me."

Cringing inwardly, Callie looked up at Third Mom. "Yes," she said, a tad more loudly.

"What about you, Miss Paws? Did you laugh at Griselda and call her ugly?"

Miss Paws looked at Third Mom, then at Callie, and then at Third Mom again. "Yes."

"Well, I would just like to tell you that you hurt Griselda terribly. She's in the bathroom right now, staring in the mirror, trying to convince herself that she's not hopelessly ugly. And thanks to Suki, she's just about convinced herself."

Callie and Miss Paws looked at each other in surprise. Griselda in the house? Suki actually trying to make another cat feel better? Their surprise turned to consternation, however, at Third Mom's next words. "This is what you're going to do. You're going to march yourselves to the bathroom and apologize to Griselda. Don't just say you're sorry either. Mean it. Start moving."

Like all creatures, cats have a difficult time apologizing for anything. Callie and Miss Paws were no exception. They looked around for help, but none appeared to be forthcoming. So shoulders drooping, they began slowly trudging to the house.

"A bit more lively, girls. I know you can walk faster than that."

The two cats, their dread of the impending confrontation increasing with every step, picked up their pace slightly for a few steps before gradually slowing again, each one trying to think of what she was going to say to Griselda without looking foolish.

When they reached the bathroom, neither one had come up with any face-saving words of apology. Thankfully, Third Mom took pity on her two beloved miscreants. Picking them up and putting them on the counter, she said, "Griselda, will you please tell Callie and Miss Paws how you felt when they called you ugly?"

The two cats glanced at Griselda to find Griselda glancing sideways at them. Ashamed, the two lowered their heads as Griselda spoke up in a timid voice. "I felt like crying when Suki told me what it meant."

"And Callie and Miss Paws, did you hear your consciences telling you not to call Griselda names?" The two cats nodded. "And how did you feel when you called Griselda ugly? Did your hearts feel happy and contented? Or hard and mean?"

The two cats answered together in a subdued tone, "Hard and mean."

Third Mom was relentless. "Did you like yourself at that moment?"

"No."

"Do you have something to say to Griselda that might make you like yourself a bit better? And make her feel better too?"

"Yes."

"Well, go on. Say it."

Heads still lowered, the two cats said in barely audible voices, "We're sorry."

Third Mom was not satisfied. "I don't think she heard you. And look at her when you talk to her."

Raising their heads slowly, the two cats looked at Griselda. "We're sorry." Then they burst into tears. A few seconds later, Griselda and Suki joined them.

Third Mom let them cry for a few moments before interrupting. "I'm proud of you both, Callie and Miss Paws. Now I want you to touch noses with Griselda and Suki."

Still sobbing slightly, the four cats touched noses, Griselda and Suki so overcome with emotion that they touched each other's noses as well.

Third Mom smiled with delight. "I just want you to know that all four of you are a step closer to your halos. Apologizing is hard, but sometimes, accepting an apology is hard too. I'm proud of all four of you. Now outside with the lot of you."

Relieved that the ordeal was over, the four cats lost no time in making their exit. Once outside, Griselda and Suki looked at Callie and Miss Paws, and Callie and Miss Paws looked at Suki and Griselda. What were they supposed to do now? Walk away from each other as if nothing had happened? Hang around a few minutes for the sake of politeness? Tails twitching, the four cats stepped from one foot to another as they tried to make up their minds. Finally Griselda spoke up. "How about a game of Gotcha!? I'll be the pouncer."

Suki frowned. Apparently, Griselda didn't know that she never played games, especially outside ones. But she didn't want to hurt Griselda's feelings by refusing the offer. Her feelings had already been hurt enough for one day. Amazed that she was considering how another cat might feel, she nodded to Griselda that she would play.

Callie and Miss Paws looked at each other. Evidently, Griselda didn't know that they detested pouncing games. And Gotcha! was definitely a pouncing game, like hide-and-pounce. The only difference was that in hide-and-pounce, the pouncer hid behind a shrub while in Gotcha! the pouncer hid in tall grass. But to them, a pouncer was a pouncer, no matter where, and they hated pouncers. However, the very least they could do after hurting her feelings was to accept her offer, even though they had much rather spend the rest of the morning playing chase-the-tail-around-the-tree. So they squared their shoulders for the ordeal ahead.

Unfortunately for the three other cats, Gotcha! was Griselda's favorite game, one she put all her heart into, especially if she were the one pouncing. Crouching in the grass, the tip of her tail vibrating ever so slightly, eyes fixed unwaveringly on the cat or cats strolling unwittingly toward her, she would tensely wait for the right moment to spring out and roar, "Gotcha!" She could conceal herself so well in the grass that the other players were never sure where she was or when she was going to leap out. But as she had explained, "I should be good at hiding and pouncing. It's how I earned a living most of my life."

On that particular afternoon, however, the game did not work out as usual. Griselda, hiding herself in the tallest grass she could find, waited gleefully for the other three to approach. The other three, however, took their time, huddling together, looking cautiously around at each step, and then pausing to collect their wits before taking another one, constantly alert for the slightest quiver of the tall grass. After their fifth step, they began to feel more confident. Relaxing a bit, they took a sixth step, then a seventh and an eighth. Suddenly, seemingly from out of nowhere, the grass parted and out leaped Griselda, paws, claws, sharp teeth, and all. "Gotcha!"

Suki screamed, and Callie and Miss Paws fainted dead away. Looking down at the two cats prostrate on the ground, Griselda was dumfounded. All she had done was yell, "Gotcha!" What was there to faint about in that? But there the two cats lay, reviving only when Third Mom, summoned by a desperate Suki, came running with a vial of vinegar in her hand. Unstoppering the vial, she waved it under the two felines' noses. Wrinkling their nostrils, the two cats sneezed themselves conscious to find Griselda looking down at them while saying over and over, "I'm sorry, I'm so sorry."

So gratified were Callie and Miss Paws to find Griselda apologizing to them that they immediately forgave her. Regrets had been given and accepted on both sides, so they could once again hold their heads high. Their pride was saved. Even better, all four spent the rest of the morning playing chase-the tail-around-the-tree.

Homecoming

W HEN THE OTHER CATS SAW the four playing together that day, their eyes widened in astonishment. They were doubly astonished when the four, with Sweet William in the middle, snuggled down together for the night. Prissy voiced their sentiments: "Like Third Mom says, 'Miracles happen every day.'"

The other cats nodded at these words of wisdom as they did at all of Third Mom's sayings, although they rarely had the slightest idea what they meant. Their pride, however, kept them from admitting the fact. They knew cats had a reputation for being wise and enigmatic, and they intended to do their utmost to preserve the image.

As for Sweet William, with three more moms to snuggle with at night, he was in seventh heaven. He had never had any proper mothering. When he was two weeks old, the human his mother owned had wrenched him from her and dumped him in a field. Fortunately, the field adjoined Second Mom's yard and Second Mom was outside feeding the birds at the time. Hearing the kitten's cries of despair and terror, she threw down the cup of birdseed she was holding, ran to the fence, climbed over it, tearing her jeans on the bob wire in the process, and tore across the field toward the cries. What she found was a tiny kitten, so young that its eyes had not yet opened nor its ears unfurled. She could not believe one so little could have made all that noise. She adopted him immediately.

For two weeks, she had to bottle feed him every two hours. That added up to twelve times a day. Doing so meant rising at twelve and two in the morning, then again at four and six in order to keep his tummy full. And eight more feedings during the day! As his tummy grew, however, the time between feedings increased gradually to four hours. Was Second Mom ever relieved! She had to feed him only five times a day and once during the night then. By the time he was six weeks old, he was ready for kitten food. Second Mom felt as if a milestone had been passed in both their lives.

For the first three weeks, he stayed in a basket. Second Mom put a hot water bottle wrapped in a towel next to him to help him stay warm. She also added a clock wrapped in another towel. Its muffled tick reminded him of the beating of his mother's heart. He slept curled next to it. Second Mom kept the basket by her all day and on the desk next to her bed at night. She liked to pat the kitten gently ever so often, checking his breathing to make sure he was still alive while at the same time reassuring him with her touch.

Sweet William thrived under so much love and care. By the time he was four weeks old, he was able to jump out of his basket. Tottering around, he spent his time learning to walk, jump, and tussle with the rugs and blinds. By the time he was six weeks old, he was prancing around the house as if he owned it. Second Mom began taking him outside for short walks around the house every morning and afternoon. When he was outside, Sweet William was beside himself with excitement. The chirp of a bird! The smell of a flower! The tickle of grass on his paws! Everything he saw, smelled, felt, and heard was new.

One morning, Second Mom inadvertently left the front door slightly ajar on her way to the mail box. The open door was an invitation Sweet William could not resist. Squeezing through the door, he eagerly gamboled outside, where he proceeded to have a grand time, exploring every nook and cranny he saw, chasing every leaf that blew across his path, pouncing on every blade of grass that tickled his nose. Suddenly a cloud passed overhead. Looking up, he saw the talons and beak of a hawk zooming down upon him. Then his world went dark. The next thing he knew he found himself in a basket remarkably like the one he slept in. However, the basket was not on Second Mom's desk or kitchen counter but on the back porch steps of a house.

Standing up and putting his front paws on the side of the basket, he immediately began meowing. His meows caught the attention of Suki, who was going out the cat door for a rare foray through the backyard. Staring in the direction the sound had come from, she beheld a kitten climbing out of a basket. Immediately, she claimed him for her own. She had always wanted a toy kitten; here was one waiting for her.

Unfortunately, Suki was not experienced at tussling, playing games like hide-and-pounce, or chasing mice and rabbits, behavior in which good mother cats instruct their kittens. Nor was she interested in teaching her small charge the good manners kittens are supposed to learn at their mother's paws. She had much rather give Sweet William a bath, curl up with him for a nap, or regale him with descriptions of her beauty and grace and tales of all the tomcats who had lost their hearts to her. The rest of the time, he was on his own. Naturally, Sweet William suffered in the bargain. Prissy would have lent a paw, but all her paws were busy looking out for Little Cat.

Once she had made friends with Suki, however, Griselda lost no time in taking charge of Sweet William. Giving him the proper raising that Suki either couldn't or wouldn't reminded her of the times she had had kittens of her own. She told Third Mom, "I still remember all my kittens, what they looked like, what I named them, how I cried when they left to make their way in the world. Now I have another kitten. Only this one is staying. I do hope all my kittens ended up in a home like this."

Third Mom smiled at Griselda in reassurance. "I don't think you need worry about that, Griselda. God takes care of all His creatures. And when something bad happens to one of them on earth, it ends up in heaven that much sooner. And in heaven, all homes are good ones. One day you might want to take a journey to find all your kittens that are in heaven and see how they are doing. They could visit you too. How would you like that?"

"That's every mother cat's dream. But I can't leave yet. I want to be here when Second Mom arrives. Besides, I haven't taught Sweet William all he needs to know. He's dreadfully deficient in cat etiquette. And he has no idea at all about how to stalk a bird. He gets confused when he tries to catch one. So do the birds. But he's coming along."

More weeks, months, and seasons passed. The cats ate, slept, played, and grew in goodness. Some took a few steps toward their halos, some many, while a few backslid a step or two, before righting themselves. In short, life in heaven went on as it was meant to.

Late one afternoon, almost a year after Griselda's arrival, Third Mom told Black Bart to round up all the cats and bring them to the back porch. Within minutes, Black Bart had herded them onto the back porch, a few grumbling about having their tussling and tumbling and their hide-and-pounce games interrupted, a few indignant about being awakened from naps. But the look on Third Mom's face quieted their complaints.

With a glance at Hon, who was mowing the side yard, Third Mom began to speak. "Don't say anything to Hon. No sense getting him overly excited and anxious. I want you to all go down to the edge of the field. Second Mom is going to be coming through it soon. She may be a little confused and frightened, being in a strange place. You need to be there to welcome her. Once she sees you, she'll be all right."

The cats sat in stunned silence. They had longed for this day to arrive. But now that it had, they didn't know how to react. Suddenly, Neiki burst out in a quavering voice, "But what about you, Third Mom? How are you going to get along without us?"

The other cats spoke up. "Yes, Third Mom. We love Second Mom, but we love you too."

"You're going to be lonely without us. What will you do?"

"I want to live with you and Second Mom, both. Why can't I spend one night with you and one with Second Mom, the way we do with you and Hon?"

To quell their litany of concerns, Third Mom held up her hand. "It's all right to be sad because my time with you is coming to an end. I'm sad too. I'm going to miss all of you. But I'll also be happy knowing you're with Second Mom again. Besides, I won't be too lonely. I still have Sweetie Pie. And I bet I have another cat by tomorrow evening. Who knows? Maybe it will be a stray cat or one that's never had a home, one that I can keep forever. And I can visit you anytime I want. You can visit me too. I'm sure Second Mom won't mind. Now let me say good-bye to all of you. I might not have a chance later."

The cats set up an immediate clamor to be first to say good-bye. With tears in her eyes, Third Mom picked up each one, hugging it and touching its nose to hers. When she was finished, the cats teemed around one another, tails twitching in excitement, feet treading the porch in anticipation. Third Mom cautioned, "Remember. I don't want Hon to know what's going on yet. He might try to find Second Mom before it's time for her to be found. Go quickly now and quietly. Don't look back."

Heeding Third Mom's words, the cats gathered at the edge of the field, still muddling around, peering in every direction, each one hoping to be the first to spot Second Mom. Hon could not help but notice them as he rounded the back of the house on the lawn mower. Stopping the mower, he yelled at Third Mom, "What's up with the cats? I've never seen them behaving this way before."

Straightening up from the flower bed by the back porch, where she was busying herself in order to keep a close watch on the cats, Third Mom shrugged her shoulders. "You know how cats are. No one can ever guess what they're going to do next."

Laughing, Hon said, "You're telling me. I've lived with cats for some seventy years and they're still a closed book." Shaking his head, he resumed his mowing while Third Mom returned to her work in the flower bed, still watching the cats out of the corner of her eyes. As for the cats, they continued to wait for Second Mom, still twining around one other in confusion, trying to see over the field's summer growth of grass that was higher than they were.

Finally, Tibby said in exasperation, "How are we going to see Second Mom coming with all this grass in our eyes? The rest of you can stay on the ground if you want, but I'm going to jump on a fence post so I can have a better view."

Soon all the cats were lined up on the fence posts along the fence that divided Third Mom's yard from the field. In spite of their vantage point, however, they smelled Second Mom long before they saw her. Turning their heads in the direction of her scent, they soon spotted a figure in the distance, glancing around as if bewildered. Then they heard Second Mom's voice.

"How did I get here? The last thing I remember is going to bed after lunch for a nap. Have I started sleepwalking? How ridiculous. I've never walked in my sleep in my entire life. Maybe I'm dreaming. I'll pinch myself to see."

By this time, all the cats could see her wading through the grass in their direction. They saw her pinch herself on her neck. "Well, I could feel that a little, so I'm not dreaming."

She looked down at herself. "How in the world did I get on jeans and a shirt? It's been years since I've worn jeans and a shirt. I *know* I had a gown on when I went to bed. Why, look at my hands! They're not wrinkled anymore. They look so . . . so . . . so smooth and young! Strange, I feel much better too. I'm not tired. And I don't ache anywhere either! Oh, I wish I had a mirror so I could see what the rest of me looks like. Is my face as young looking as my hands? I hope so. I would love to look young again. Even if I am ninety-five."

By this time, all the cats had jumped down from the posts and were bounding toward Second Mom, yelling at her as loudly as they could. Before long, the noise reached Second Mom's ears. First, she heard one voice.

"It's me, Second Mom. It's Tibby. Don't be afraid. Just stay right there. I'm coming to you."

Then another voice reached her ears. "Second Mom, Second Mom, don't go anywhere. I'm coming to help you. It's me, William."

Next she heard Black Bart and Big Tig and Rufus. Then Elvira and Pretty Polly and Louis Little and all the others. She could even hear the kittens, Neiki and Little Cat and Sweet William. A look of wonderment lit up her face. Within seconds, all the cats that she had loved were pressing against her legs, twitching their tails and meowing in welcome.

Disbelief and wonder written on her face, Second Mom knelt down and reached out to them. "My cats, my cats! How I've missed you! But here you all are and I can understand what you're saying! What's going on?"

"You're in heaven!" the cats shouted in unison.

"In heaven?" A look of incredulity crossed Second Mom's face.

"Yes! In heaven!" shouted the cats again. "And we can understand you too."

"In heaven! I'm really in heaven?" Second Mom's face wore a mixture of belief and disbelief. She looked around her. "And you're here with me. Let me look at you. Are all of you really here? Let me see. Here's Prissy. What a glow you have!"

"That's because she's perfect. She's earned her halo," said the other cats, still shouting in joy.

"Perfect? Prissy's perfect? How wonderful! I'm so proud of you, Prissy. And what about my little Crazy Cat? Is she perfect yet?" said Second Mom, spying Neiki.

"I'm afraid not," drawled Suki. "She's got a long way to go. And with two patches of catnip to roll in, she's not getting there very fast."

Neiki hung her head in shame.

"That's all right, Neiki," said Second Mom. "I'll help you become perfect."

Neiki beamed in gratitude. Second Mom could do anything.

Second Mom looked around at the other cats, counting them off on her fingers as she recognized them. "Here are the two Toms. You still look just alike. And Dorca One and Two, my sweet little inkblots. Oh, here's Callie and Miss Paws and Black Bart and Big Tig. Just as big as ever, I see. Why, here's Louis Little. How I missed your visits! And Rufus and Pretty Polly. How pretty you still are, Polly. And Shala, my little beauty.

"Oh, look who we have here. Elvira, my sweet pea of a sweetie pie." At the mention of her name, Elvira squeaked and lay down on her side, squirming with pleasure. Tears sprang to Second Mom's eyes. "You have four legs again. I had forgotten what you looked like with four legs."

Tibby, annoyed at not having been noticed, butted her head against Second Mom's legs. Second Mom laughed. "Here's my Tib Wib cat. She's not going to let me overlook her. How magnificent you look, Tibby. I had forgotten you were so big.

"And Little Cat and Sweet William. What precious kittens you are."

Little Cat and Sweet William turned somersaults over each other, so filled with happiness that they had to show off. Laughing at their antics, she spotted William, sitting still with an anxious expression on his face.

"William, my little worrywart. What are you looking so worried about now?"

"I was afraid you wouldn't remember me."

"Oh, William, I could never forget my little glum-wum." Overcome with joy, William toppled prostrate onto the grass, covering his eyes with his front paws and peeking out at Second Mom between his toes.

Suddenly Second Mom spied a boxy-looking cat with a snub face. "Griselda, you're here! How I missed our lap time together. But we'll have plenty of lap time now." Griselda, who had been afraid that Second Mom might decide that she was one cat too many or was simply not pretty enough to keep, heaved a sigh of relief before wrapping herself around Second Mom's legs in happiness.

After Second Mom had satisfied herself that all her cats were there, she picked each one up in turn, holding it close to her heart, knowing they would never again be parted. Tears of joy rolled down her face. Putting down the last cat, she dried her tears on her shirt. Standing up, she looked around. "But where's Dave? He's in heaven too, isn't he? I have to find him."

"Don't worry! He's mowing Third Mom's yard," said Neiki. "And guess what?"

"What?" said Second Mom, laughing at the eager expression on Neiki's face. "What is it you can't wait to tell me? And who is Third Mom?"

"Third Mom has been taking care of us. We've been living with her all this time. And Hon's built a house for us and you!"

The other cats immediately turned on her. "Neiki! That's supposed to be a surprise!"

Neiki hung her head in shame for a second time.

Second Mom patted her head. "That's all right, my little Crazy Cat! You're just so excited to see me that you forgot. And I don't know what the house looks like. So it will still be a surprise."

Neiki looked gratefully at Second Mom again. Second Mom always made things right.

Glancing around the field again, Second Mom said, "Well, where is he?"

The cats, each eager to lead her to him, raced toward Third Mom's yard, beckoning to Second Mom with their voices. "He's over here. Just follow me."

Laughing, Second Mom said, "Slow down, my little cats. I can't run as fast as you." She began walking as rapidly as she could, the cats stopping ever so often for her to catch up. Suddenly, halfway across the field, she saw Hon standing by a gate at the edge of a yard, looking in her direction. Screaming his name in joy, she ran toward him, the cats bounding ahead.

Transfixed at the sound of her voice, Hon could not move for a moment. Then, collecting himself, he leaped over the gate and raced toward her. When he reached her, he swept her in his arms, hugging and kissing her as if he would never stop, crying, "Jane, oh Jane, you're here, you're really here." Finally both stepped back, tears rolling down their faces as they looked at each other tenderly.

Second Mom said, "If this is a dream, I hope it never ends. Is it really you? Is this really heaven?"

Hon smiled. "It's not a dream. It's really me. And we're really in heaven. And it will never end."

"I've missed you so," said Second Mom, voice quavering as she wiped her eyes. "I imagined this moment so many times after you died. It's what kept me going. That and my cats. And now it's here."

"And I've missed you. But no more," said Hon.

Second Mom smiled. "No, never again." Her eyes widened. "You're so young. You don't have gray hair anymore. Or any wrinkles. You look like you did when I married you."

Hon laughed. "You don't have any wrinkles either. And your hair is brown again. You look like you did when I married you."

Second Mom smiled in delight as she touched her hair and face, joy written on her face. "How wonderful heaven is! I'm young again, all my cats are here, and we're together. Forever! What could be more perfect than that?"

"Nothing."

Suddenly, she clutched at his arm, tears beginning to stream down her face again. "Oh Dave, my parents . . . and my grandparents . . . I'm going to see them! And my brother and sister and all my friends. I'm really, really going to see them all again. And your parents too. And your brothers and sisters. And one day, our children and grandchildren and our great-grandchildren will be here. And on and on until the end of the world. I . . . I'm so happy I don't know what to do."

"Well, for a start, we could go home," said Hon.

"That's right. I almost forgot. We have a house. And we'll never have to leave it. What's it like?"

"Almost like the one we built all those years ago."

"Exactly what I wanted. Yes, let's go home," said Second Mom. She took a step forward and then stopped. "With my cats?"

"No," said Hon.

Second Mom's face fell, while the cats murmured in consternation.

Smiling broadly, Hon said, "Let's go home with *our* cats."

Second Mom's face lit up as the cats muttered, "That's better."

Pulling Second Mom close against his side, Hon put an arm around her. Talking excitedly, they walked toward the yard, the cats following, to begin the rest of their lives.

About the Author

LYNDA HAMBLEN LIVES WITH HER husband and her cat, Elvira, in a small gray house on a hill on a farm outside of Union City, Tennessee. Having lived a life blessed with cats, she decided to write a novel about a cat's view of life, heaven, and eternity. She is a published essayist and poet, but this is her first novel.

CPSIA information can be obtained
at www.ICGtesting.com
Printed in the USA
LVHW09s0011181018
593997LV00001B/279/P